The Faberge Flute

by

Maeve Maddox

The Faberge Flute

COPYRIGHT © 2021 by M. J. Maddox

Cover Art by *Debbie Taylor*

The Wild Rose Press, Inc.
PO Box 708
Adams Basin, NY 14410-0708
Visit us at www.thewildrosepress.com

Publishing History
First Crimson Rose Edition, 2021
Trade Paperback ISBN 978-1-5092-3381-6
Digital ISBN 978-1-5092-3382-3

Published in the United States of America

Sallie retraced her steps to the zebra crossing. What was going on? She'd mentioned Kassim to Dave and Dani at least twice. As for Kassim, the time she'd mentioned the Kings to him, he'd waited for her to explain who they were. If the Kings and Kassim knew each other, why pretend they didn't?

Thoughts whirling, Sallie took her place with a group of people she thought were waiting for the light to change, but as they surged forward, she realized that she was at a bus stop. As the huge red hulk of a Number Nine hurtled toward the curb, she felt the pressure of a hand at the small of her back and found herself being propelled forward into the street. For the first time, she noticed that red London buses have black fenders and that one of them was inches from her face.

Dedication

To Amanda.
She got me to the end.

Chapter One
Beginnings

Erzurum, Turkey, 13 April 1915

The gold and jewels of the ancient reliquaries lanced bright bursts of color with each movement of the lantern in the shaky hand of the Armenian monk. The monk's outfit with its pointy hood reminded Armstrong of a Klansman's robes, only black.

A professional soldier, Buck Armstrong had been attached to the American consulate in Erzurum for the past year, but the way things were going, he wouldn't be there much longer. Just two days ago, the order to close the consulate had come from the US Ambassador in Istanbul. Most of the American staffers were already on their way out of Turkey. His own luggage, with the exception of a rucksack he'd kept with him for last-minute souvenirs, was with the exiting convoy. The only reason he and his boss were still standing here listening to the old monk recite his spiel for a gaggle of American tourists was that the consul owed a favor to a US congressman whose mother was in the group.

Armstrong glanced at the boss. As usual, he was pretending to listen, but today he kept shifting weight from foot to foot and stealing looks at his watch. The beads of sweat on his forehead in the cool cave chamber were a clue that he might be regretting his decision to delay his departure. Earlier that morning, the market in Erzurum was buzzing with rumors of a massacre of Armenians at Van, a town not far from there. Rumor had it that Turkish soldiers were on their way to Erzurum with similar intentions and would be there next day. Knots of fleeing Armenians stopped in a steady stream on their way out of town at the house of an American missionary family, dropping off valuables and insurance policies for safe-keeping. The American ambassador in Istanbul was reported to be on the verge of resigning because he couldn't persuade government leaders—Turks or Americans—to do anything about the ethnic killings.

A scoffing sound escaped Armstrong's throat. He knew a thing or two about ethnic killings. He'd been with General Jake Smith in the Philippines back in '01. He reckoned the Armenians were to the Turks what the Filipinos had been to the Yanks sent to pacify the islands after the Spaniards left—inconveniences to be got rid of.

The black-clad monk stood in front of a curtained alcove, displaying relics that were usually hidden in a vault behind the curtain. He spoke in an English so accented he might as well have been speaking Armenian. Armstrong had heard it so many times he knew the gist of it.

The four objects he showed to the tourists were all associated with Saint Gregory the Illuminator, founder of the Armenian Christian Church and patron saint of the Armenian people. For the longest time, Armstrong thought Gregory's title had something to do with illuminated manuscripts. Making conversation with the consul's wife at a reception one time, he'd made the mistake of remarking that he'd like to see some of Gregory's illustrations. When the snooty cow finally stopped laughing, she told him the saint was called "The Illuminator" because he'd "brought light" to the pagan Armenians by converting them to Christianity, not because he illuminated manuscripts.

The monk droned on. He'd reached the part where the visitors were permitted to touch the relics, not with their hands, but with scarves, gloves, or whatever lightweight objects they had about them. According to the benighted superstitions of these people, a piece of cloth that touched one of the relics had the power to heal cuts, sickness, even broken bones. Armstrong turned another scoff into a cough. He'd left his own religion behind with childhood, but nevertheless, a sense of Protestant repugnance stirred in his soul as he watched the hocus-pocus with the gorgeous reliquaries and their ghoulish contents. His eyes caressed the exquisite objects. Such sublime materials deserved to be put to better use.

Three of the objects were reliquaries made of gold, not the yellow gold Armstrong was familiar with, but a distinctive rose-colored variety he'd never seen before.

One of the containers was a long jewel-studded box shaped like Noah's ark. It contained the arm bone of a second century female saint with an unpronounceable name. A container shaped like a life-sized human hand held two of the Illuminator's fingers. The third container, a rose-gold cross studded with pearls and sapphires, held a piece of the True Cross, a gift to Gregory from some Roman emperor or other.

The fourth object was not a reliquary, but Gregory's golden chalice. Like the bones in the reliquaries, the cup, set with one large cabochon ruby, was said to have the power to heal.

The scraping of the heavy entrance door announced the arrival of a late-comer. Armstrong recognized the consul's driver, who pushed his way to the boss and whispered into his ear. The consul jerked to attention and moved toward the exit, speaking to the monk as he went. "Pardon me for interrupting, Father." His voice sounded unnaturally loud. "An emergency has arisen. Our visitors must return to their bus immediately."

Without waiting for a response, the consul exited, leaving the driver to herd the puzzled tourists from the crypt. The Turkish soldiers from Van must have made better time than expected.

Armstrong moved to follow. He glanced at the old man, who was gathering up the holy vessels to return them to their place behind the curtain. Poor fool. As an Armenian monk, he had only a few more hours to live. His precious relics would be spoils of war before his body cooled.

Glancing around the chamber, empty now except for him and the monk, Armstrong decided to act. He drew a souvenir dagger from his rucksack and stabbed the monk from behind, quickly and efficiently, the way he'd learned to do it while serving with General Howling Jake in the islands.

He wiped the blade on the black habit and turned his attention to the thousand-year-old reliquaries gleaming in the lantern light, waiting for their next owner. Might as well be him. He knew a place he could get them melted down, no questions asked.

Armstrong grabbed the chalice first, drawn by the huge ruby set in its side. He placed it carefully at the bottom of the rucksack. Then he reached for the reliquaries. Before stowing them, he emptied their grisly contents onto the dirt floor. A flicker of motion caught his eye and he froze. Holding his breath, he stared at the curtain in front of the storage alcove. Had it moved? Nothing now. Imagination. Or possibly a draft from some crevice open to the outside.

Armstrong drew a deep breath and slung the knapsack over his shoulder. It didn't matter if he had been seen by someone lurking behind the curtain. In a few hours, he'd be with the rest of the delegation, safely aboard an American cruiser with his precious haul. Once the jewels were separated from their settings and the rose gold melted into a single ingot, old Gregory's magical reliquaries would be unrecognizable, their healing mumbo-jumbo a forgotten fable. Best of all, Buck Armstrong, mercenary soldier, would be a very rich man. Grinning with satisfaction, he exited the crypt.

****

DeSoto Springs, Arkansas, 31 October 1985

The old armory rang with the clang of folding chairs and music stands being set up. Sallie Dunbar joined the DeSoto Springs Community Band shortly after returning to her hometown when her life in Dallas fell apart. Weekly band practice was one of her few pleasures, a refuge from the stress she called her life. For two blissful hours, totally insulated from the frustrations and worries of teaching high school English and French and living in her mother's basement, she didn't have to think or interact. All she had to do was count, stay in tune, and try to keep up.

By day, the armory served as a senior center. Sallie

didn't need to read the posted menu to know that cabbage had been on today's menu. She wandered over to the bulletin board to wait while the flute section was set up.

A bright orange border of jack-o-lanterns made the ancient announcements look more faded than usual.

FREE HEARING TEST
FREE SCOOTER CONSULTATION
SUPPLEMENTAL DEATH BENEFITS

A pair of arms reached past Sallie, forcing her to step aside.

"You might find this more interesting reading than that old junk, Sallie."

Band secretary Nadine Lightfoot removed the thumbtack from a hearing-aid placard and used it to fasten a glossy three-color sheet of paper over it.

Come to London!
INTERNATIONAL
OBOE AND FLUTE ASSOCIATION
CONVENTION
November 25-30.
Registration Deadline November 1

Sallie looked at the deadline date and laughed. "Kind of short notice, don't you think? Today's Halloween. The deadline to register is tomorrow."

Nadine shrugged. "Guess I've been carrying it around for a while."

The poster was illustrated with the picture of a gorgeous golden flute set with gemstones. "I saw that picture in the flute magazine," Sallie said. "It has a name, but I can't remember what."

"The Fabergé Flute."

Sallie knew without looking that Delphine Pringle

had joined them. An aura of cigarette smoke clung to her, the only smoker in the band. Eighty-three years old, Delphine was a founding member and a town character. She'd never learned to drive and was a familiar sight pedaling around hilly DeSoto Springs in all weathers.

"That's right," Sallie said, "Fabergé. Like the eggs. I should have remembered. I've seen pictures of the eggs." She looked back at the poster. The flute, an artist's rendering and not a photo, was a riot of color. The golden tubing had an unusual rosy cast. Colored gems were set in some of the keys. She turned to Delphine. "It's beautiful, but according to the article in the IOFA magazine, it doesn't exist."

Delphine turned on the heel of a red tennis shoe and headed for the flute section. "It exists."

Sallie followed, eager to know more.

The four chairs for the flute section were in place. Delphine sat in the first one and Sallie in the fourth. The two high school students who would occupy the other two chairs were still chatting with youngsters from other sections. The community band leader also led the high school band and offered extra credit to students who played in both. Considering the average age of the adult band members and frequent bouts of flu, padding the sections with teenagers was good insurance.

Sallie spoke across the empty chairs as they assembled their flutes, continuing the conversation about the jeweled flute. "According to the article, the only person who believes in its existence is an eccentric London flute collector."

Delphine shrugged. "I know it exists. When I was a

child, in Marseilles, my aunt told me about this flute." Delphine was a French war bride, brought to Arkansas in the 1940s by Private First Class Orville Pringle. She leaned toward Sallie. "This man, this 'Duby,' he knows things."

Delphine pronounced the flute collector's name as if it had air quotes around it.

"What 'things'?"

Delphine executed another superbly French shrug. "Things."

The high school students took their seats. Sallie lapsed into band mode, concentrating on the music. Between numbers, however, her thoughts returned to the poster on the bulletin board. Come to London! The words made her ache.

London had figured in Sallie's fantasies from the time she read *The Prince and the Pauper* at the age of ten. Her favorite childhood books all had English settings. *The Little Princess. The Secret Garden. Master Skylark. Black Beauty.* In ninth grade, after seeing her first Shakespeare play, she'd opened a savings account she called her "England Fund" and put every cash gift she received in it. By the beginning of her senior year in college, she had enough money to pay for a three-week stay. Only the trip never happened. Three weeks before graduation, she'd married Nick Patillo, and the money for England went to buy Nick a new red Mustang.

At break, Sallie bee-lined for the bulletin board. The London convention was scheduled for Thanksgiving week. Registration, hotel, and airfare were all included in the posted price. She weighed the possibility. In the three years since Nick's death, spending money had become painful, every dollar like a

8

physical cut. Nick's death left her not only penniless but drowning in debt. Come to find out, he'd been skipping insurance payments and other essentials. More, he'd run up thousands on scuba gear and weekend diving trips with his set of rich friends from work.

Nick died on one of those trips when he ran out of air in the Eagle's Nest Sinkhole in Florida. It was the day of their tenth wedding anniversary. When the phone rang, Sallie thought it would be Nick, phoning to wish her Happy Anniversary. Instead it was one of his diving buddies, calling with the news. Two days after the funeral, she learned she'd not only lost her house and her car but had also inherited a credit card debt in the thousands.

Sallie sighed, brushed her fingers longingly against the beautiful flute on the poster, and headed back to her section. Thanks to her mother, she had a place to live, and thanks to an uncle who co-signed the loan, she had a car. She even had enough in a savings account to cover the cost of the IOFA convention. She toyed with the idea. The dates fell during Thanksgiving week. She'd be off two days anyway. A lot of teachers called in sick Thanksgiving week. She always complained about them for doing it. She never could bring herself to lie about being sick. Still, London…

Rehearsal closed with the Barnum and Bailey march, leaving Sallie feeling energized and optimistic. On the way out, she filched the announcement from the bulletin board, folded it, and slipped it into a back pocket of her jeans.

Another thing Sallie liked about weekly band practice was the chance to trade professional garb for tennis shoes and jeans. Her principal, Mr. Huysman, was Old School. All women teachers and staff were required to wear skirts and nylon stockings. Even the P.E. teacher had to change clothes whenever she left the gym to go to another part of the school. Sallie grimaced. Mr. Huysman and her mother had a lot in common. The concept of personal choice for others was lacking in their worldview.

Practice ended at nine, so it was already dark when Sallie left the building. She quickened her steps, glad that she'd taken the precaution of parking under a security light. Halloween was not the best of nights for teachers. As she reached the back of the building, she heard laughter and what sounded like a series of rapid-fire slaps. Then came the pounding of feet on pavement. She ran the rest of the way to her car, dreading what awaited her and finding what she feared.

Glistening in the yellow vapor light, the shattered remains of at least two dozen eggs gleamed on the surface of her less-than-three-years-old blue Escort.

By the time Sallie got home from the all-night car wash, it was close to midnight. Too late to watch Rockford. She'd be embarrassed to admit it, but the high point of her weekdays was watching eleven o'clock reruns of *The Rockford Files*. She loved the character played by James Garner. She liked his looks, of course, but what attracted her the most was the way he accepted people for what they were, even a miserable specimen like Angel Martin.

Nick never liked anyone the way they were, including Sallie. Especially Sallie. He disliked all her friends "because they were stupid." He tried to change everything about her. The way she dressed, the way she talked, the kind of books and movies she liked. In her fantasies, Sallie was married to Jim Rockford, who liked her just the way she was.

Sallie stopped the car at the end of the driveway to retrieve the mail, pulled up the rest of the way, and parked. Expecting a notice, she switched on the dome light to look at the envelopes. Finally! Of all the things she hated about working at her old high school was the in-service requirement. Every year, teachers had to sit through thirteen hours of "professional development" programs, harangued by motivational speakers telling them they must be all things to all children, but not going into much detail as to how to do it. To spare herself from a few hours of the yearly drivel, she'd taken a three-hour summer correspondence course in Latin. She tore open the envelope from Huysman's office and read the contents: "Request to count Latin course denied. Not sufficiently related to employee's job description."

Sallie crumpled the letter and threw it over her shoulder into the back seat. Damned Huysman. Some asinine course in statistics would count but learning more about the source of eighty percent of the English vocabulary "wasn't sufficiently related to teaching English." She took a few deep breaths before getting out. This had not been a good day.

The front porch was in darkness. Mother's Halloween rule forbade the use of any lights that could be seen from the street. To ensure that a light couldn't be switched on accidentally, she always unscrewed the porch and hall bulbs.

Sallie unlocked the front door and groped her way along the darkened hallway. "Damn!" She kicked the solid lead doorstop in the shape of a sleeping cat that usually stood outside the back door. Pain exploded in her big toe. Mother always brought Kitty in at Halloween so that no trick-or-treaters could steal or damage it. As if anyone could lift it!

As she rubbed her throbbing toe, the day's frustrations washed over her. The desire to chuck everything for a week and go to London gripped her more strongly than it had in the armory. A whole week away from DeSoto Springs and Huysman and high school students and her mother. She might even meet someone interesting. Someone like Rockford, who would like her for herself.

Light gleamed in the doorway of the room Momma called her "den." Sallie looked in. Momma was asleep in her chair, lighted faintly by the 1960s seashell TV lamp. Thursday was beauty shop day. A bouffant halo of bluish-white hair framed her face. Her mouth sagged open and her breath came in little snorts. Sallie's feelings of rebellion dissipated in a surge of affection. She couldn't afford a trip to Dallas, let alone London. Besides, how could she think of leaving Momma to celebrate Thanksgiving alone? She fished the IOFA flyer from her back pocket and dropped it into the wastebasket by the door. Another time maybe. She flipped on the overhead light. The snoring stopped and her mother stirred.

"Time for bed, Momma," Sallie said gently.

Her mother's pale blue eyes opened and looked up at her. Her gaze traveled from Sallie's head to her feet and back again. A frown creased her papery forehead.

"Did you go out dressed like that?"

Sallie sucked air as if she'd been punched. She

retrieved the convention flyer from the wastebasket.

"Yes, Mother," she said. "I did. And by the way, I'm going to London for Thanksgiving."

Chapter Two

London's East End, 23 November 1985

Whoever was ringing the bell this time was not going to give up. It couldn't be the Buyer. They'd agreed that the Buyer would ring the bell at three p.m. Precisely. It had just gone two.

Morris tried to ignore the ringing, but the damn thing continued to jangle, and the dog, shut in the kitchen after the last visitor, added his annoying noise to that of the bell.

Obstinate as he was, even Morris Duby had his limits. Cursing, he put down the instrument he was working on, an open-holed silver Haynes flute in need of new pads. Before getting up, he pulled a polishing cloth over the fine leather flute case that lay beside the telephone on his worktable. Satisfied that it was concealed, he went to the door, muttering his annoyance.

"Mannerless nincompoops, can't they read? Don't they know what 'Closed' means?" He'd fastened only the top lock after the last visitor. Now he unfastened it and, bracing his foot against the bottom edge, opened the door a crack. "Can't you read?" He jabbed a gnarled finger at the tattered pasteboard sign that hung swinging against the glass, the red "CLOSED" side outward.

"Please," said the visitor, "I've come all the way

from Central London on the bus." He stuck a paper through the crack and waved it under Morris's nose. "The IOFA Conference information says you're open until six on Saturday." Morris slapped the paper away and squinted through the crack. A man, he supposed. They all dressed alike these days, men and women, in hooded jackets. Like young Derek from next door.

"Please let me in," the person repeated. "I must talk to you."

Morris moved to shut the door, but the visitor stopped it with the toe of his shoe. "I'll pay you for your time."

Morris shrugged and held the door open wide enough for the stranger to enter before shutting it. The dog's barking became more frantic. On his way back to the worktable, Morris let him out of the kitchen. The little white terrier dashed into the room, leaping and pirouetting almost as high as Morris's head. He rushed to sniff the stranger's shoes. The young man backed away. The dog lost interest and stretched out under the bench on a litter of old instrument cases and discarded polishing rags. Morris plopped back down on his stool, stirring a draft that sent a small bit of paper over the edge of the workbench. He saw it fall but made no move to catch it. The dog snapped at it as it fluttered past.

Outside, the watery November sun illuminated the shabby East End street, but the room was dim. Morris had drawn the blinds earlier. The only light came from a lamp clamped to the workbench. He was expecting the Buyer and had wanted to discourage random visitors. It hadn't worked. First that officious business type showed up, demanding this and that. Now this one.

"Well?" Morris snagged a pad between the pincers of a long pair of tweezers and went on with his work. The man leaned toward the bench but kept his feet away from the dog.

"I heard…I was told…someone said you have come into the possession of a very special flute."

Morris grunted, his version of a laugh.

"I'm in possession of a great many very special flutes, but since you couldn't read a CLOSED sign, I expect you missed the one that says DUBY RARE FLUTE MUSEUM."

Keeping his eyes on the repair, Morris waved an arm in the direction of the wall in which a doorway had recently been cut. Thanks to the death of his longtime neighbor, whom he never liked, Morris now owned both sides of the semi-detached house just off the Roman Road in Tower Hamlets. His living quarters and workshop remained on one side while the other now housed his collection of rare and unusual flutes. The Collection. The only joy in his bitter existence.

Unwanted as he was, the visitor fueled Morris's pleasure in boasting about his treasures.

"Got a spy flute, I have. Uses .22 caliber bullets and can kill a man at twenty paces, if you know how to aim it. Got a sword flute, as well, 1738. Can't tell it from a gentleman's fine walking stick. Ever see a glass flute? Or one made of a dinosaur's bone?"

"I've heard about your collection. I've a friend who has seen it."

Morris looked up and peered at the visitor, but the hood obscured the face. All the young people wore them. As if they had something to hide. No matter. One face was like another. Morris didn't pay much attention to faces. Only to the flutes brought to be mended. Forty years he'd done the work for the money, money he needed to provide a place for his flutes. After today he wouldn't have to mess with strangers. After today, the future of the Collection would be secured. One treasure sacrificed for the sake of the many.

Morris's fingers crept beneath the cloth that concealed the flute case beside the telephone. They traced the pattern of the embossed morocco leather. He smiled. After all these years, to possess again the beautiful hateful instrument that disrupted his life when he was a boy of fourteen. He'd shown them, shown them both. He'd taken it from them and left. But then someone took it from him. Long ago. Before the war.

Morris shook his head furiously at the memory. He never should have trusted that man. That's what happens when you trust people. They pay you back all right. He trusted him, and he took it. Stole it from him. But it came back. After all these years, it had come back.

"Mr. Duby?"

Morris had forgotten about the visitor. "Well?" he snapped. Say what you've come for or go on your way. I've work to do."

"I want to know if it's true that you've found..." The stranger's voice trailed off. Morris squinted up at him. The hood slipped back a little. Unusual eyes. Irises such a pale blue they seemed almost white. Eerie.

"Found what?" Morris snapped.

The young man inhaled audibly, as if to summon enough breath to speak.

"Have you really found the Fabergé Flute?"

Morris grinned and ran his tongue in and out of the

gaps between his teeth. His fingers stroked the case under the cloth. He felt a growing urge to take it out, show it off. The same urge had possessed him the night the American phoned. That had been a mistake. Bragging to the American about it. The American had seen the magazine article. Had asked Duby if he believed such a flute could have ever existed. He hadn't been able to resist. Existed? Not only did it exist, I have it!

A stupid thing to say. Still, in an hour or so the flute would be out of his life again. No one would have the chance to rob him of it this time. If the American did come to investigate, Morris would say he'd been pulling his leg.

He squinted at the man in the hood. "You're not so daft as to believe what you read in the IOFA magazine, are you?"

"If anyone would know about this flute, you would, Mr. Duby."

The words stroked Morris's ego. His tone softened. "What have you heard about it?"

"That it's not only the most beautiful flute in the world, but that it has the power to heal."

"Beautiful, yes, but the power to heal? Tripe!"

"They say that playing it gave Goldblatt three more years of his career after his hands were crippled with arthritis. They say Hindenberg was going deaf, but when he played the Fabergé Flute his hearing was restored."

Morris laughed. "You heard wrong." Beneath the cloth the leather case grew warm under his caress. The urge to show the flute, to revel in his brief possession of it was growing stronger, as if the flute were calling to him. The Buyer would be there soon. What harm in bragging just one more time? At his age, and especially after that last stroke, Morris could never expect to have such a chance again. His days were running out. The money he would get in exchange for the fabulous treasure would ensure that the Collection would stay together after his death. Too bad he couldn't have the money and the flute. Too bad Father couldn't know who had got some good from the beautiful, damned thing after all.

The man waited. The strange eyes bored into Morris as if willing him to admit to having the flute.

"I don't have it, I tell you."

Shoulders sagging, the stranger turned toward the door. "I suppose it was too much to hope for," he said. "Sorry to have troubled you."

Prodded by a spirit of contradiction, Morris jerked the polishing cloth away, revealing the antique case.

Holding the case in both hands like some holy vessel, Morris stood and took it round to the visitor's side of the worktable. The dog jumped up briefly and resettled. The old instrument-maker laid the flute case down directly under the lamp. Unsnapping the bronze clasps, he opened it. He wasn't sure if the gasp he heard came from the visitor or from himself.

No matter how many times he'd opened the case since the day Derek brought it to him, Morris was unprepared for its exquisite beauty. Under the lamp the reddish gold of the tubing glowed against the dark green velvet. Crown gold it was, seventy-five percent gold alloyed with silver and copper. Copper for the rosy color. Morris held up the head joint to show the single cabochon ruby at the stopper end. He rolled it in his hands to show the elaborate design engraved upon the silver embouchure plate.

Gently replacing the head joint in its velvety bed, Morris lifted the middle joint and turned it to catch the light. More engraving, a riot of inlaid colored enamel; not the pale blues and pinks of most nineteenth and early twentieth century enamelers, but the resplendent yellows, mauves, salmon, and greens that could have come only from the workshops of Carl Fabergé.

Five of the keys were closed with little cat's-eyes in removable settings. When Morris was a boy at home struggling with flute lessons, he'd asked Father for a flute with closed keys. He could still hear the anger and indignation in his voice. Closed holes are for amateurs! Your brother would never play a closed-hole flute!

All these years later the criticism stung. "Your brother this." "Your brother, that." Brother, indeed. Guttersnipe, more like. Cuckoo in the nest, shoving out the trueborn son.

The young man reached out, but Morris snatched the piece away and put it back into the case and snapped the lid shut. He could hardly imagine what the flute would bring in a legitimate auction at Christie's. In the 1960s an American collector had paid over a million for a single Fabergé egg. No telling what one would go for now. The flute had to be worth at least ten of the eggs.

"There," Morris snapped. "You've seen it."

"It's breathtaking, but I'm not interested in its beauty."

"What then?"

"I have a friend. A flute player. Doctors cannot help him. I believe that this flute could."

"You are a superstitious fool."

Morris put the case back by the telephone and covered it with the cloth and some papers. He'd never believed the story about the flute's healing powers. It had the power to make him play better than he could on any other flute, but healing powers? Poppycock.

"Perhaps," the stranger said, "but I would be willing to pay you a hundred pounds a month for the rest of your life if you would lend me the flute, if only for a fortnight. A week, even. I was told that its healing power is so great that it acts in a short time."

"A hundred quid a month, is it?" Morris studied the face under the hood. The expression was earnest. The words were sincere. Too bad the flute had eluded Morris until he was old and ill. He might have been able to keep it for the Collection, renting the use of it to such fools as this. Too late now. The Buyer was bringing the cash, not literally in a bag, but as paperwork that would transfer the sum of three million American dollars into Morris's name. No questions asked about the flute's provenance. Still, Morris was curious.

"Who is this friend that you would offer so much to heal him?"

The visitor uttered a name. A sharp pain stabbed over Morris's right temple. A sound like a high whine invaded his ears and his breath came rapidly. He clutched at the table, head spinning. That hated name. Never. Not for a hundred thousand pounds a month would he so much as offer a cold cup of water to that hateful man. He felt his knees give way.

"Mr. Duby? Mr. Duby? What is it? Are you all right?"

Morris felt hands clutch his arms, easing him to the floor. He heard the click and whiz of the telephone dial and the frenzied barking of the dog—the last sounds before losing consciousness. And his last thought: the Flute.

****

Above the Atlantic, 23 November 1985

Sallie settled into her seat on the 5:30 plane to London. She'd asked for a window seat, assuming it would be an advantage to be able to look out. The aisle and middle seats in her row were still empty. Passengers streamed past her, struggling with their bags. She hoped that the passengers who had the seats next to hers would be congenial companions for the eight-hour flight from Dallas to Gatwick. Maybe one would be a good-looking single guy.

Sighing deeply, Sallie tried to grasp the idea that she was really on her way to London. She'd come close all those years ago. Even when they'd started getting serious, she'd told Nick she still planned to go to England before the wedding. He'd offered no objection. Said he understood how she'd want to fulfill a goal she'd set before meeting him. But then the chipping away began, the mild reproaches, the if-you-really-loved-me's. In the end, the trip to England dissipated, along with all the other pre-Nick dreams and post-Nick expectations.

Sallie shook her head so violently that her hair whipped against her face. *Nick is dead, dammit. Isn't it time you stopped letting him control your thoughts?* Her seat shook, jolting her out of the bitter memories of her youthful stupidity. A large man in a boxy red plaid overshirt had dropped a carry-on bag onto the empty aisle seat and a balled-up raincoat and briefcase onto the middle seat. He was squinting at a boarding pass.

"Looks like this is me." Without looking at Sallie, he shoved a coffee cup at her. "Hold this a minute, little lady." Then he rared back into the aisle, stopping traffic while he manhandled the carry-on into the overhead bin. His head still out of sight, he flailed a hand over the aisle seat. "O.K., little lady, now the raincoat."

Clod! Sallie handed him the coat. He shoved it into the bin after the carry-on and then dropped onto the end seat, sending shock waves through the row. Still without looking at her, he placed the briefcase under the seat in front of him and leaned back. Sallie's feelings of happy anticipation shrank into a ball of annoyance centered in her stomach. Eight hours next to a rude chauvinistic pig. Maybe someone better would come for the middle seat. Finally, he turned to make eye contact, and Sallie's mouth opened in amazement.

He was a James Garner look-alike! Gleaming black hair, square jaw, dazzling smile.

"Name's Harry Slocum," he said. "You are?"

Sallie closed her mouth and proffered her hand. "Hi. Sallie Dunbar."

The eye contact was short-lived. He threw his head back against the headrest, his eyes staring unfocused in the direction of the reading light/air vent console above them as he groped down the side of his seat. Sallie assumed he was feeling for the lever that moved the seat back and forth. He found it and shoved the seat back as far as it would go. Behind them, a woman yelped. "Sir! Sir! Could you move your seat forward a little?"

Slocum made a show of complying, but all the seat

did was bounce a little. Sallie leaned against the window, instinctively trying to distance herself from him. She felt foolish for having offered to shake hands. She never did feel comfortable offering her hand to men. To women either. Thirty-three years old and a teacher who controlled her classroom with an iron hand, but when it came to meeting people at large, she was what her students would call lame.

Fishing in the pocket on the seat in front of her, Sallie pulled out the flight magazine and flipped through it. The heck with Harry Slocum. She had been hoping to meet an attractive man on this trip, but he obviously wasn't the one, no matter how much he resembled James Garner. She'd be in London for a week. Surely she'd meet someone more civil than this lout. What a waste of looks.

An explosive sound made Sallie jump and jerk her head toward the source. An attendant was moving along the aisle shutting the overhead bins. Most of the passengers were seated now, giving her a better view of the plane's interior. She was astounded at the number of people. If the 747 went down, it would be as if a small town had perished. Great! Now she was thinking like her mother. Why do you want to waste all that money? What if the plane crashes? You could be murdered by a terrorist like that poor man on the cruise ship Achilles Something. You won't know anyone there. You'll get lost.

Momma had still been trying to talk her out of the trip as she climbed into the airport shuttle that morning, but, like Christian in *The Pilgrim's Progress*, Sallie put her fingers in her ears—figuratively of course— determined not to be called back from her journey. She laughed to herself. Like the fictional character, she was in search of salvation of a kind, or at least a respite from the dreary sameness of her life in DeSoto Springs.

Two blue-uniformed attendants stationed themselves near the bulkhead between Economy and Business Class. Sallie paid strict attention as they mimed recorded emergency instructions. She touched her seat cushion at the mention of flotation devices and cast an anxious look above her head to see if she could tell where the yellow oxygen masks would emerge. When the demonstration was over, she slipped the instruction card back into the seat pocket and leaned back. That's when she became aware of Slocum regarding her with an expression of amusement.

"First-time flier?"

Her face grew warm. She still felt rebuffed and didn't want to be friendly, but she was too well brought-up to ignore him.

"First time out of the country," she said. "I have flown before." He didn't have to know that this was only the second time. The year before, she'd attended a teachers' conference in Washington DC.

Sallie studied his face. Eyes set a little closer together than Rockford's. Laugh crinkles at the corners. Nose had been broken. Football probably. Had the build for it, though running a little to fat. His belt, if he was wearing one, was out of sight under belly bulge. In his late forties, probably, with thick black hair carefully combed and held in place with shiny hair gel. A few strands falling over his forehead gave him a boyish look.

"Business or pleasure?" he asked.

Lost for context, Sallie stared at him with what was

surely a dopey expression.

"Your trip," he prompted. "Business or pleasure?"

"Oh. Pleasure, I suppose. At least I expect to enjoy myself." She'd intended to let the conversation stall, but, predictably, she continued it with a reciprocal question.

"What about you?"

"Business. I'm headed to a convention. Work-related."

"What kind of work?"

Slocum leaned back, his eyes half-closed. He hesitated a beat before answering. "Musician. I'm a musician. I'm heading to the IOFA convention in London." He pronounced the initials like a word rhyming with "sofa," I-OFA. Sallie's surprise spoiled her efforts to remain aloof.

"What a coincidence! So am I!"

It was his turn to express surprise. "Really? What do you play? Oboe or flute?"

"Flute," she said, feeling like a fraud. She looked him over again. It probably wasn't fair to judge him by that first impression with the raincoat. They were both going to the same place in London. And he did look like James Garner.

"Where do you play?" he asked.

"Oh, I'm not a professional musician. Just an amateur. I probably have no business going to a flute convention at all, but the group rates for the hotel and the flight were so much less expensive than I could get traveling on my own, I couldn't resist. All I really want is to see a little of London."

Harry smiled. He had a really nice smile. "Well then, what do you do for a living?"

"I'm an English teacher."

Harry gave an exaggerated shudder. "Uh-oh. Guess I'd better watch what I say."

Sallie smiled mechanically. She was used to this kind of reaction to her profession. Like Kipling's Elephant's Child, she was hot, but not at all astonished. "Don't worry," she said. "I don't try to correct the speech of anyone but my students." They sat in awkward silence for a few seconds. Then, in an effort to show she hadn't been insulted, Sallie asked what instrument he played.

"How about you? Oboe or flute?" Sallie didn't wait for an answer, however, because at that moment the plane's engines throbbed and more explosions signaled the attendants' final walk down the aisles, slamming the overhead compartments. No one had claimed the middle seat, so she retrieved the shoulder bag she'd stowed under the seat in front of her and put it where it would be handier. She took a jumbo-sized package of Big Red gum from the outside pocket in preparation for take-off. The first time she'd flown, she'd suffered a stopped-up ear for weeks afterwards. This time she'd come prepared. She smiled at the thought of how her eighth-graders would react to the sight of her jaws working furiously as the plane gathered speed down the runway. One of their names for her was "the Gum Nazi." Nobody chewed gum in "Miz" Dunbar's room. She'd once made a guest speaker spit his out.

Sallie felt a touch on her hand. "You can open your eyes now," Slocum said. "We've reached flying altitude."

"It's not the flying that scares me," Sallie said, and spat the gum into its wrapper. "It's the going up and coming down."

"Married?" Harry asked.

"Widowed."

"Sorry."

"It's been three years," Sallie said quickly. She was as uncomfortable as ever with the assumption that she was grieved by an event that had improved her life a thousand percent. "You?"

"Divorced."

They sat in silence for a while. Sallie caught the smell of his aftershave, something like Old Spice, but not quite. She liked it.

"Ever heard Bernini play before?" Slocum asked. Sallie must have looked puzzled. "The featured soloist," he prompted. "Alan Bernini. At the convention."

"Oh. I must have seen his name in the convention materials, but no, I'd not heard of him before."

"He'll be playing the *Syrinx*." Slocum looked at her closely, as if expecting her to react to the name of the piece. When she remained silent, he prompted her some more. "Debussy? *Syrinx*?"

Sallie shrugged.

"I'm afraid I don't know it."

"It's one of the most difficult solo pieces for flute. Truffaut was famous for it."

Again Sallie greeted Harry's information with what she knew had to be a blank stare.

"You really don't know much about the flute scene, do you?"

A fresh flash of annoyance sent the heat to Sallie's face. There was that tone of condescension he'd used when claiming his seat.

"I told you, I don't pretend to be anything but an amateur." She counted to ten. When she spoke again, her voice was normal. "You never did say whether you play oboe or flute." Slocum smiled as if enjoying a private joke.

"Flute," he said emphatically. "I play the flute."

"With an orchestra?"

He nodded.

"Which one?"

"Ever hear of the California Symphony?"

"No."

"Figured you wouldn't have."

Harry's whole manner changed. Where before he'd been cautious about what he said, answering only to specific questions, he became garrulous. He told her he lived in San Francisco and played first flute with the California Symphony there. He mentioned flutists she'd never heard of and told her what kind of flutes they played and how much they were worth. He seemed to be more interested in flutes than in music, rhapsodizing about William Bennett's "Louis Lot" and James Galway's "gold Muramatsu" and telling her in pounds and dollars how much had been paid for each.

"Betcha didn't know flutes could cost so much." He reached across the empty seat and poked her in the arm with a thick forefinger. "I know a guy had a $9,000 Muramatsu stolen from him last year in Santa Monica. Poor slob hadn't insured it. Hell, he hadn't even finished paying for it."

Sallie tried to think of something she could contribute to the conversation. She thought of the beautiful flute on the conference poster and what she'd read about it in the IOFA magazine.

"How much do you suppose the Fabergé Flute is worth?" she asked.

"The whatsit flute?"

"The Fabergé Flute."

"Never heard of it."

Sallie reached into her carry-on and fished out the IOFA magazine.

"Here," she said, turning to the article. "It's in an interview with a man called Morris Duby. He runs a flute museum in London. He says he has collected some of the most unusual flutes in the world, but what would make it complete is the Fabergé Flute. There's a special sidebar about it. It was made by Fabergé for Nicholas II, the last Russian Tsar." Sallie thrust the magazine at Slocum, but he waved it away.

"Sorry," he said. "Gotta check out the head."

When Harry came back, the conversation returned to his litany of notable flutists and their instruments. Sallie wanted to talk about the Fabergé Flute, but he didn't. Bored with the catalogue of expensive flutes, she tried to change the subject. "Will you be performing at the conference?"

"Huh? Nah. It's all politics who gets on the schedule for those things. Bernini, now, people are always asking him to play."

Sallie frowned, trying to remember where she'd heard the name Bernini.

"Alan Bernini. Remember? The featured soloist at the convention. Plays a platinum flute worth $70,000. Wouldn't I just like to get my hands on that one! They say he's the next Truffaut." Harry didn't wait for Sallie to ask him to explain who Truffaut was. "Truffaut's an old guy, about the age of Marcel Moyse—Moyse is a famous flutist too. Truffaut doesn't play anymore. Had a stroke a couple of years ago. Messed up his facial muscles. You can hardly understand a word he says. Like I said, his signature piece was Debussy's *Syrinx*. Now he can't play 'Twinkle, Twinkle, Little Star.' "

The one-sided conversation droned on, Sallie drifting in and out of sleep, until the evening meal.

Sallie took a single miniature bottle of wine, but Harry put away three or four before settling down to sleep out the remainder of the flight. Once he was asleep, Sallie's own drowsiness left her. She rummaged in what she called her "Needments bag" in the seat between them. Sallie smiled to herself. One of the things that used to drive Nick crazy was the way she associated ordinary things with literature. She called the well supplied shoulder bag she carried everywhere her "bag of Needments" after the line about Una's dwarf in *The Faerie Queene*:

Behind her far away a Dwarf did lag,
That lazy seemed in being ever last,
Or wearied with bearing of her bag
Of Needments at his back.

Sallie pulled out the only book she'd brought, a thick, one-volume edition of Jane Austen's novels. She'd debated between taking several small paperbacks but decided that one big book would be easier to keep up with than several small ones. She hadn't anticipated how awkward it would be to hold such a heavy book in the cramped economy class seat. She opened it to *Northanger Abbey*.

An hour or so later, Sallie put away the book, too sleepy to continue. She cast another speculative glance at Harry. The broad shoulders and plaid overshirt made him look more like a lumberjack than a flutist. He'd made a bad first impression, but first impressions could be misleading. It would be nice to have an acquaintance at the convention. She decided to reserve judgment. After all, the man was a flutist. Granted, he was bossy and sarcastic, but how coarse could anyone be who played the flute? And he wasn't married.

Chapter Three

A London hospital, 24 November 1985

Morris Duby woke to the smell of antiseptic and the sound of hushed voices. He lay in a curtained-off hospital bed.

His thoughts fluttered disconnected for a moment until they took shape around the last thing he remembered. "The Flute!" The young man with the hood and the funny eyes. Talking about healing. Morris struggled to sit up. "Damned bloke in the hooded jacket probably took it," he shouted.

A nursing sister pushed through the curtains that surrounded his bed and beamed a big smile at him. Her two front teeth were as broad as a pair of clarinet reeds. "Are we feeling better," she asked in a sing-song hospitally voice.

Morris felt his lip curl. "I don't know about you," he snapped, "but I feel like bloody hell." He tried to swing his legs over the edge of the bed, but they struck a railing. "Let me out of here," he shouted. "I've got to go home. I've got to see to something."

"There, there, Mr. Duby," she said. "You're quite ill and need to rest. I'll be happy to phone someone for you."

Phone someone. Who the hell could he trust with the business of the Flute? The nursing sister waved a piece of paper under his nose. "We found this in your wallet."

There was that "we" again.

"It's a list of names and phone numbers," she cooed. "Which shall I call?"

Morris squinted at the writing on the paper. Last time he was in hospital the admitting clerk made him come up with three people to notify in an emergency. Friends or relatives. He didn't have any friends or relatives. He'd had a brother once. Or thought he had. The names on the list were all customers. Strangers, really. Too bad the American wasn't in London. He might be able to trust him.

The summer before, Morris had taken the American on as an apprentice in instrument repair. For the money. The American had been in some kind of accident and couldn't do what he'd been doing any longer. Needed to learn a trade. Said he'd always wanted to learn instrument repair and had heard about Morris. If he were in London, he'd trust him to go to his house and check on the Flute. But he supposed the American was back home in Chicago. Morris needed somebody now. He stabbed a finger at the first name on the list.

"Phone that one," he told the sister. "If he doesn't answer, phone the next one."

****

Alan Bernini, featured soloist for the IOFA convention, lay beside his lover on the bed of the convention hotel, thinking idly of where he and Teddy might go for supper. He'd taken the train into London from his house in Royal Tunbridge Wells on Friday afternoon so as to be at the convention hotel when

Teddy got there.

That had not been the original plan. The original plan was for Teddy to travel straight to Tunbridge from Heathrow. The convention didn't begin until Monday, so they would spend the weekend in the country and travel into London Sunday night. But then the Maestro asked Teddy to meet him at the hotel "on the weekend," but neglected to give a time of arrival. Not wishing to inconvenience the Maestro, Teddy decided to go directly to the hotel, skipping Tunbridge altogether. Now, here it was, four o'clock in the afternoon on Sunday, and the Maestro had yet to arrive.

Bernini chided himself for feeling resentment. After eight years in their relationship, he felt certain he needn't fear a romantic rival, but sometimes he felt a twinge of jealousy toward the Maestro.

On the bed beside him, Teddy murmured into his ear. "How about dinner at Simpson's-in-the-Strand? After all this exercise, I could use some good Scottish beef."

"Simpson's! You know it'll cost pounds and pounds."

"Not to worry. The father of one of the students auditioning for the Hoffman Prize has offered to pay me £100 a pop for as many lessons as I can fit in before the convention finals."

"Never!"

"Hope to die. I've already given the boy two lessons. The father wanted me to give one this afternoon, but I told him I had a pressing engagement."

"Very pressing," Bernini agreed. He probed Teddy's ear with his tongue, and they were on the way to another bout of exercise when the phone in the other room rang. Not wishing to call attention to their relationship by sharing accommodations, they'd booked connecting rooms. The phone was ringing in Bernini's room.

"Blast." They said it at the same time.

"Let it ring," Bernini said.

Teddy murmured assent and nuzzled Bernini's jaw, but then, abruptly, he scrambled to a sitting position. "It could be the Maestro."

"Wouldn't he ring your room and not mine?"

"Maybe they mixed us up at the desk. You'd better go answer it."

Bernini sighed and got up. "Very well." The moment had passed. "It'll probably stop ringing as soon as I get to it."

The ringing continued until Bernini got there, but it wasn't the Maestro. It was a nursing sister from the London Hospital in Whitechapel, calling on behalf of Morris Duby.

"Duby?" Bernini's first impulse was to refuse. It wasn't as if he had any personal connection to the old man. Duby was his instrument repairman. Running to his hospital bedside hardly qualified as an obligation.

As if sensing his thoughts from the other end of the line, the nursing sister spoke quickly. "You're the third name on his list of who to call in an emergency, Mr. Bernini. The first two refused to come. Said he's nothing to them."

Bernini hesitated. Going would mean a long train or bus ride or expensive taxi fare to the East End, standing around in hospital corridors, and possibly having to go to Duby's house to feed the dog. He seemed to recall that the old man had a dog.

The sister's next words put an end to his hesitation.

"The old boy hasn't any blood relations at all, sir. And yours is the last name on the list."

Bernini remembered with a pang of sadness how his own family had cut him off when they found out about Teddy. For a moment he pictured himself alone at the end, in some barren hospital room. If anything happened to Teddy, he'd have no one. "I'll be there as soon as possible."

Teddy was standing by the bed when he returned to the other room. "I heard what you said. Do I take it that I may as well give another hundred-quid lesson?"

"I'm sorry, dear one." Bernini put his arms around his friend. "It's old Duby the instrument maker. He's been taken to hospital and has no one else."

Teddy returned the embrace. "The old boy needs you. I wouldn't expect you to do anything less."

****

The taxi driver dropped Bernini outside the hospital's main entrance. He hated hospitals with their sterile surroundings, antiseptic smells, and aura of suffering.

A desk clerk directed him to a four-bed bay where Mr. Duby lay in a narrow curtained enclosure hooked up to an array of tubes and wires. The old man lay staring at the ceiling. Bernini went to the side of the bed and looked down. Duby's milky gray eyes fixed on his face, and one claw-like hand reached over the railing and clutched his wrist with unexpected strength.

"Mr. Bernini! I'm glad it's you that's come. You'll understand the importance of what I have to tell you."

Bernini listened, first in humoring disbelief, then, beginning to realize that the old man might not be raving, in rapt excitement. Duby claimed to have recovered the Fabergé Flute.

Bernini had been chasing the Fabergé Flute for two decades, ever since coming across a reference to it in an old French newspaper. He'd interviewed dozens of people connected with the Fabergé company and with more than one government. The consensus was that if the flute did exist and were ever found, more than one claimant would come forward. He looked down at the old man in the bed and shook his head in wonderment. He knew from the recent article in the IOFA magazine that Duby believed in the flute's existence, but he never dreamed that he could possibly have acquired it. Against all probability, it had been brought to the old man's East End doorstep by a neighborhood tough. The Fabergé Flute. In England. Bernini's heart pounded. He struggled to conceal his excitement.

The old man's eyes glittered in their sunken sockets. "I've a right to it. My father brought it home from one of his sales trips. He would have given it to me, but…" Duby paused a long time before finishing. "…things happened."

Bernini chose his words carefully. "If this is the flute that disappeared during the Russian Revolution, Mr. Duby, several individuals and at least two governments claim ownership. For starters, the Russians. Fabergé company records show that it was commissioned as a gift for Tsar Nicholas."

"And they'll see that he gets it, I suppose." Duby's cackling laugh turned into a cough.

"Fabergé's heirs also claim it," Bernini said patiently, helping the old man to a sip of water. "According to them, Carl Fabergé took it with him when he fled St. Petersburg after the October Revolution in 1917."

Duby uttered a triumphant snort. "That should prove that the Russian government has no claim to it. By then the Tsar had abdicated. His days were numbered. He never had a hope of seeing the flute, so how could it belong to him?"

"What about the jeweler's heirs?"

"What of them? If Fabergé accepted the commission to make it, you can be sure he got plenty of money up front. If the Flute wasn't with his things when he died, the heirs have no more right to it than Russians."

Bernini nodded thoughtfully. "Did your neighbor boy say where he'd got it?"

The old man broke into a wet cough. Bernini held the yellow plastic crescent tray for him to spit.

"Of course he didn't," Duby croaked as soon as he could speak. "But it's not too hard to guess, is it? His old man's a thief. I reckon he picked up the flute along with other artsy stuff breaking into some stately home. He gave the flute to his spawn or the kid nicked it from him."

"There's an American claimant as well," Bernini said.

Another coughing spell choked the old man. When he could speak, he shouted. "How could an American claim it? It's never been to America."

"According to the claimant, his grand-uncle provided Fabergé with the gold and jewels from which the flute was made."

Duby squeezed Bernini's wrist. The bony fingers hurt. "Please. None of these people has a claim to

39

compare to mine. None of them has even seen it. My father brought that flute home from his travels when I was a boy. I took possession of it when I was fourteen years old. It was stolen from me. And now it has come back to me. It's mine."

Bernini disengaged his hand and laid it over Duby's. He knew the old man would not be swayed by any claim but his own, but he had to state one more, the one that mattered most to him.

"The British government also claims the flute, Mr. Duby. I've been told by someone at the Home Office that Carl Fabergé gave the flute to the British in gratitude for a consulate's help in getting him and his family to safety."

Bernini's mind raced. If the British could claim it, the flute would be a national treasure. And he would get the credit for securing it. He tried to keep the whine out of his voice. "Wouldn't you like to see your flute on display in the British Museum? Wouldn't you like for everyone to be able to see it? Think of it, Mr. Duby. Your name, like Mrs. Pretty's on the Sutton Hoo Treasure, 'benefactor to a grateful nation.' "

"Bother the nation." The old man's eyes filled with tears. "The Collection is what matters. I have a buyer who will give me enough money for that one flute to set up a museum to preserve the entire Collection after I'm dead. I can't just give it away."

"I know people," Bernini said, "people in the government. I've worked with them on cultural projects. I'm certain they would agree that something as unusual and precious as the Fabergé Flute would merit a special display in the British Museum."

The old man's fingers found their way around

Bernini's wrist again. Bernini flinched, but continued to cajole in a quiet, steady voice. He'd seen Duby's flute collection. It contained several interesting specimens. He persisted.

"What if the finer pieces of your collection could be included in an exhibit alongside the Fabergé Flute? Would you be willing to turn it over to the government if that could be arranged?"

"The Collection would remain intact?"

"That could be made a condition of your gift."

Duby let his hand fall back onto the bed. His entire body shuddered with the sigh he drew. "Go to my house. The flute is on my workbench, by the telephone. It's covered with papers and polishing cloths. It's in a green leather case, very old, beautifully embossed."

Bernini almost ran from the hospital. The Fabergé Flute for Britain. A grateful nation might just reward the man who had made it happen. He wondered if there would be time to add another name to the Queen's list of New Year's Honors. Sir Alan. To think he'd almost told the nursing sister to phone somebody else.

Bernini's feelings of elation lasted until he arrived at Duby's house and found the beautifully embossed case lying open and empty on the floor of the workshop. The next-door neighbor, a slovenly woman wearing house slippers with holes cut out for her bunions, could provide little information, just that Duby's dog had refused to let the ambulance attendants go in at first. Then a man in a "foreign-looking hat" had come along and talked to the dog and it hushed up "just like that." Then the ambulance men got old Duby and took him away. For all she knew, they'd taken the dog as well.

His stomach a lump of lead, Bernini thanked the woman and directed his steps back to the high street where he found a taxi. So close, but he'd missed it. Still, he couldn't help feeling a little fillip of excitement. The Fabergé Flute was not the myth so many of his colleagues insisted it was. Teddy would be amazed.

****

Eager to tell Teddy about the flute and too excited to wait for the elevator, Bernini took the stairs to the fourth floor. Unlocking the door to his room in a fever, he crossed to the connecting door and turned the knob two or three times before realizing the door was locked from the other side. Knuckles poised, he stopped, arrested by the sound of voices, followed by the muffled click of a softly closing door. Whoever had been in Teddy's room had gone into the hall.

Jealousy had never been a factor in Bernini's relationship with Teddy, but at the moment it flooded his throat with the taste of bile. He knocked. After a few ticks, the door opened.

"Alan! You're back. How is the old boy?"

As they embraced, Bernini looked over the other man's shoulder and scanned the room behind him. Teddy had remade the bed since their afternoon interlude, but the bedspread was slightly disarranged, as if someone had been sitting on the edge of the bed.

"I thought I heard you talking to someone. Anyone I know?"

Teddy gestured at the dresser. "Must have been the radio. I had it on a minute to see if I could catch tomorrow's weather. So tell me about your Mr. Duby. Is it very bad?"

The Fabergé Flute lost all importance as Bernini wrestled with the unfamiliar idea that his lover could be capable of infidelity. They'd been together for nearly eight years. Bernini had alienated his family over what he expected to be a lifelong relationship.

"Duby seemed frail and weak, but I think he'll survive. I shouldn't wonder if he has to go into a nursing facility, though, at least for a while." The news he'd been so eager to tell Teddy stuck in his throat. The locked door. The voices. Radio be damned. Someone had been in there. He forced himself to make conversation.

"So, how was the lesson? Is the child as good as the father thinks?"

"Pretty good."

"Is the Maestro here yet?"

"He'll be here later tonight. He's asked me to set up a tape recorder for him in his room. I was just about to go do it. Says he wants to listen to some of his old recordings." Teddy glanced at the door, then at the bed and back again to the door. "So, I reckon I'd better go get that done. His room's on this floor too, but way at the other end."

Bernini sensed that Teddy was waiting for him to leave. "Oh, right then. I'd better go back to my room. You'll be wanting to lock the joining door again."

"No! Not at all. No." Teddy picked up an old-fashioned Grundig tape recorder and opened the door. "Don't know how I happened to lock it earlier." He mimed a kiss. "Back later."

Bernini stared at the closing door until the lock clicked. Mystified, he glanced around Teddy's room. The rumpled bed offended his sense of order, so he went over to smooth the covers. His hand encountered something solid under the spread. He reached underneath and pulled out a flute case. Bernini knew that Teddy's flute, like his own, was locked away in the convention security room. He looked with distaste at the cheap imitation leather case, worn white at the corners, its handle repaired with wire. Having no interest in seeing whatever piece of junk lay inside, he placed the case on the dresser next to the radio and finished straightening the bed. He was going to leave it at that, but the thought occurred that some clue to the owner of the shabby case might be found inside. He went back to the dresser and opened it.

"My God!"

Bernini stared at the incongruous contents, his eyes dazzled by the rich gleaming colors wakened to life by the overhead light. He knew without any doubt that he was looking at the Fabergé Flute.

He gazed at it, trying to make sense of its presence in Teddy's room. Surely Teddy hadn't stolen it from Duby's workshop. Yet here it was. Teddy would have told him about something this momentous. Yet he hadn't.

Staggering, the flute case still in his hands, Bernini returned to his own room and locked the connecting door from his side. He sank down on the edge of the bed. Was it possible that Teddy hadn't known it was there? Could whoever was in his room have slipped it under the covers without his knowing? What nonsense! Teddy must have concealed it there before opening the door. He knew it was there and didn't want Bernini to know.

His mind in turmoil, Bernini found himself

wanting a drink, something strong to settle his nerves. He wished this were the kind of hotel that supplied liquor chests in the rooms. He looked at the treasure lying across his knees. He brushed his fingertips across the head joint, hardly daring to touch it. It must be his imagination, but the rosy gold felt warm. He gazed at it for another moment before shutting the case. He couldn't check it into the security room. No one would be on duty at this hour. Besides, if Teddy had stolen it, Bernini didn't want to implicate himself by checking it in under his own name.

Too agitated to think, Bernini stood and paced. He had to speak to Teddy but was too agitated to wait for him to come back. God, he wanted a drink. He'd hardly touched anything but wine and beer during the past eight years, but now the old craving clamored to be satisfied. The hotel bar might be open. Having been abroad for the past six months, he was finding it difficult to remember the ins and outs of the licensing laws.

The pacing stopped. Bernini had made a decision. The flute would not leave his possession until he got it to a safe place. He grasped the case by the handle, but immediately thought better of it. Better not trust the repair. His glance fell on the goodie bag he'd received for the convention, a small canvas bag with the silly convention logo. He emptied the tacky contents onto the bed. A sound came from the next room. Teddy was back, unlocking the door from the hall. Any second he'd be turning the handle of the connecting door.

Bernini couldn't face the inevitable confrontation. He needed a drink first. Grabbing the flute case and the canvas bag, he waited until he heard Teddy shut the hall door. Then he slipped out of his own room and hurried to the elevator.

Chapter Four

Sunday, 24 November 1985, Central London, the Strand

Bossy or not, Harry Slocum proved an asset at Gatwick as he steered Sallie through the ordeal of disembarkation. He swung her second shoulder bag down from the overhead bin and used his broad body to funnel her into the slow shuffle toward the plane's exit door. He led her confidently through the correct custom lines and showed her where she could change traveler's checks into English money. He kept her calm and entertained when a bomb scare caused the police to evacuate part of the airport, detaining them until late afternoon. By the time he'd helped her hoist her bags up the steep steps of the train to Victoria Station, she'd completely forgiven him for the rudeness and arrogance he'd shown on the airplane. She didn't know how she would have managed without him.

From Victoria they shared a taxi to the convention hotel in the Strand, not far from the famous Savoy Hotel. Harry had two large bags of his own, so Sallie didn't expect him to manage hers as well. While he paid the taxi driver, she wrestled the two big bags and the two shoulder bags as far as the lobby. The strap of the bag containing her flute and stand dug painfully into her shoulder. She comforted herself with the thought

47

that in a few minutes she'd be able to turn the heavy lifting over to a bellhop. She let the shoulder bags slide to the floor and got her passport and papers out of the fanny pack at her waist.

The desk was staffed by a tall black youngster who looked just like Pooky Washington, one of Sallie's ninth-graders. She was absolutely enchanted to hear a Cockney accent coming out of a Pooky look-alike. Elbows on the check-in desk, he rested his chin on his clasped hands as if to demonstrate his inability to help them with their luggage.

"Between shifts now, aren't we? Be a hour 'fore anyone can take up your bags, won't it?"

Sallie didn't want to wait. She took a deep breath, readjusted the shoulder straps, and braced for the ordeal of getting the luggage from the desk to her room.

Sallie and Slocum squeezed into the narrow elevator. Both their rooms were on the fourth floor, but at opposite ends. The midway point was the elevator lobby.

"Wait here," Harry said. "I'll drop my stuff and come back to help you with yours."

Not wishing to impose, Sallie ignored his instructions and set out on her own. The straps digging into her shoulders had become so painful that she tried balancing a bag on each suitcase, but they kept sliding off. Harry rejoined her before she'd made it halfway to her room. He took the handles of both suitcases and lifted one of the bags to his own shoulder.

"Whatcha got in this one, bricks?" By the time she unlocked the hotel room door, she was strung to the breaking point with frustration and fatigue. All she could think of was getting unharnessed from the strap digging into her neck and shoulder. She let the bag drop onto the bed.

"Thanks, Harry," she said, rubbing her shoulder. "Maybe next time I'll listen when someone tells me to take more money than I think I'll need and fewer clothes." All she wanted to do was drop down next to her bag and sleep for a couple of days.

Harry came close and kneaded her shoulders. She felt a twinge of erotic pleasure and speculated idly whether he might be the "shipboard romance" Momma warned her against. He concluded the brief massage with a comradely slap on the back.

"There." He walked to the door and smiled that Rockford smile. "You could use a drink even more than me, Sallie, and I sure can use one. Come on, I'll show you an honest-to-goodness London pub."

Pub. Suddenly rest became irrelevant. She could rest when she got back to Arkansas. "Give me some time to catch my breath and clean up a little."

Harry looked at his watch. "I'll meet you in the lobby at six-thirty."

Sallie hurried to get ready to join Harry for their pub excursion, washing her face and lightening her bag of Needments by dumping *The Complete Jane Austen* and folder of uncorrected essays onto the bed. Then she slung the strap over her shoulder and left the room.

A man stood in front of the elevator, a dapper little man in a blue blazer, white turtleneck, and gray slacks with knife-edge creases. He was hunched over, concentrating on something in his hands. The elevator button wasn't lighted so Sallie reached around him and pressed it. Even then, he didn't look up. She could see that he was struggling to push a flute case past the zippered opening of a canvas bag. She could understand why he might want to get it out of sight. It was a nasty-looking thing that not even an amateur like her would keep a flute in. Its handle had been repaired at one side with what looked like dirty string. Besides concealing it, putting it in the bag would eliminate the danger of carrying it by the damaged handle.

A soft grunt escaped the man's lips as he finally succeeded and zipped the bag shut, the stretched canvas showing the shape of the case. He became aware of Sallie and looked up. He recoiled, clearly startled. Sallie gasped when she saw his face.

He was beautiful, with the kind of beauty one associates with a Greek statue. His sandy hair looked sculpted, the slightly wavy hair fitting the contours of his head as if it had been painted on. His head and features were perfect, but he was at least two inches shorter than Sallie's five-three. His head, so perfectly shaped, looked too big for the rest of his body.

"Hello," Sallie said.

The beautiful head jerked backward. "Oh, I say, uh, hello. I was just, excuse me, I find I don't need the lift after all." As the elevator door glided open, the man nodded to Sallie and retreated. The doors jerked shut. She hoped that Harry would be waiting for her in the lobby.

Stepping off the elevator, Sallie scanned the lobby for her "date."

No Harry, but a drama in progress by the front desk. Pooky's look-alike had been replaced by a more mature man with a disapproving scowl.

A woman in an emerald green raincoat stood imperiously in the midst of a sea of luggage, like Venus rising from the waves. A little behind her, leaning on a cane and gazing around at nothing in particular, as if to indicate that the drama with the desk clerk had nothing to do with him, lounged a tall, slightly stooped man in a brown trench coat and a black Russian hat with the ear flaps up. At the woman's feet, leash tangled in the luggage, tongue lolling agreeably in a canine grin, sat a small white terrier. A confrontation with the clerk was in progress.

"He's a perfect gentleman, I assure you," the woman rapped out in a crisp, no-nonsense Yankee accent. "He goes everywhere with us, stays where we stay, and no one has ever complained."

Frowning dubiously, the clerk chewed his lower lip.

"You'll have to pay a carpet deposit. And we can't have him disturbing the other guests. Does he bark?"

"Of course, he barks. He's a dog."

"Not to worry," the man in the trench coat offered. "He only barks when provoked."

The clerk shook his head, but relinquished the keys, casting a disapproving look at the dog, which was now noisily engaged in grooming its private parts. "Room 412."

Great. Sallie was in Room 414. A barking dog in the room next to hers. She looked at her watch. Six-forty-five. She'd set it to London time before getting off the plane. Harry had told her to meet him at six-thirty. She whirled at the sound of the elevator bell. The doors slid open and three people got off. Harry was not one of them.

Feeling conspicuous, Sallie decided to explore the lobby. The hotel had two street entrances separated by a large planter. Near the elevator, double glass doors opened onto a side street. A more elaborate main entrance featuring a revolving door flanked by regular push doors opened directly onto the Strand.

The front desk occupied the wall inside the main entrance on the right as one entered. Just past it, the lobby widened into an area with scattered furniture groupings and doorways leading to restrooms, stairways, and the hotel restaurant with the quaint name of "the Hunter's Den."

Sallie looked at her watch. Seven o'clock and still no Harry. When the next hum of the elevator caught her ear, she went back to that part of the foyer, summoning magical thinking on the way. Be on it this time, Slocum. Be on it.

It worked. Harry was on it. And with him was the handsome little man she'd seen upstairs. He had the canvas bag slung across his body bandolier-style. The bag bulged with the outline of the battered case she'd seen him stuff into it.

"There you are, Sallie!" Harry called, as if he'd been the one kept waiting.

Choking back an indignant comment, Sallie joined them, looking pointedly at her watch. If Harry noticed, he gave no sign.

"Sallie Dunbar, meet Alan Bernini."

Alan Bernini. The flute player with the $70,000 flute. Sallie extended her hand, staring at the bag that contained the shabby case. Surely he didn't keep his $70,000 flute in that thing.

"Pleased to meet you," Bernini said. His handshake was more of a slide than a grip. He took a couple of steps and stopped, as if uncertain where he wanted to go.

"Sallie and I are on the way to a pub," Harry said. "Come have a drink with us."

Bernini turned his head, looking for someone or something. The tall, complicated planter did not totally cut off the line of sight between the side and front entrances. Bernini's gaze shifted from one to the other, as if trying to choose which to leave by.

Harry steered him toward the side exit. "Come have a drink with us," he said again.

Bernini pulled away, when the elevator bell announced another arrival. He stiffened and stopped resisting, permitting Harry to propel him toward the side exit.

"Just a quick one, perhaps," he said.

Sallie followed the men out the side door. Glancing back, she saw a tall slim man in a duffle coat with the hood up leave the elevator and hurry across the lobby to the revolving door. Like Bernini, he seemed to be looking for someone.

Chapter Five

The Four Moons was situated two long blocks from the hotel, fronting on the Strand, with an alley entrance marked by a small, lighted sign spelling out PUB in green letters. At the street entrance, Sallie and her companions stepped aside as a group of young people erupted, pulling their jacket hoods up against the misty drizzle. Hooded jackets everywhere.

Next to the front door, a dingy stained-glass window permitted customers to look inside. Sallie could make out enough to see that all the tables visible were occupied, as were the stools along the bar. She doubted they'd find a place to sit.

The laundry blast of hot air that hit them as they entered made Sallie claw at her jacket, desperate to get it off. About twenty tables crammed an area the size of her mother's basement. Finding it impossible to walk in normal fashion between the tables, customers and the two waiters sidled crabwise.

"Yoo-hoo, Mr. Bernini! Over here, Mr. Bernini!"

A high-pitched whiny voice cut through the pub noise. Sallie traced it to a frantically waving gray-haired woman half standing at a table along the back wall. "Yoo-hoo! Mr. Bernini! Come sit with us." The "us" included an elegantly dressed man.

When they'd managed to weave their way to the back, Sallie got a closer look at the woman. Her haircut was a no-nonsense pageboy resembling a silver helmet. In bizarre contrast, her face displayed jet-black eyebrows, bright red lipstick, and white face powder. She looked like a Japanese doll or a fossilized Flapper.

Flapper Lady trapped Bernini's extended hand in both of hers. "I'm Alice Pinkerton, Mr. Bernini, IOFA president and Conference Director this year. We've spoken on the phone several times." The man at the table stood and offered his hand.

"This is Max Paulson," Alice said. "He's at the convention with his extremely gifted son, Orlando." She released Bernini's hand so he could shake with Max, who bowed slightly.

Taller and older than Harry Slocum, Max exuded dignity and wealth. An expensive gray suit matched the silvery gray of his hair. He looked to be in his early sixties, about twenty years too old for Sallie, but definitely attractive. He shook hands all round and resumed his seat. Sallie stowed her shoulder bag under the table.

Harry scooted his chair to make room for the bag. "Why the heck did you bring that thing with you? Don't you have your money in your fanny pack? That thing weighs a ton."

"I did lighten it," Sallie said defensively. Her face grew hot. Explaining was too complicated. She just felt better with her "stuff." Flashlight, Band-Aids, antiseptic wipes—she never knew what might come in useful. "Force of habit, I guess." She turned her attention to the others at the table.

Alice was still gushing over Bernini. "I'm so looking forward to hearing your performance of the *Syrinx*. Maestro Truffaut will be so proud of you." She looked around the table to include everyone in her explanation. "Mr. Bernini is a student of Monsieur Truffaut."

"Was." Bernini said.

Alice showed no sign of having heard him. "Before his stroke and accident," she went on, "the *Syrinx* was Monsieur Truffaut's signature piece." She turned back to Bernini. "The Maestro will be pleased to hear you perform the extremely difficult piece he was famous for. Don't you agree?"

"I can't say whether he will be pleased or not," Bernini said.

Conversation lapsed.

A gaunt elderly waiter arrived with their drinks, slapping down the glasses as if they were too heavy for him to hold. As he placed a beer in front of Sallie, she jerked away to avoid being spattered. He looked so frail that she fought an urge to stand up to give him her seat. He studied their faces, as if committing them to memory. Then, when he noticed that Sallie was looking at him, he moved away.

Sallie lifted her glass and almost spat her first sip of English beer onto the table. She expected beer to be cold. She looked at Harry for his reaction. He was drinking without any apparent surprise so she didn't say anything. Bernini downed his Scotch in two gulps and waved the empty glass in the air.

The elegant Max was drinking red wine. He leaned toward Bernini. "Please don't think me presumptuous, Mr. Bernini, but I would like to ask if you have time to schedule a lesson for my son during the coming week. I brought him to London early for the express purpose of trying to fit in lessons with some of the excellent flutists

I knew would be here for the convention."

Before Bernini could reply, Alice put her oar in.

"Oh yes, do, Mr. Bernini. You must meet Orlando. He is absolutely amazing." As before, she addressed the others with backstory. "Mr. Paulson's foster son Orlando is one of the finalists for the Hoffman fellowship." She put a hand over Paulson's. "This man is a philanthropist, a real saint. He found Orlando living in the streets of Rio and rescued him. He's brought him up as his own son and given him the finest musical training."

Sallie thought she saw a flicker of distaste cross Bernini's face as he looked away from Max to take another glass from the waiter.

"My answer must be 'no,' Mr. Paulson," Bernini said. "My schedule is quite full for the next six days."

Alice Pinkerton continued to dominate the conversation with a nonstop monologue about people Sallie had never heard of. She churned out her words in a stream, like an old-fashioned tickertape machine spitting out an endless strip of paper, leaving no interval for anyone else to insert a remark. Sallie stared at Alice's mouth in fascination, wondering how she breathed. The IOFA magazine had contained an article about a flute technique called "circular breathing." Maybe that's how she did it.

Losing interest in the "conversation," Sallie looked idly around the noisy, smoky room. The eight stools at the bar changed occupants at a rapid rate as places at the tables became available. The only other waiter was the antithesis of theirs, a chubby cheerful youth who looked too young to be in a bar, let alone work in one. Both waiters were in constant motion. The older one tended to hover near the tables after delivering drinks, as if he might be listening in on the customers. At the moment, he was hovering next to a table occupied by two men engaged in earnest head-to-head conversation.

Sallie could see only the back of one of the men but had a good view of the other. Dark, possibly of middle-eastern origin. He looked like a young Omar Sharif. She felt her face grow hot as she realized that she was sizing up every man she saw for romantic potential, like someone in the market for a new car. When you're content with what you're driving, you don't pay attention to other cars, but once you're looking, you notice them all. Becoming aware that "Sharif" was returning her stare, she quickly turned back to her companions.

Alice was still talking. She leaned forward conspiratorially. "I've heard the most delicious rumor." She licked her crimson lips and looked eagerly from face to face. If she'd expected an interested response, she was disappointed. The others returned her excited gaze with indifference. Slocum and Max leaned back easily in their chairs. Bernini sat ramrod straight on the edge of his, like someone waiting for a bus that should arrive at any minute.

When no one responded, Alice tried again. "They say that the Fabergé Flute has been discovered in London and that someone at the conference actually has it in his possession."

Max, who had his handkerchief out to dab his lips, ran it across his forehead before folding it and returning it to his pocket.

Harry Slocum made a scoffing sound. "Fabergé Flute! Everybody knows there's no such thing."

Sallie stared. When she'd mentioned the Fabergé Flute to him on the plane, he'd acted as if he'd never heard of it.

"A myth," Max said.

"Now, Mr. Paulson," Alice said coyly, "I know ever so many people who are convinced it exists. Maestro Truffaut for one."

Max's thin lips formed a condescending smile. "Every in-group has its Flying Dutchman, its Wandering Jew, the elusive Eternal that is out there somewhere, always there, but never caught up with." He cast a people-like-us-know-better look round the table. "The Fabergé Flute is a myth. You can be certain of it."

Pink under the powdered pallor, Alice slapped her head in mock dismay. "Good Heavens! Here I sit squandering time in social niceties when I have a meeting with the audio-visual committee." She stood. "It has been enjoyable, gentlemen," she said, overlooking Sallie in her parting remarks. Her departure left a perceptible sense of relief.

"Insufferable woman!" Max said.

"Must believe everything she reads in the IOFA magazine," Slocum said. "Fabergé Flute, my hind foot." He avoided Sallie's attempt to catch his eye.

Bernini spoke, his voice barely audible against the background sounds of the pub. "It exists."

Goosebumps rose along Sallie's arms. The words echoed Delphine's cryptic remarks that night at band practice back in DeSoto Springs.

Bernini's small body leaned forward, taut with intensity. His eyes took on a faintly wild look. He still had the canvas bag slung bandolier-style across his

59

chest, its strap bunching his natty blazer. He pressed the bag against his chest protectively with a forearm. Sallie remembered the shabby flute case she'd seen him force into the bag. If it contained the $70,000 flute Harry told her about on the plane, it surely deserved a better case.

Another full glass of Scotch had materialized under Bernini's fingers. This time he sipped rather than swigged and turned his attention to Slocum. "How much do you know about Russian history, Mr. Slocum?"

Harry laughed. "No more than necessary. I know they used to have Tsars and now they have Commies. And that Fabergé made fancy eggs, not flutes."

"Fabergé didn't make the flute," Bernini said. "He designed it, as he designed the Easter eggs and other jewelry that came out of his workshops. He employed smiths and technicians to do the actual manufacturing."

"Even if Fabergé designed a flute," Max said, "it couldn't have been more than a trinket, a curiosity, perhaps, but nothing a professional could actually play on—a glorified tin whistle for the Tsarovich."

"It's a real, working flute," Bernini said. "Made by a German instrument-maker who learned the craft from his father who had worked with Boehm in Munich. Fabergé brought him to St. Petersburg especially for the purpose."

"Yes, yes," Max said dismissively. "And he made the flute out of some mysterious magical golden treasure that can do everything but raise the dead. I also read the article."

Bernini's face flushed bright red. The heat of the pub would be enough to account for it, but Bernini was on his fourth Scotch, and Max's sarcasm was clearly ruffling his composure.

"Some do believe that the flute has the power to heal," he said. "Of course that's nonsense. But it was made from the gold and precious stones of a holy relic taken from a church somewhere. The American who brought the materials to Fabergé wouldn't say where he'd got them. He was an American foreign service employee. Before going to Russia, he'd been assigned to a U.S. consulate in Turkey. He knew that the Tsar was an amateur flutist, so he decided to turn the gold and gems—which he'd doubtless stolen somewhere in Turkey—into a magnificent bribe. He was after certain Russian mineral rights."

Slocum guffawed, spraying beer and winking at Sallie.

"How'd you happen onto all this intriguing information, Bernini? At a séance?" Sallie looked away in an attempt to distance herself. Harry was not deterred. "Fabergé Flute my ass! Maybe you can get Sallie to swallow that kind of hocus-pocus, but I'm wise to you."

Bernini's beautiful face took on such a stricken look that Sallie wanted to throw her glass at Harry. How could he be unaware of his outrageous rudeness? Tiny droplets of beer glistened on Bernini's lapel, next to a little jeweled flute pin. She tried to think of something to say that might take the sting out of Slocum's words.

"The Fabergé Flute sounds like a real treasure, Mr. Bernini. Why isn't it in a museum somewhere?"

Bernini's expression softened and he looked as if he might go on with his story. He cast an appreciative look at her, but then his glance shifted to something behind her. He stood abruptly, jostling the table. "I must go." He fished a bill from his pocket, threw it onto the table, and made his way toward the pub's back entrance. He clasped the canvas bag to his chest as if he didn't trust the strap to hold it.

Immediately, Max Paulson stood to leave.

"Orlando will be wondering where I've got to," he said. "So nice to have met all of you." He threw money on the table and exited out the front.

Sallie turned around in her chair, trying to see what had sent Bernini scrambling so quickly. He'd had a view of the front door and the grimy little window next to it.

Just inside the door, a thin man in a duffel coat with the hood up stood looking around. He walked over to the bar and claimed a vacant stool. When the bartender offered to take his order, he shook his head and swiveled the stool. His back to the bar, he scanned the room. For a moment his eyes met Sallie's. The yellow bar light illuminated the planes of his face. Sad, bulging eyes made her think of Tolkien's Gollum, perpetually mourning the loss of his Precious. The face, though young, displayed haggard fatigue. Breaking eye contact, he continued his slow, systematic search of the room.

"Last orders, please, last orders, please." The young waiter threaded his way among the tables, reminding customers that closing time was near. The old waiter was nowhere to be seen.

"Guess we'd better hurry," Sallie said. "Soon they'll be calling, 'Hurry up please, it's time.' " Harry might ridicule her about her lack of flute-related knowledge, but she doubted he'd catch her reference to

The Wasteland.

Harry upended his glass, finishing off the beer in one long draft and glancing at the front door. The table lurched, upsetting Bernini's almost but not quite empty glass, spilling the residue into Harry's lap. He jerked his head around angrily, but when he saw the cause of the impact his attitude instantly altered. A young woman with black lipstick and fishnet stockings had stumbled into their table while rising from her own. Derrière less than an inch from Harry's left ear, she shimmied enthusiastically to adjust her skirt, then staggered against him.

"Sorry!" She giggled. "Somebody's making the bloody floor move." Slocum stood and steadied her, again glancing toward the door.

"There's a nice chap." She laid hold of his arm. "Fancy helping a girl find a taxi?"

"Sure thing," Harry said. Much too eagerly, Sallie thought. He added another bill to the money already on the table and said, "Here, Sallie. That ought to take care of both of us. You can find your way back to the hotel, I guess." Without waiting for a reply, he escorted the young woman out the door, saying something close to her ear that caused her to throw her head back and emit a braying laugh as they exited the pub.

Sallie sipped a little more beer. In less than five minutes, she'd gone from having three men at her table to none. The young waiter, rushing to fill last orders, paused to right the chair the girl in the fishnets had overturned. He glanced at Sallie's unfinished beer but didn't bother to ask if she wanted another round. He scooped up the money and moved on. Like Sallie's erstwhile companions, the other waiter had vanished as well.

A burst of laughter came from the bar, and Sallie fought the irrational feeling that it was directed at her. The young man with the Gollum eyes had gone. The table where the Omar Sharif look-alike and his companion had been sitting was vacant. Fighting old feelings of vulnerability and lack of worth, Sallie pushed away the awful beer and stood to go. Get a grip. If you can fly off to London for Thanksgiving week by yourself, you can find your way back to the hotel alone. She shoved open the heavy door and stepped out onto the busy Strand.

Traffic rolled along the famous thoroughfare as thickly as if the time were eleven in the morning instead of eleven at night. The big black London taxis were busy with the theater trade from nearby Aldwych. Sallie marveled at the way they maneuvered swiftly and aggressively in and out of the lanes of traffic, yet always managed to slam on their brakes if a pedestrian only so much as looked as if he were going to put his foot into a zebra crossing. Back home in DeSoto Springs, even in the marked crosswalks, pedestrians took their lives in their hands as soon as they stepped off the curb. She took a deep breath. The exhaust fumes smelled better than the close, beery air of the overheated pub. She felt a little leap of excitement. London. She was in London!

The momentary depression ebbing, Sallie looked across the street at the façade of the Savoy Hotel. The golden figure of a knight lighted by baby spots stood guard on the marquee. She got the connection at once. Most of her knowledge of English history came from historical fiction and Shakespeare's plays. She knew about the Savoy from Anya Seton's novel *Katherine*, the story of John of Gaunt's mistress. The original Savoy had been Gaunt's fabulously beautiful palace on the Thames—until rebelling peasants burned it down.

Sallie loved the way the English incorporated the past with the present. On her own and away from the intensity of Bernini and the others arguing about the existence of some mythical flute, she remembered that it was England and not the IOFA convention she'd come for. She wished she had six months in London instead of six days. The klaxon of a passing ambulance startled her into an awareness of her immediate surroundings. She might be asking for trouble leaning against a pub wall in the theater district so late at night.

As she stepped off the curb to cross the alley, a figure hurtled out of the darkness, colliding with her and pushing her toward the traffic on the main road. Frightened into a state of infantile terror, she yelled "Momma!" and pushed back at the figure with all her strength, scrambling to get back onto the sidewalk. Heart pounding and breath coming in gasps, Sallie stood frozen as her perceived attacker slumped to the ground at her feet. She looked down on a familiar oversized head.

"Mr. Bernini! What's happened? Are you all right?"

The little flute player accepted her hand and struggled to his feet.

"Did you see anyone run out of the alley ahead of me?"

"No. No one. Just you. What happened?" In the glare of headlights she saw streaks and smudges of dirt on his blazer and slacks. One arm hung limply at his side. The canvas bag was no longer slung across his chest.

"Where's your bag?"

Without replying, Bernini walked a few steps back into the alley. Sallie followed. The green sign saying PUB flickered out, leaving the back doorway in deep shadow.

"Hang on," Sallie said. "I have a flashlight." Fishing in her shoulder bag, she brought out a six-inch flashlight and activated its powerful beam. With Bernini in the lead, they walked down the alley to where it opened onto another street. Sallie played the light along the sides of the alley, but there was nothing to see. When they reached the end of the passageway, Bernini stopped, shoulders sagging in disappointment. "That's that, then," he said.

As they retraced their steps to the Strand, Sallie kept sweeping the flashlight from side to side but saw nothing that looked like the bag Bernini had been carrying.

They returned to the hotel in silence. Outside, Bernini offered his hand, but quickly withdrew it, as if it hurt.

"Excuse me for not shaking hands," he said. "I seem to have banged my fingers."

"You're limping as well," Sallie observed. "Maybe you ought to go to the emergency room."

"No, I'll be fine." Bernini took a step toward the entrance and winced. "I have turned my ankle a bit, but I'm sure it will be all right in the morning."

Sallie rummaged in her bag and pulled out a rolled Ace bandage. "I twisted my ankle at school about a week ago and had to wear it for a few days. I brought it along just in case I had a relapse. Please, take it. It's been washed."

Bernini tried to refuse, but Sallie insisted until he took it.

"So what happened after you left us?" she asked. "Were you mugged?"

"Oh no, nothing like that. I shouldn't have gone out the back way. The steps into the alley were narrow and steep and not very well lit. I suppose I tripped over my own feet. Clumsy of me, but there it is." He looked at her earnestly. "I'd be most grateful if you'd say nothing about it. Embarrassing you know." He looked down at his soiled clothing. "I'm not fit to be seen! I'll go in by way of the service entrance. Good night, Miss Dunbar. And thank you for your help."

Sallie frowned. If he'd simply tripped on the steps, why had he come tearing out of the alley asking if she'd seen anyone? And what had been the purpose of walking the dark alley with the flashlight if he hadn't been searching for something?

"What about the flute?" she asked. "What happened to it?"

Bernini stared at her.

"Flute?"

"The one you had with you in the pub. The one in the canvas bag."

"You're mistaken, Miss Dunbar. My flute is in the security room. I had no flute with me in the pub."

Sallie watched until Bernini disappeared past the dumpster. No flute in the pub? She'd seen him put it into the bag while she waited for the elevator. In the pub he had clutched the bag as if afraid it would jump out of his hands. And now, apparently, it had. Very well. If that was the way he wanted it. The IOFA convention hadn't even started and already she'd had enough of flute players. Maybe she should just skip the music scene and be a tourist.

Dismissing Bernini from her mind, she thought of the landmarks she'd like to visit. According to convention publicity, the hotel was a short bus ride from Trafalgar Square and the National Gallery. The British Museum couldn't be too far away. She definitely wanted to see the Sutton Hoo Treasure.

Eager to plan her sightseeing, Sallie entered the hotel by way of the side entrance.

****

Still trembling from the attack behind the pub, Bernini left the American woman to go in the side door, hurried past the dumpster to the service entrance, and took the back stairs to his room on the fourth floor. Unlocking the door as quietly as he could, he pulled it shut behind him and crossed to the connecting door to make sure it was still locked. Then he went into the bathroom to see what kind of damage his attacker had done.

His slacks were ruined where he'd been knocked to his knees. He could see his abraded flesh through the tears. The jacket would probably be all right with a cleaning. He reached for a washing flannel with his right hand and yelped with pain. His wrist had begun to swell and discolor. He tried to flex it, but the pain stopped him.

"Damn and blast." He'd have to tell that cloying Pinkerton woman to find someone else to play for the opening session in the morning. He hoped he could still play the *Syrinx* at Saturday's closing banquet. He looked at his watch. Nearly midnight. He lifted the phone with his left hand, rang the switchboard and asked the woman who answered to be put through to Mrs. Pinkerton.

Ring followed ring with no answer. Still at her meeting, no doubt. After the fourth ring, a recording device activated. Good. He wouldn't have to talk to her. Briefly, he told the machine that he'd hurt his wrist, not badly, but he needed to rest it so as to be ready for the closing solo. Despite leaving a message, he felt uneasy. What if she didn't hear the message in time? As insurance, he consulted his list of IOFA officers and made a second call to the IOFA vice-president. She didn't answer either, so he left her the same message.

Ordinarily Bernini would have not hesitated to go straight through to Teddy's room and ask him to substitute for him in the morning, but things were no longer ordinary. How could he be sure that it hadn't been Teddy in the shadows behind the pub? A sob escaped his throat. Had it really been only a few hours since Teddy and he were lying on the bed in the adjoining room, talking idly of where they might go for supper?

Favoring his right wrist as much as possible, Bernini changed into his pajamas. The slightest movement sent him into paroxysms of pain. Remembering the bandage the American woman forced upon him, he retrieved it from a pocket in the ruined trousers. What a curious thing to travel with. That and a powerful electric torch! He wondered what else she carried in that enormous bag of hers.

Wrapping his wrist as best he could, Bernini turned out the light and went to bed. The Fabergé Flute lost all importance as he wrestled with the unfamiliar idea that his lover could be capable of infidelity.

He had to calm down. He had to sleep. In sleep he could find relief from this anguish of uncertainty. For a little while, at least.

Somewhere on the fourth floor, a flute began to play. The notes massaged his rigid muscles like invisible fingers. The tension eased, and Bernini drifted into sleep.

****

Sallie entered the elevator in the lobby with her mind seething with sight-seeing plans, but by the time she got to her room, fatigue hit her like a slaughterhouse mallet. Not only did she lack the energy to pore over brochures, she barely had the strength to retrieve the nightgown she'd packed in one of the carry-ons. The suitcases would have to wait. She did manage to wash her face and brush her teeth before falling into bed.

Lying down was bliss. Too late, she realized she couldn't reach the switch on the bedside lamp without getting up again. Oh well. Momma wasn't there to complain about her running up the light bill. Let it stay on.

Somewhere a flute was playing. The notes washed over her, floating her into sleep.

Chapter Six

Monday, 25 November 1985, Day One of the IOFA Convention

The first sound Sallie heard when she woke Monday morning, like the last she heard as she dropped off to sleep Sunday night, was the playing of a flute. She stretched luxuriously. Despite the fact she'd slept only about six hours after being awake for twenty-four, she felt completely refreshed. The clock on the nightstand read seven-thirty. Registration began at eight a.m. No time to unpack, but it didn't matter. She had a change of clothes in the carry-on. The suitcases could wait a little longer.

Sallie showered and dressed in record time and strapped on her fanny pack. She lightened the Needments bag as much as possible and slung it over her shoulder. Would she need her flute and stand? It was a flute convention, after all. Sighing, she hoisted the heavy bag to her other shoulder and set out.

Registration was on the mezzanine. The crowd in front of the registration tables boded a long wait, but she didn't mind. Sallie often entertained herself by observing the people around her, making up stories about them and giving them names.

A beautiful, dark-skinned girl with glossy straight black hair down to her waist stood beside a stocky red-faced man in a conservative business suit. She'd often seen that bewildered, long-suffering expression on the face of Kimberly Cartwright's father. Kimberly—never plain "Kim"—was an affluent and spoiled ninth-grader. This father-daughter pair bore the same air of doter and dotee. Sallie christened them "Big Daddy" and "the princess."

The princess's beauty was marred by an exaggerated pout on her narrow lips. Big Daddy's unexceptional suit was accessorized with tooled western boots and a leather string tie with a silver slide set with a large irregularly shaped turquoise. The unbuttoned mud-colored jacket gaped to reveal an elaborate silver belt buckle carved with a design Sallie wasn't close enough to make out. The princess's whine, however, carried nicely.

"I don't want to try out for the Hoffman Youth Prize, Daddy. I just can't get any kind of tone out of my old flute!"

"Now, honey, your audition's not until tomorrow. Try out one of them high-priced flutes in the exhibit hall and find you one that you like better than the one you have. Though I'd think for what it cost, the gold one you have ought to be good enough for the heavenly choir."

Sallie smiled and let her gaze drift to a short elderly man in a soiled yellow suit who was speaking a foreign language in a loud wheezing voice. A Toscanini mane of white hair flared around his leathery face. The language sounded to Sallie like a cross between Spanish and French. He was talking to Max Paulson, the man she met at the pub.

Next to Max stood a young man with beautiful

almond-shaped eyes and skin a delicate shade of café au lait. He must be the Brazilian orphan that Flapper Lady had been going on about. Sallie tried to remember the boy's name. Orpheus? Omar? Something poetic. The boy stood unsmiling, face set in a polite mask of attentiveness. The indirect way he looked at Max reminded Sallie of Tasha Reed, a ninth grader who screamed at Sallie once for touching her shoulder in a friendly gesture.

Flailing his hands in broad gestures, the man in the yellow suit leaned into the personal space of his listeners, driving them backward. Once he put an age-spotted hand on the youngster's wrist and the boy recoiled as from something poisonous. The man with the mane spoke not in sentences, but in explosive exclamations. He had a lascivious air, something unclean and predatory. Sallie couldn't quite identify what it was that caused the impression. She decided to call him "the Dirty Old Man."

The registration line moved ahead. The woman in front of Sallie was wearing earrings that looked like silver sticks. Looking more closely, she saw that the little sticks were tiny flutes. She supposed that tiny oboes would look like sticks too. Woodwinds were not the best instrument shape for a jeweler to work with. Violins maybe. Or harps.

Sallie's turn came. The man sitting behind the A-D box wore a tiny silver flute on his lapel. He handed her a heavy white plastic bag printed with the IOFA convention logo: a line drawing of Nelson on his column in Trafalgar Square. Unlike the real statue, which shows Nelson with an empty right sleeve and his left hand resting on a sword pommel, the drawing depicted the naval hero with his right arm restored. In the version on the bag of convention materials, the hero of Trafalgar was holding the middle joint of a flute like a telescope to his blind eye.

As Sallie turned to leave, she noticed a transaction at the E-K box. The person registering received more than a bag of materials. He was given a bright green blazer.

"Hey," Sallie said. "Don't I get one of those?"

"Are you eighteen or younger?"

"Obviously not," Sallie said.

"Then you don't get a jacket. Next, please."

Sallie was ready for breakfast. She looked around for Harry Slocum as a possible meal companion but remembered that he'd abandoned her to find her own way back to the hotel. Her interest in finding him shifted to the hope that he wouldn't see her.

The Hunter's Den offered a complete English breakfast that included shiny golden fish she guessed must be kippers. Promising herself to try them at least once during her stay, she fell back on the familiar, taking some scrambled eggs, two link sausages, and a bowl of grapefruit segments. She seated herself at a small table and skimmed the convention program. Alan Bernini was scheduled to play at the opening session, but she doubted he'd be able to. Not after the way he'd yanked his hand back from his proffered handshake when they parted outside the hotel.

The chink of crockery being cleared caused Sallie to glance up. Her eyes met those of the cadaverous waiter who had worked their table in the pub the night before. He looked away quickly. Poor man. Having to work two jobs at his age.

"Don't tell me you're schlepping both of them around the hotel." Without asking if he could join her, Harry Slocum heaved Sallie's bags off the second chair, set them on the floor and seated himself in their place. "I see you got back all right last night."

She resisted the obvious response of *No thanks to you!*

"No reason why I shouldn't have," she said. "How'd your date turn out?"

Harry gave a short laugh. "Date schmate. I'm not into cradle-robbing. I put her in a taxi outside the pub and took a little walk before coming back to the hotel."

Sallie felt disproportionately pleased to know that Harry hadn't dumped her for the girl in the fishnet stockings. She didn't even like the man, but after sitting with him for eight hours across the Atlantic, she'd developed proprietary feelings.

"So," she said, "what did you make of all the talk last night of the fabulous flute? Do you think it exists?"

Harry picked up Sallie's remaining piece of toast and managed to grin while chewing. "Just the sort of fairy tale to please the amateurs. I could tell you were falling for it hook, line, and sinker. Hey, where are you going?"

Sallie left her coffee unfinished, retrieved her bags, and quit the table without bothering to respond. She hadn't traveled 3,000 miles to be treated like a moron. That she could get at home.

****

The morning after the attack in the alley, Alan Bernini woke to hear Teddy rapping on the connecting door and calling to him.

"Alan, dearest! Open the door, please. We have

need to talk."

Bernini pressed his lips together. He was not ready.

Teddy continued to knock and call for about five minutes, then stopped. After a few beats, he loosed a stream of curse words and kicked the wall. "Very well, *mon cher*. I haven't time to play this game at the moment. The Maestro waits."

As soon as Bernini heard Teddy's door to the corridor shut, he got out of bed, taking care not to jar his injured wrist. Gingerly, he began to unwind the bandage, expecting pain to return. He stared at his hand. Not only had the swelling gone down, the bruising and discoloration had disappeared completely. He flexed each finger in turn. Not a shred of pain. He could have played for the opening session after all.

Since he had nowhere to be for a while, Bernini showered leisurely, rinsing out the Ace bandage as he did so. When he was dressed, he blotted the bandage in a towel and draped it over the curtain bar to dry. He wanted to return it to the American woman in the same state he'd received it. Then he brewed a cup of coffee and sat down at the little table to think what to do.

He couldn't avoid Teddy forever. They needed to talk about the Fabergé Flute, what it was doing in Teddy's room, and who had snatched it in the alley behind the pub. Bernini didn't want to believe that Teddy could be so rough with him, pulling him down the steps, yanking the strap over his head, and hurting his neck that way. No. Somebody other than Teddy must have followed him to the pub from the hotel. Someone who knew what he had in the canvas bag. Anyone watching him in the pub lounge would have had time to leave by the front door, go round to the alley, and wait.

Still, Teddy lied about having someone in the room when Bernini returned from the fruitless visit to Duby's house. Radio be damned. Teddy was talking to someone behind the connecting door. Possibly the unknown person slipped the flute case under the bedclothes without Teddy's knowledge. Not likely, but possible. Bernini was willing to believe any explanation that would absolve Teddy from the charge of disloyalty.

Whatever the truth of the matter, Bernini was certain the unknown person was no secret lover. Teddy was the most loyal person in the world. Last year, when a childhood friend was arrested for manslaughter and abandoned by his wealthy family, Teddy refused to believe in his guilt. He cancelled a tour, paid for expensive counsel, and stayed at his friend's side until the acquittal.

Teddy's loyalty to Maestro Truffaut ran deeper still. After the stroke, when all the students—including Bernini—left Maestro Truffaut for other teachers, Teddy stayed with him.

Bernini slapped his head. Of course! Truffaut had to be the answer. It wasn't the instrument's beauty or value that would lead Teddy to keep the Fabergé Flute a secret from his partner. The flute was supposed to have healing powers. The only thing that would cause Teddy to conceal the flute would be his desire to cure the Maestro.

Bernini almost shouted with relief. Sylvan Truffaut was the only person in the world Teddy loved more than he loved Bernini. He would do anything to reverse the effects of the stroke and burning accident that had destroyed the Maestro's ability to play.

He stood and paced the room. Dear romantic, sentimental Teddy. Trust Teddy to believe the mumbo jumbo about the healing powers of the Fabergé Flute. That was the only explanation. Somehow Teddy had obtained the flute. He hid the fact because he knew Bernini would want to take it straight to British authorities. If anything would cause Teddy to deceive his partner and skirt the law, it would be his desire to heal Truffaut. Once the flute had done its work, Teddy would have no further use for it.

Once it had done its work.

Bernini laughed. Now he was thinking magically. The flute had no supernatural powers. It belonged in the British Museum. If he waited until the flute cured the Maestro, it would never happen. He could forget about any reward from a grateful nation.

But who snatched the flute in the alley? Teddy would not have used violence against him, not even for Truffaut. If he'd been holding the canvas bag in the ordinary way, with the strap over one shoulder, he wouldn't have been pulled off balance. If Teddy was the one who snatched the bag, he hadn't intended to hurt him.

Bernini went to look at his face in the bathroom mirror. The cut over his eye was completely gone. He went back to the table and scanned the Monday morning schedule of events in the program. He checked the time. The opening session would be over in about twenty minutes. Following that, the Maestro was giving a master class.

Bernini voiced his thought. "If Teddy won't tell me what's going on, I'll catch the Maestro after the master class and find out what he knows about the Fabergé

Flute."

****

Leaving Slocum at the table, Sallie stormed her way as far as the restaurant entrance and stopped just outside in the lobby. She was more annoyed with herself than with him. It would be obvious to anyone with good sense that Harry Slocum was an arrogant, insensitive jerk not worth the time of day.

Something was going on by the planter partition that separated the elevator alcove from the main lobby. Sallie recognized the woman who'd had the confrontation with the desk clerk over the dog when checking in. Today she was dressed like someone out of a 1930s movie, Rosalind Russell in an orange pants suit and matching turban. At the moment, she was poking the narrow tip of an umbrella through the lattice of the divider.

Sallie moved closer and heard a disembodied male voice.

"That's not doing the slightest bit of good. It's only making him go farther from this end."

Sallie looked down and saw someone's legs sticking out from under the partition. The woman's husband lay on his stomach, peering into the tunnel-like gap made by the two planters that formed the base of the divider. "Come on, Tacet," he wheedled. "Come here. Good dog. Come out, you wretched animal."

The woman leaned down. "Maybe I should ask in the restaurant if they'd let me have something else."

"We've already tried sausage, bacon, and kippers. The kippers only made him go farther back. Can't say that I blame him."

Sallie pulled a small plastic package from her

Needments bag. "Maybe these will help." She tore open the packet and handed it to the man on the floor. "Dog treats."

Within seconds, the dog was out and his leash firmly back in the grasp of its master, who struggled back to his feet with the help of a cane.

"Lucky for us there was another dog owner in the place," the man said. He transferred the cane to his leash hand in order to shake. "I'm Dave King and this is my wife Dani."

Sallie saw the unconventional spelling "Dani" on the woman's nametag. She touched her own tag as she introduced herself.

"What kind of dog do you have?" Dani asked.

"I haven't got a dog."

The Kings' bewildered stares prompted an explanation.

"Last time I was at Walmart, someone was handing out dog treat samples. I forgot about them until just now."

Dave laughed. "You never know what might come in handy, right?" He kissed Dani on the cheek. "I'll meet you at the registration table at noon." To Sallie he said, "Gotta see a man about a dog." Pulling Tacet along with him, he left by the side door.

Dani looked at her watch, a large gold circle dangling from a heavy gold chain attached to her lapel. The pin holding the chain in place was shaped like a flute. "Almost time for the opening session. It's in the ballroom upstairs. We'd better hurry." Pleased to have someone to sit with, Sallie followed as Dani moved quickly through the crowd.

"Stupid dog," Dani said. "We'll be lucky to find a

seat."

Sallie kept up with difficulty, her bags weighing more heavily with every step. Ahead of her, Dani carried only a handbag and the convention program.

****

Morris pushed the nurse call-button again. This time he held it down. The nursing sister was taking longer and longer to respond. When she came, she stuck her head past the curtain without coming to the bedside.

"What is it this time, Mr. Duby?"

"Bernini. Has he come yet? Has he phoned?"

"Not in the past five minutes, no. I'll be sure to tell you if he does, Mr. Duby. Now, please don't press the buzzer again unless you're in distress." The curtain fluttered back into place.

"I *am* in distress, dammit!" he shouted after her.

Surely it had been days since he'd told Alan Bernini about the Flute, but according to that hulking brute of a nurse, it was only yesterday. Still, Bernini could have telephoned by now. Bloody cheek, taking advantage of an old man tied to a bed. He'd probably sold it by now. Couldn't trust anybody.

Duby fell into a hacking coughing fit. When it had passed, he sighed. How could he expect a complete stranger to be trustworthy when his own father had betrayed him? His thoughts drifted to his childhood. They'd wandered there a lot since he'd been stuck in a hospital bed with no more freedom to move than a pot of ivy.

Morris's father, an antiques dealer, traveled often and brought back splendid gifts from the places he'd been. Morris never knew his mother; she'd died giving birth to him. Her absence had been filled by a live-in housekeeper he called Nana, a large, comfortable woman with red cheeks and a cheerful disposition. Childless, widowed by war, she'd mothered him as if he'd been her own. Nevertheless, he'd been a lonely child. Always in the company of adults, he prayed every night for God to send him a brother. On his seventh birthday, his prayer was answered.

Morris groaned. Be careful what you pray for.

Between business trips, Papa would take Morris to a large park where they watched puppet shows and other entertainment. His favorite performer was an organ grinder whose costumed monkey collected coins in a brass cup. Papa always gave Morris a coin to give to the monkey. One day, passing the cup among the spectators in the animal's place, was a little boy. Their eyes met over the cup. As young as he was, Morris recognized depths of sorrow and deprivation in the other child's gaze. On the way home he asked his father if the boy could come live with them and be his brother. Of course, Papa told him how impossible an idea that was, but every time they visited the park, Morris renewed his plea. "Please, Papa! He looks so hungry! Please, Papa, he looks so sad."

Besides collecting the money, the little boy performed on a pennywhistle, conjuring extraordinary music from the cheap little instrument. Month followed month, Morris never failing to end every visit to the park with a plea to bring the little flute player home with them to be his brother.

At last, Papa relented. He made inquiries, discovered that the organ grinder had no legal claim to the child, and made arrangements to foster him. On

Morris's seventh birthday, the boy from the park came to live with them. And though the boy had a name, Morris called him simply, "Brother."

An indescribable ache filled Morris's chest as remembered happiness dissolved into remembered misery.

They'd grown up devoted to each other and united in a desire to please Papa. In turn, Morris' father devoted the same attention to the adopted child, bringing identical gifts from his trips: embroidered waistcoats, golden cufflinks, tortoiseshell brushes.

When Brother taught Morris to play the pennywhistle, Papa bought them both real flutes and hired a music master.

The adopted son quickly revealed himself as the more gifted musician. One day, the music master told Papa that Brother had the makings of a Taffanel. From that moment, things changed. Morris's father continued to bring them gifts from his trips, but, although the gifts looked the same, Brother's would be of better quality. Then, when the boys were about fifteen, Papa came home with only one gift in his bag.

"Here it is."

A woman's voice jolted Morris out of his bitter reverie. The nursing sister was leaning over him to plug a telephone extension into one of the outlets. "Here's that telephone call you've been waiting for, Mr. Duby. Only it's not that nice Mr. Bernini." She placed the phone beside him on the bed. "It's someone with an American accent."

****

The convention's opening session was in a ballroom with crystal chandeliers and gilded columns along the walls. Sallie was surprised to see such an attractive room in a budget hotel. Rows of gold and white folding chairs faced a low stage. She and Dani found two vacant seats about midway, not side by side, but one behind the other. Sallie sat and lowered her bags to the floor with a relieved sigh. The squeal of a microphone being adjusted pierced the air, sending muscle contractions through Sallie's shoulders. On the stage, a rotund figure in a dark blue suit fiddled with sound equipment.

Dani leaned forward and put her mouth close to Sallie's ear. "That's Dimitri Durrell. I recognize him from his pictures in Dave's *Double Reed Quarterly*. He's first oboist with the Prague Symphony. Dave's going to take a master class with him. I have one with T…" The last word sounded something like "Tofu." Sallie didn't know what a master class was but didn't think it was the time to ask.

The mike squealed again, this time in the hands of Alice Pinkerton. "Good morning everyone," she said, in her plummy private school accent. "Welcome to the sixteenth annual convention of the International Oboe and Flute Association. The official figures are not in, but we estimate that attendance this year is expected to pass the five hundred mark." When the applause subsided, she continued. "Before we get on with business, I have a program change to announce. Our featured soloist, Alan Bernini, was scheduled to start us off with 'The Carnival of Venice Overture.' Unfortunately, Alan had an accident last night and sprained his wrist."

Sounds of surprise and dismay went up from the audience. Alice tapped the mike, sending another ear-torturing whine through the room and turning the murmurs to groans. "Not to worry. Mr. Bernini assured me that by Friday he will play the *Syrinx* at the closing banquet as scheduled."

Sallie grinned delightedly at the way Alice pronounced *scheduled* as *sheduled*. Judging from the enthusiastic applause, Bernini had plenty of fans among the convention-goers.

As soon as she could make herself heard again, Alice announced Bernini's replacement.

"Playing 'The Carnival of Venice' for us this morning is a young man who deserves to be better known in the flute world. Ladies and gentlemen, please welcome Monsieur Benoît DeLille."

Alice stepped away and a slightly-built young man in a tux took center stage, followed by two men in khaki jumpsuits who rolled a baby grand into place. The piano was followed by dark man with a tousled black mane of hair who seated himself on the bench with a theatrical flourish of tails. Sallie stared at Benoît DeLille. The soloist's peroxided hair and long sideburns made him look more like a rock star than a flute player. Apart from the hair, there was something familiar about him. Where had she seen him before? On the plane? In the hotel?

DeLille raised his flute and began. The tuxedo changed his appearance from scruffy to respectable, and the bleached hair was a surprise, but Sallie placed him. At the Four Moons he'd been wearing a hood, but she recognized the strange Gollum eyes. This was the man who left the pub by the front door about the time Bernini went out the back to be mugged for the flute he claimed he never had.

Chapter Seven

As soon as the opening session ended, Dani invited Sallie to go with her to her master class.

"What's a 'master class'?" Sallie was beginning to regret having plunged herself into a world she knew so little about.

"It's called a 'master class' because it's taught by a master flutist. Students have to be advanced players to be admitted. They're there to learn from the master, but they're also being observed by an audience."

"But where's your flute?"

"In the security room. On the mezzanine. Come on." Dani led the way to what the program referred to as "the moving stairs," *escalator* in American English. Unbalanced by her bags, Sallie staggered a little as she stepped on. Dani put out a hand to steady her.

"What in the world are you carrying in those bags?"

"Among other things, my flute and folding stand."

"You need to check them into the security room. For a one-time fee of five pounds you can check your bag in and out as many times as you want. It's well worth it. That way you don't have to carry it everywhere, and your flute will be safer than in your room."

Sallie made murmuring noises to be polite, but rejected the idea, unwilling to spend the five pounds.

She'd undertaken this trip on a shoestring. By the time she'd paid for the conference package, she had hardly any cash left for spending money. Charging was not an option because the credit card companies had revoked her cards when Nick died. Never mind the fact that she'd been the one making the payments every month. As an unmarried woman, she had no credit. The bills and traveler's checks she had in her fanny pack and the money belt under her clothes would have to last.

A line snaked out of the security room on the mezzanine. They took their place at the end and Dani expanded her explanation. "The class is limited to five participants. Everyone had to send an audition tape. Alice Pinkerton told me that at least fifty players applied for this one." Dani's excitement was evident.

The line moved quickly, and they were soon within sight of the counter where a heavily-fleshed woman with a thick neck and square unsmiling jaw presided. After every transaction she sat down, breathing hard, masculine shoulders straining against her blue gabardine uniform. Dani's turn came. The woman snapped out a syllable.

"Chit?"

Sallie turned an uncomprehending look at Dani to see if she'd understood the woman's utterance.

Dani laughed.

"TCH-it," Dani pronounced carefully, emphasizing the first consonant sound, the sound in *church,* and not the one in *shirt*. She placed a flat white piece of plastic with a black number onto the counter. The chit resembled a room-key tag. Retrieving Dani's bag from a numbered cubbyhole, the attendant returned promptly to her chair, ready for the next in line.

Pivoting on her heel like a guard at Buckingham Palace, Dani marched out of the security room and led her troop of one to their destination. Unlike the uncertain conference-goers who milled about, clutching programs and gazing hopefully at the signs outside the meeting rooms, Dani led the way with confidence.

"You seem to know where you're going," Sallie said.

"I came up before breakfast to look for the room. I don't believe in leaving things until the last minute. Especially not something as important as a lesson with Sylvan Truffaut."

"I've heard that name a lot since I've been here," Sallie said. "I guess he must be pretty famous in the flute world."

"Just about all of the modern flute players of any importance have studied with him. And his life story is absolutely amazing. He was an abandoned orphan living in the streets of Marseilles when an organ grinder made him a part of his act after his monkey died."

Sallie broke into laughter, tickled by the image of a child replacing an organ grinder's monkey. Dani cast her a stony glance.

"Sorry," Sallie said. "It just sounded so funny the way you said it."

"Truffaut was about seven or eight years old when a wealthy businessman took an interest in him, took him into his home, raised him with his own son, and paid for the best musical education money could buy." Dani stopped abruptly. She fixed Sallie with a solemn look. "He studied with Ravel."

Goosebumps rippled across Sallie's arms and she understood what it was that so excited Dani about her upcoming lesson. Truffaut represented the continuity of human endeavor, the laying on of hands from one generation to the next, a line of people like the kings in *Macbeth*—stretching out to the crack of doom. In a sense, Ravel still played the flute, just as some remote ancestor lives in the color of one's eyes or some trick of speech or gesture.

They came to a door marked by a sign taped to the door frame.

MASTER CLASS WITH M. TRUFFAUT
SPECTATORS MUST REMAIN SILENT

Dani hurried into the room and claimed one of the five folding chairs reserved for the participants. Sallie found a seat behind a woman wearing a yellow rain hat. If they weren't wearing hoods, they were wearing hats. She scooted one seat over to sit behind a little girl, presumably the woman's child, who offered the advantage of being short and hatless.

Glancing toward the doorway, Sallie saw Princess and Big Daddy engaged in an agitated conversation that ended abruptly as the princess swept away to claim the chair next to Dani. Big Daddy backed sheepishly out of the room. The daughter must have given him marching orders. Sallie could sympathize. Her own father was a vague memory, but her mother was a critical presence she never felt comfortable having around when she had to do anything in front of an audience.

Max Paulson's beautiful adopted son with the poetic name took the seat next to the princess. He whispered something into her ear that made her smile. Sallie looked around for Max but didn't see him.

The five chairs for the participants faced an armchair and a tall stool. An elderly man in a dark green V-neck sweater and green corduroy slacks sat in the chair. Beside him, Alice Pinkerton squatted awkwardly, her gray helmet of hair at the level of his head. This must be the venerable Truffaut. Alice leaned forward, an intent listening look on her chalky face. Truffaut's lips made exaggerated movements, as if speaking were difficult. Hoisting herself to her feet Alice beckoned to a young man with a video camera who proceeded to set up his equipment.

Idly, Sallie let her gaze follow Alice to the door. As Alice left, the handsome man from the pub, the one who looked like Omar Sharif, entered. He took a seat at the end of a row and sat on the edge of the chair, as if not intending to stay long. Sallie felt heat rising in her face and looked away before their eyes could meet. She turned her attention back to the stage area and studied Truffaut, looking for signs of his disability. He was a Charles De Gaulle-type of Frenchman with an eagle nose that dwarfed the rest of his features. A woman with the same kind of nose had joined him and half-sat, half-leaned on the stool next to him. Truffaut turned his head to speak to her and Sallie gasped.

The left side of his face was comely for an old man, but the right side was grotesque. The mouth that on the left half was mobile enough for speech, on the right was a pencil line of immobility. The right eyelid, swollen, hung almost shut. His skin, which on the left side of his face was reasonably smooth, on the right was blotched and bubbly, like a burnt marshmallow without the charring.

"For chrissake!"

Harry Slocum dropped onto the seat behind the woman with the hat. The expletive was delivered in an explosive whisper. "I'd heard he was pretty messed up, but I had no idea it was that bad. Surprised he'd want to be seen in public."

Sallie whispered back. "Didn't you say he'd had a stroke? I never knew of a stroke that could cause that kind of disfigurement."

"It wasn't just a stroke. He was playing in a period gig at the time. Everyone was dressed up like their favorite composers, not just the performers, but the audience too. Period instruments, candles for footlights, the whole schmere. Truffaut was wearing a wig. The stroke caused him to fall into the footlights, and the wig caught fire."

"How can he give lessons?"

"His daughter Melisande. She can understand what he's saying when nobody else can. He makes the comments and she translates them for the students."

Truffaut turned his head again, concealing the deformed side and Sallie realized with a qualm of shame that she was glad to have it out of sight.

Melisande Truffaut stood and addressed the five class participants.

"It is time." Her words were colored by a slight French accent. "Who will begin?"

Dani, the princess, and Max's son had been joined by an Asian youth in slacks, shirt, and tie, and a short-haired person of indeterminate gender in jeans and a voluminous T-shirt. The Asian volunteered to go first. He played a few measures of *The Afternoon of a Faun*, beautifully, Sallie thought, but Truffaut struck his forehead with his left hand and waved his right hand like a man directing traffic.

"Non, non, non!" he shouted and said something

that Melisande proceeded to translate for the reddening student.

"Any fool can wiggle his fingers. Soul. Where is the soul?"

The student began again from the beginning of the phrase. Truffaut marked time with his hands and uttered odd sounds to indicate the rhythm: "emm-paa, emm-paa, détaché, détaché. NON! No crescendo, now. Fullness of tone, not force!"

Sweat stood out on the young man's forehead. His eyes were squeezed shut and his whole body showed the tension of concentration. Again and again he repeated the measures, then a single phrase. Again and again. Every time it sounded beautiful to Sallie, but again and again Truffaut shouted "Non!" and demanded a sound, an intonation that the student had yet to give him. The student played it again and this time Truffaut remained silent, a slight smile touching the mobile side of his mouth. The student lowered his flute and looked at the master, his sweating face revealing the knowledge that this time he'd got it right.

"Please, Mummy! I can't wait any longer!"

Every head in the room swiveled. A moment earlier and no one would have heard the desperate plea, but coming as it had in the silence, it soared like a shout. Melisande Truffaut glared icily at the offending child. Maestro Truffaut uttered an incomprehensible tirade that ended with a word Sallie recognized: "DeLille."

Materializing from somewhere, the loosely jointed figure of Benoît DeLille made its way to Truffaut's side and put his ear near the master's mouth. He'd traded his tux for jeans, T-shirt, brown corduroy blazer with patches on the elbows, and loafers. Nodding, he turned to the audience and relayed the maestro's instructions.

"This class is no longer open to the public. You will all please to leave as quickly and quietly as possible." Ignoring the indignant protests, DeLille herded them to the door and out into the corridor. The offending child was dragged away by her outraged mother.

"How can you expect to be a world-class flautist if you can't control your bladder? I've never been so humiliated, and Truffaut, of all people. Haven't you any idea how lucky you were to have a chance…"

The mother's harangue died away, but Sallie's sympathies went with the poor child. If her mother were anything like Sallie's, recriminations would continue until suppertime.

When the last spectator was out of the room, DeLille closed the door and placed a folding chair directly in front of it, clearly intending to remain as sentry until the class ended. Pulling over a small table, he sat on the chair with his back against the door and his feet propped on the table.

Harry Slocum, who had exited with Sallie, moved off. "See you later, Sallie. Gotta see a man in the Exhibit Hall."

Sallie wrinkled her nose. *As if I cared.*

Not far from DeLille's sentry post, Sallie leaned against the wall and leafed through the convention program to see where she might go next. An authoritative voice caused her to look up.

"Move your chair, please, M. DeLille. I've come to hear Orlando play. I want to hear for myself how much he's benefited from yesterday's lesson with you."

Max Paulson, impeccably dressed as before in a tailored suit of some shiny, expensive-looking fabric, stood over DeLille. Orlando. That was the name of Paulson's adopted son. She knew it started with an O. Evidently, Orlando had taken at least one flute lesson with DeLille. Max had mentioned at the pub that he was trying to set up lessons with as many virtuosi as he could.

DeLille crossed his ankles on the table top. The scruffy, off-white loafers with their tacky leather tassels, one of which was missing, contributed an ingredient of insolence to his demeanor. If the shoes were any indication, he needed money, so it was surprising to see him act like that to a man who could pay for lessons.

"*Je regrette*, M. Paulson. The Maestro has closed the session. Nobody must go in."

Max's urbane smile froze. A muscle pulsed in his jaw. "You don't understand. Orlando is my—" slight pause "—protégé. I have the right." His steely eyes held an unspoken threat, but DeLille met his look placidly, chair firmly planted against the closed door.

"The rights are with the Maestro, M. Paulson. Please to come back in about forty minutes and then you may fetch your—" exactly the same pause that Max had made "—protégé."

For an instant the urbane composure flickered, but then Max's face relaxed into the kindly expression that had charmed Sallie in the pub. She couldn't be sure she'd actually seen the gleam of pure venom in his eyes. He glanced around as if looking for an ally. As if on cue, Alan Bernini approached from around a turning in the corridor.

"Mr. Bernini," Max called. "I need your support here." He glanced coldly at DeLille. "According to this young man, I've arrived at Maestro Truffaut's master class too late to be admitted. Surely, as Orlando's guardian, I've a right to sit in."

Bernini's eyes met those of DeLille. Sallie would not have been able to point to anything specific, but a look full of some kind of meaning passed between them.

"I would need to know the particulars," Bernini said. "Is it an open session?"

"It was," DeLille said, "but the Maestro had the room cleared because of a disturbance."

"I wasn't in the room when the disturbance occurred," Max said. "The exclusion cannot, therefore, apply to me."

Bernini moved his shoulders in a gesture not quite a shrug. "If the Maestro sent the audience out, he does not want an audience."

Max looked as if he was going to argue but instead pressed his lips into a thin line and drew himself up with such dignity Sallie expected to hear his heels click. He nodded curtly to Bernini, cast another icy look at DeLille, turned, and stalked away.

DeLille and Bernini watched Max's retreating back until it disappeared. Then Bernini spoke, very formally.

"I wonder, M. DeLille," he said, "if you could arrange an appointment for me to speak to the Maestro. Only for a few minutes, of course. In private."

DeLille considered before answering.

"Certainly, Mr. Bernini. Where can I reach you?"

"I shall be in my room." Bernini walked back the way he had come.

Sallie had been observing the scene with undisguised interest and had unconsciously moved closer to the center of action. DeLille noticed her staring at him.

"Do I perhaps know you, mademoiselle?"

"No," Sallie said, "but you may have seen me before. Last night, in The Four Moons. You were there when I was."

DeLille looked at her coldly.

"You are mistaken, mademoiselle. I was not there."

"You weren't there very long, but I saw you come in and sit at the bar. You were looking for someone."

DeLille turned away and stared at a point on the opposite wall.

"You are mistaken, mademoiselle," he repeated. "I never left the hotel last night."

Sallie was tired of being told she hadn't seen what she knew good and well she had. First Bernini, telling her she hadn't seen him with the battered flute case, and now DeLille insisting that he hadn't been at the pub when she'd seen his goggle-eyes under the hood of his ratty duffle coat at the bar.

Were all flute players a creepy lot of liars? She wondered if oboe players were any more reliable. She'd been glad enough to have company on her first visit to a pub, but she'd still ended up alone when they all decamped at the same time. It had been as if Bernini's abrupt departure had signaled everybody to leave— Max, Harry, even the hollow-eyed waiter. A plague on all of them. She'd finally gotten to London and was going to enjoy herself. After all, the conference wasn't her main objective in making the trip. If she was going to be alone, all the better. She could go where she pleased and make the most of being in the city that had fed her imagination since she was a child.

Sallie took the escalator to the main floor, planning to leave the hotel and enjoy a little sightseeing, but on the other side of the revolving door, the sky was so overcast as to turn day to night. Heavy drops fell on her head as she stepped out from under the marquee. A jagged white lightning bolt cut the black sky. Sightseeing in the midst of a thunderstorm was probably not a good idea. She returned to the lobby and looked about for something else to do. Her glance fell on a large placard with the word EXHIBITS and an arrow. The arrow pointed to a broad staircase leading to a lower level. *I know! I'll go find myself some flute earrings!*

The commercial exhibits filled a vast hall partitioned into rectangular cubicles along the walls and back to back to form several aisles. For sale were not just flutes, oboes, sheet music, and accessories such as metronomes and tuners, but every conceivable product that could incorporate a musical motif, no matter how incongruous.

She stopped in front of a display of china. The plates depicted a Baroque scene in which a bewigged gentleman was playing a flute, surrounded by an attentive crowd of men in green and orange knee-breeches and women in tall hairdos and puce gowns.

"Frederick the Great and his courtiers."

Sallie backed away from a dumpy, aggressive woman with thick false eyelashes and coal black hair with a white streak like a skunk.

"Only £500 including VAT and shipping anywhere in the States or Canada."

"It's very nice, but I already have plenty of dishes."

Damn. There I go again. Sallie was sick of apologizing for what she thought. Especially to sales people, with polite inanities, explanations, and excuses. She didn't think the dishes were "nice." She thought them grotesque. She wouldn't have wanted them if they were free and if she hadn't anything but boards to eat from.

Moving quickly away, she stopped a few booths down at one selling musical recordings. She stayed away from the new CDs because she didn't have a player for them. She did have a little cassette player. She picked up a selection at random, something by Mozart.

"Good choice!"

Harry Slocum brushed up against her and jabbed the plastic case with a finger. "Marcel Moyse conducted that one. Let me tell you, it was a great experience playing under his baton, even if it was only the second flute part."

Sallie couldn't help but be impressed. She read the insert. The recording, by the Marlboro Winds, was one of Mozart's wind serenades. She decided to buy it so she could say she knew one of the performers. When she looked around for Harry, he'd moved on. Slipping her purchase into her bag, she turned into the next aisle.

A gigantic red mushroom decorated with musical notes for spots loomed over an area enclosed with white lattice panels and dedicated to things garden. Flute and oboe wire sculptures with pointed ends to be skewered into flowerbeds were threaded through the openings in a cast iron outdoor chair with a back shaped like the treble clef. At the sight of a grimacing plaster garden gnome playing a piccolo, Sallie laughed aloud.

"My reaction precisely," said a man's voice with the lightest trace of an accent neither American nor English.

Rounding the display, Sallie saw the speaker, a salesman in a beautifully tailored charcoal suit leaning against a stool next to the lattice panel. Omar Sharif. First the pub. Then the master class, and now here. She felt herself redden with pleasure and embarrassment.

"I will never become accustomed to the Anglo-Saxon tendency to create ugly objects that serve absolutely no purpose." His tone was serious, but the dark brown eyes held amused mischief. He moved toward her and extended his hand.

"My name is Kassim. Are you perhaps in the market for a flute?" He gestured at a table that held several assembled flutes.

Sallie thrilled to his musical voice and the touch of his warm dry hand enclosing hers.

"Sallie," she said, responding in kind to his one-name introduction. "I already have a flute." Immediately she wished she'd said something else.

Wiping the mouthpiece with a disinfectant cloth, Kassim handed her one of the assembled flutes from the table.

"Try this one. See if it doesn't have a better tone than what you have."

Sallie felt a twinge of panic. She'd observed musicians trying out flutes at other tables. They picked them up with practiced eyes and hands and ran through whole sections of Ravel with their eyes closed. All she could think of to play was the F scale. It may have been her imagination, but the tone did sound richer, and the low notes came out more easily.

"This is nice." Damn, that insipid word 'nice' again. "How much does a flute like this cost?"

"In dollars, the catalog price is $4,000, but the special convention price is just $3,700."

Sallie handed the flute back as if it were suddenly hot. "That's quite a bit out of my league. I'd have to play a lot better—and be a lot richer—to buy a flute like this." Recalling the reputed price of Bernini's flute, she added, "What would make a flute worth $70,000?"

"The material would be one factor. Craftsmanship another. A platinum flute could cost that much." The intelligent eyes held her own as if she were the only person in the hall. "I believe I saw you with someone who has such a flute. Sunday evening in the Four Moons pub."

He had noticed her.

Sallie tried to keep her voice steady. "I didn't believe it when someone told me how much Bernini's flute is worth. I still find it hard to believe that anyone would pay so much for a flute."

"To a professional, playing well is all that matters. If a musician thinks that placing a diamond in the end of his head joint will make him play better, then the extra cost will be to him worth it." Kassim took the flute from her and wiped her fingerprints from the keys.

"I'd hate to think what something like the Fabergé Flute would be worth," Sallie ventured.

Kassim stopped polishing. "Beg pardon?"

"The Fabergé Flute. Some people at my table were talking about a flute that was made in the workshops of Carl Fabergé. Two people said there's no such thing, but Bernini believes in its existence."

"I say, I say!" A short man in a red velvet blazer that clashed horribly with his orange hair demanded Kassim's attention. "I want to try out the X-10 model if it's not too much trouble." The little man glared at Sallie out of little pig eyes, as if to imply that she had intruded on his right to service.

Kassim reached for the requested flute. "Certainly, sir. Try this one."

Sallie recognized with disappointment that his interest in her as a potential customer was at an end. She turned to leave.

"Sallie, wait." His accent made her ordinary name sound exotic. "I must see to customers right now. Perhaps later we could have a coffee and talk some more, yes? Sometime after lunch?"

Sallie mustered all her powers of control to conceal her excitement. "Sure. How'll I know where to find you?"

"I will be in the hotel's coffee shop at two o'clock. Look for me there."

Her quest for flute earrings forgotten, Sallie hurried to the exit. Romantic speculation kicked in. She imagined her mother's certain disapproval if she knew she was having a coffee date with someone named Kassim. She fantasized about bringing him home to DeSoto Springs and the reactions she would get, not just from her mother, but from all her relatives and neighbors. For heaven's sake, Sallie, he's an Arab or something.

Chapter Eight

At the exit, Sallie saw Harry in conversation with a bald-headed man dressed all in black. Tall, broad-shouldered Harry looked small next to him. Harry's body language was deferential. The man was huge, ominous, and unsmiling. The bald head shone in the light over the door. The rimless glasses caught the glare in such a way that his eyes looked like empty cartoon circles. If he had a kindlier expression, Sallie might have christened him "Daddy Warbucks," but his hard, mean look suggested "the Godfather." The man was holding two flute cases, one of which he handed to Harry just as she slipped past and out of the hall without being seen by either of them.

Upstairs, the lobby's glass doors and windows revealed a sky bright with sunshine. The storm had passed. Sallie decided to get rid of some of the weight she was carrying and go for a walk. When she reached her room on the fourth floor, she found her door wide open and the doorway blocked by a linen cart. Startled and annoyed, she called out.

"Hello?"

A woman in a hotel housekeeping uniform stuck her head out of the room opposite. Somewhere on the floor a flute started playing.

"I can't get into my room."

The woman smiled and nodded, the way language

learners do when they don't understand what's been said to them. The situation, however, spoke for itself and the cleaner quickly moved the cart, smiling and nodding enthusiastically.

Sallie's bed was newly made and the bathroom stocked with fresh towels, so she didn't understand why the maid left the door open. She shut it with a deliberate bang and threw her things onto the bed. The bag with the flute slid to the floor with a thump. Sallie snatched it up. "Great. Take my new flute three thousand miles to trash it."

She sat on the edge of the bed and set the case on her knees. She knew that the fall to the carpeted floor couldn't have hurt it, but she undid the clasps anyway to have a look. It was barely three months old. The $300 price tag had been an extravagance. Momma was still complaining about it. Sallie laughed shortly. Wait until Momma heard about Bernini's $70,000 flute.

The shiny silver pieces gleaming against the dark blue velvet sent the thrill of new possession through Sallie. 'Tis a poor thing, but mine own. What she was beginning to think of as "The Fourth Floor Flute" was playing "Where Sheep May Safely Graze." Under its soothing strains, her feelings of indignation at having found her room open evaporated. It was one of her favorite flute pieces, not only to listen to, but to play. It was slow and the notes neither too high nor too low for her limited skills. The haunting music drove sightseeing plans from her mind. She felt a sudden urgency to put the flute to her lips. In a rapid motion, she took the head joint and body of the flute out of the case. Too rapid. With a sickening clunk the head joint connected with the heavy bedside lamp. Damn! The head joint, perfect

103

a moment before, now had a half-inch dent just below the lip plate. Damn, damn, damn.

Sallie rubbed the dent with the yellow polishing cloth, as if rubbing might heal it. Well, it was done. Her new flute was new no longer. She replaced the pieces into the case. The Fourth Floor Flute finished the piece and Sallie no longer felt the urge to play. She snapped the case shut and laid it on top of the dresser. She'd go for that walk and put it away later. She checked to be sure she had a couple of traveler's checks handy in the fanny pack, hoisted her bag of Needments to her shoulder, and left the room.

Just as the elevator doors opened, another strain of exquisite music from the disembodied flute floated down the corridor. Sallie's fingers curled with a renewed desire to play.

Back in the lobby, Sallie joined the between-session throng of people on their way from somewhere to somewhere else. The Dirty Old Man in the yellow suit, flailing his hands and scattering spit, had someone backed into a corner. Dani and Max Paulson chatted on a settee near the restaurant. On a bench next to the side entrance, Benoît DeLille, with the princess and Orlando in their green blazers, sat bent over sheet music, their heads nodding in some complicated syncopated beat.

Dave King came through the side door, carrying numerous plastic bags and tripping over Tacet's leash. Sallie hurried over to help. She took the leash and let it run through her fingers until she found the end and could put her hand through the loop. Tacet's lolling grin was irresistible and she reached down to pat him. She'd barely touched his wiry fur when he became a snarling whirlwind and launched himself at the occupants of the bench by the door.

The princess screamed and DeLille flattened himself against the wall, shielding his face with his arms, crossing his legs, and shouting in French. Orlando leapt up and took cover on the other side of the planter.

Sallie hauled on Tacet's lead, reeling it in as fast as she could. Dave dropped the bags and grabbed the dog. Tacet thrashed wildly, barking, snarling, and treading air. Alice Pinkerton rushed over, shrieking. "Why anyone would permit a dog to stay in a hotel is beyond me." She wrapped a protective arm around the princess. "Did it bite you? Are you hurt? Your father will never forgive me if I've let you be injured."

Clutching the dog against his chest and holding its muzzle shut, Dave smiled at an approaching hotel employee whose expression did not bode well for Tacet.

"I'm sorry, sir. We can't have a dangerous animal in the hotel. We shall have to ask you to…"

Dave looked from the employee to the bench where DeLille and the two young people had been sitting. He moved his head in a gesture of confidentiality and spoke sotto voice so that only the employee and Sallie could hear. "The dog's not dangerous. He was doing you a favor."

The employee frowned. "Sir?"

Dave nodded toward the now-abandoned bench. DeLille was gone. Orlando remained standing by the planter, and the princess was still being comforted in the clutches of Mrs. Pinkerton. Dave lowered his voice to a whisper. "There's only one thing sets him off like that." The hotel employee frowned and leaned in, waiting for the explanation.

"Rats," Dave said. "The dog can't stand them."

The hotel employee recoiled, gasping.

"Don't worry," Dave said, backing away with the struggling dog. "We won't tell a soul."

Red-faced, the employee hurried back to the desk where he snatched the nearest telephone.

Dani and Max crowded around Dave and Sallie.

"What was all that about?" Dani asked.

"Nothing much," Dave said.

Sallie helped Dani gather up Dave's scattered shopping, a quantity of individual servings of yogurt, easy-open packets of dog food, and small packages wrapped in butcher paper.

"Why all the groceries?" Dani asked.

"I went to get some food for Tacet, but then I saw this little Chinese deli and then I passed a French cheese-monger's, and then there was this bakery... Anyway, I thought why not join the dog for a little picnic lunch in our room?"

Dani laughed. "Trust Dave King!" She turned to Sallie and Max. "There's enough here for half the conference. Why don't you join us?"

Sallie saw Orlando frown slightly.

"A capital idea," Max said, "but not indoors, please. The sun has come out, the clouds have passed, and there's hardly any wind. What would you think of having our picnic in one of the London parks?"

"Do you know of one near here?" Dani asked.

Sallie pulled a tourist map of London out of her shoulder bag. "The Victoria Embankment is practically around the corner." She showed them a little green area on the map.

"Perfect!" Dave said. "From the way that clerk has been eyeing us, it's probably a good idea to get Tacet out of sight for a while."

Orlando hung back.

"Well, Orlando?" Max said. "You're not too sophisticated for a picnic I hope?"

"No, sir. I wonder, might I invite Amber to come with us?"

The princess had a name. Amber.

This time the frown crossed Max's countenance, but before he could speak, Dani did.

"By all means," Dani said. "Do come with us, Amber. The more the merrier."

The girl blushed and looked at Orlando and blushed even more. "I'd love to go with you all, but Daddy told me to stay with Mrs. Pinkerton until he gets back from his day trip."

Alice Pinkerton went into flutter mode. "My goodness, I'm sure your father meant only that you should let me know where you are and that you're in good hands. I can't see any reason why you shouldn't go for a little outing with the Paulsons. Just be sure to let me know when you get back."

"That's settled, then," Dave said. "Lead on, Sallie."

Two by two the picnickers left the hotel, Sallie and Dani first, followed by Max and Dave, the latter firmly grasping Tacet's leash. Orlando and Amber brought up the rear.

"I'm surprised you were allowed to bring your dog into the country," Sallie heard Max say behind her. "There's a six-month quarantine for animals entering the UK."

"That's just for foreign dogs," Dave said. "This

dog is a British subject."

"Oh," Max said, "you've only just got him."

Curious to hear more, Sallie turned and walked backward a few steps. Dave was making a show of looking at his watch. "He's been with us exactly one day, twenty-one hours, and eighteen minutes."

Sallie blurted her surprise. "I heard you tell the clerk that the dog goes everywhere with you!"

"He does go everywhere with us," Dave said. "At least he has for the past one day, twenty-one hours and eighteen, make that nineteen, minutes."

"Watch out!" Dani pulled Sallie aside from collision with a lamp post. "I always find it best to face forward when walking."

Sallie resumed face-forward mode. "I wondered why anyone would bring an animal along to a six-day music convention. How'd you end up with him?"

"It's kind of a long story," Dani said. "And it's only temporary. Dave's keeping it for someone who's in the hospital." Dani stopped walking. "Is it much farther, do you think? These are not walking shoes I'm wearing."

"Here's Buckingham Street," Sallie said, looking from the map to a street sign ahead of them. In a quick series of turns, she led her troupe to Villiers Street and then down narrow steps to the Victoria Embankment.

"Is this it?" Dave sounded disappointed.

"It's pretty skinny for a park," Dani said.

Sallie looked again at the map. "The one at Lincoln's Fields is bigger, but according to this, it's only open in summer."

The green area on the map translated to a narrow strip of lawn that extended quite a distance along the

Embankment but was only about thirty feet in depth. Several park benches stood at intervals along the sidewalk.

"Oh well," Dani said, "at least there are plenty of benches, even if they're all lined up in a row." She commandeered a string of three vacant benches, laid the food out on the one in the center and invited the others to help themselves.

Max immediately seated himself on the nearest bench. Amber wandered off to look at a monument at the back of the park, but Orlando stayed close to Max, who told him what he wanted from the picnic supplies. Sallie watched curiously. She knew plenty of well-mannered teens in Arkansas and had seen them interact with their parents, but the kind of deference Orlando showed to Max was something new to her. There was something old-worldy about it, something found in a nineteenth century novel in which children called their parents Mater and Pater and saw them by appointment.

Having finished his serving duties, Orlando made his own choices and sat at the opposite end of Max's bench. Dave tied Tacet behind Orlando, got his provisions, and took the middle space.

With the men taken care of, Sallie and Dani took their turn at the yogurt, Baby Bels, egg rolls, and croissants and went to sit on the third bench. Just like school. Girls at one table, boys at the other. Amber was still at the back of the park. As the benches faced the river, Sallie twisted on the bench to see what was going on behind them.

A vendor taking advantage of the pleasant break in the weather strolled across the grass with a bunch of helium-filled balloons. He was soon surrounded by children. Most made their choices fairly quickly, but one little girl, whose down-at-heels mother looked as if she could ill-afford spending fifty pence for such a luxury, considered long and hard before settling on a blue-green balloon with a silvery sheen. She took the string with an expression of utter rapture.

Tacet made short work of his dog food and ran back and forth along the length of his leash, flicking his stub of a tail and looking hopefully at his human companions.

Amber returned from inspecting the monument and filled her plate. "Want some water, Orlando?" At his nod, she handed him a bottle of Perrier and went to join the women on their bench.

Orlando had just peeled a Baby Bel of its wax. Requiring both hands to open the water, he set the unwrapped cheese on the wooden armrest.

So fast that Sallie could hardly be sure of what she was seeing, Tacet snatched the cheese, but before the dog could chew or swallow, Orlando let go of the water, clamped the dog's neck in the crook of his right arm, and pried the cheese from its jaws with the fingers of his left hand. Tacet's astonished yelps drew Dave and Dani to the rescue while Max's deep authoritative voice burst into the language he used at the hotel in speaking to the Dirty Old Man.

"*Orlando! Pense bem! Tem bastante comida pra todo mundo, até mesmo pro cachorro. Não te trouxe aqui pra você fazer esse papelão.*"

Sallie's knowledge of French and smattering of Spanish weren't enough to make sense of the language that sounded like a mixture of the two, but Max's tone made it clear enough that Orlando was being castigated for taking food from the dog.

Hurling the cheese to the ground, Orlando, his face dark with emotion, strode toward the back of the narrow park. Amber picked up the still-sealed water bottle, looked uncertainly at the adults, and followed.

"Please excuse the boy," Max said, spreading both hands in a gesture of placation. "Not even ten years of a gentler existence have been sufficient to erase the hardships of his early life."

Neither Sallie nor the Kings asked for an explanation, but the question hung in the air. Max waved his hands in a swimming motion that implied "Gather round," so she and Dani remained standing to listen.

"I adopted Orlando when he was eight years old," Max said. "A Brazilian friend of mine, Senhor Gomés, you may have seen me talking to him at the hotel, short gentleman with remarkable white hair, Senhor Gomés brought Orlando to my attention." Max paused to take a sip from his bottle of water.

Sallie shuddered. Senhor Gomés was the man she'd christened "the Dirty Old Man." Senhor Gomés gave her the creeps. For that matter, her friendly feelings toward Max had slipped considerably since the scene outside the master class. She hadn't forgotten the venomous look he cast at DeLille before resuming his habitual look of benign urbanity. Could be that Max Paulson wasn't the kindly philanthropist Mrs. Pinkerton and the Kings took him for.

Max continued his explanation. "Senhor Gomés noticed Orlando among the *meninos de rua*, the 'street kids' of Rio. He was struck by his beauty and the haunting way he played the little Indian flute he'd made for himself. Senhor Gomés knew of my philanthropic work and sent me a photograph. I flew to Rio to look into the boy's background and have him examined by a doctor. We learned that Orlando had been living with his mother until a few weeks before Senhor Gomés first noticed him in the street playing his flute."

Max twisted his body on the bench, checking to see that Orlando was still at the back of the park with Amber. Sallie followed his glance. The two young flutists stood close together, talking animatedly. Near them, the little girl with the silvery balloon ran back and forth in front of a white monument that looked like a gateway to nowhere.

Satisfied that Orlando couldn't hear, Max continued. "We learned that Orlando's mother had been beaten to death by her *amigo*, her boyfriend, who then turned Orlando out of the house. The child lived in the streets long enough to learn to fight for every mouthful of food, but not, thank God, long enough to become hopelessly diseased or addicted to sniffing glue."

Max patted his lips with a paper napkin. Then he held the napkin and his empty water bottle out to Sallie. She took it and immediately flushed with annoyance at his assumption that she was there to serve him. Not so much as a "please" or "would you?"

Sallie put his bottle with the empties and went to sit by Dani. Max went to join his foster son at the back of the park. Dani had kicked off her shoes and was rubbing her feet.

"I wish I'd thought to change my shoes before coming out," Dani said. "Heels are fine in the hotel, but not so good for walking this far."

Dave came to sit with them, Tacet's lead looped

securely around his wrist. The dog put his paws up by Dani and licked her exposed foot.

Dani shoved him away. "Ugh! Go away, Tacet! You've no idea how strange your tongue feels through nylon."

A piercing cry from the back of the park brought them to their feet. Turning, they saw Max gripping Orlando by an arm and shouting with the same show of fury he'd shown over the cheese incident. The shriek had come from the little girl with the balloon. Defiant, Orlando yanked his arm away and ran to the screaming child. The little girl stood at the foot of the white monument, wailing piteously as she watched her helium-filled prize float upwards to the freedom of the skies.

The trailing string snagged on a projection near the top of the monument. The child's mother ran up and tried to lead the girl away, but the child held her ground, reaching toward the balloon and screaming piteously. Orlando knelt beside her with his wallet in his hand. He offered her a bill, money to buy a new balloon, Sallie assumed, but the child pulled away in refusal. Orlando put away the money and whispered into her ear. Whatever he said caused her screams to diminish into hiccupping sobs.

In the next instant, Orlando was clambering up the side of the monument toward the top where the string remained caught. The child squealed delightedly as her champion retrieved the balloon, returned to the ground, and presented it to her with a gallant bow.

Max seized Orlando's arm and loosed another volley of Portuguese. This time his foster son did not struggle but allowed himself to be led away.

The girl's mother came over to Sallie and Dani. "That was a very kind thing for that young man to do," she said.

Sallie thought so too. Reputations and first impressions are often deceiving. Certainly Alice Pinkerton's introduction of Max Paulson as "saint" was not holding up. And now her impression of Orlando as selfish rich kid had shifted.

The blow-up over the balloon terminated the picnic. Amber stood staring after the Paulsons. Dani and Dave were packing up, so Sallie went to help. With a jolt, she remembered her two o'clock coffee date with the handsome flute salesman. She glanced at her watch. One-thirty. Plenty of time.

Dani, Dave, and the dog led the way back to the hotel. Sallie walked behind with Amber, covertly studying the girl's profile. High forehead, lush black eyelashes, and full, pouting mouth. Poor little rich girl, whom daddy could never quite make happy. Sallie may have been wrong about Orlando, but Amber displayed all the signs of being a spoilt child. Sallie often wondered about the children who are showered with material gifts from the time they're born. What's left for them to want when they grow up and find themselves on their own? The thought brought her back to the scene between Orlando and Max. Amber might be able to shed some light on their relationship.

"Any idea why Mr. Paulson hustled Orlando away like that?"

Amber made a noise with her lips that sent saliva flying.

"Orlando was being 'undignified.' " Her brown eyes flashed anger mixed with pain. On the brink of tears, she wiped her eyes on the cuff of her sleeve. "That's what Mr. Paulson was calling him. 'Undignified.' He was so mad he was shouting half in English and half in Portuguese. He said if Orlando wanted to help the little girl, he should have given her money to buy another balloon and not make a monkey of himself and risk arrest by climbing a public monument." Amber stared at Sallie, her face contorted with disbelief. "He couldn't understand that the little girl didn't want just any balloon. She wanted that balloon." Now the tears fell unchecked. "Why can't grown-ups understand that money isn't the answer to everything?"

Another first impression dashed. Sallie didn't attempt to respond to Amber's anguished question. She gave the girl what she hoped was a look of understanding. That's all it took. The teenage angst burst out to the sympathetic ear.

"I don't want to be a professional flute player, Miss Dunbar! I'm not good enough. Not like Orlando. It's not what I want. It's all Daddy's idea. All I want is to get married and have babies."

"Why don't you tell your father how you feel?"

"I've tried. He doesn't want to hear it. My momma was a professional flutist. When they met, she was playing with a symphony orchestra. He's never said, but I think I was an accident. Momma had to leave the symphony to have me. And then she got sick and died and Daddy felt guilty about taking her away from her music. So now he's making up for it. Only I'm not my momma and I don't want a career in music."

Back at the hotel, Sallie returned Amber to the custody of Alice Pinkerton, but only after a crushing hug from the girl. Sallie looked at her watch. It was ten to two.

At the elevator, Dani leaned heavily on Dave. Clearly her feet were giving her intense pain. She smiled a bit wanly as Sallie joined them. "We're going up to the room to rest for a while. Why don't you meet us for dinner? Our treat. To make up for the unpleasantness at lunch."

Sallie forced a smile, feeling the minutes ticking away. "You might be better off staying upstairs for the rest of the day and ordering room service."

Dave laughed. "She's tough. Give her an hour or two to put her feet up and she'll be ready to go again."

"OK. What time?"

"Seven's good," Dani said. "Knock on our door when you're ready, and we'll go down together."

As soon as the elevator doors closed on the Kings, Sallie headed for the coffee shop and her date with Kassim the gorgeous flute salesman.

Chapter Nine

Kassim was already there, sitting at a small, round table for two. As soon as he saw Sallie, he stood to pull out her chair. The gesture flattered and flustered her. She wasn't used to such treatment. At home she was the one to offer attentions to her mother. At work she was lucky not to have the chair pulled out from under her in the lunchroom.

"So, tell me, Sallie, as you are not a professional musician, what is it that you do in life?" He looked at her from liquid brown eyes that set her insides dancing.

"I'm an English teacher," she said, waiting for the usual negative response, the Ugh, English! I was never any good at English.

If the look of interest that sprang into those beautiful eyes was feigned, he was a better actor than the Oscar nominee he looked like. "An English teacher! How splendid. Since I was a young boy, the study of English literature has been one of the greatest joys of my life."

Sallie felt her mouth drop open and quickly shut it.

"My father wanted me to study Western economics," he said. "Of course, I did as he wished, but always I managed to slip in at least one literature course every term."

Sallie listened in a delighted daze as Kassim told her about himself. He'd been born in Istanbul, but his father's business took the family all over the world. He spent his childhood in Damascus, Paris, and Leningrad. He'd studied at Cairo in Egypt, Montpelier in France, and Keele University in the north of England.

"My love of English literature began while I was still a boy in Turkey," he said, leaning forward. "My father insisted that I study English, as a business tool, of course, not for aesthetic reasons. I began my study of the language with the same attitude as I did economics and the other courses required of me—a duty to be accomplished. Then, one year, the teacher assigned my class a novel by Dickens—it was *David Copperfield*. I became enchanted by the literature. Every year I try to read the collected works of one principal English author. Some, of course, have taken me more than a year to get through. Dickens, for example, and Trollope."

Sallie caught her breath in delight. She knew fellow English teachers who'd never even heard of Trollope, let alone read all of his novels. Why couldn't she have found someone like Kassim twelve years ago, instead of ending up with a Philistine whose idea of a good book was one with short sentences, lots of pictures, and not too many pages?

Sallie listened, hypnotized, as Kassim talked about the same books she loved. When they got to *Madame Bovary*, they talked awhile in French, Sallie feeling nervous from lack of practice, but managing to keep up.

A sudden crash of breaking glass and an exclamation that sounded like "Kuk!" shattered Sallie's happy trance. A waiter had dropped a tray of cups. The coffee shop was carpeted, but the adjacent walkway was tiled. The tray landed on carpet, but the cups had hit the tile. The waiter was on his knees gathering the shards. Kassim left his seat and knelt to help.

Sallie had to look twice. It was the waiter she'd seen in the Four Moons and later in the Hunter's Den. Did he ever sleep?

Kassim and the man were speaking some language Sallie didn't recognize, although a couple of times she thought she heard something that sounded like "American" and once a word that resembled "Bernini." Once, they both looked in her direction, as if talking about her, but she knew that had to be her imagination. In a few minutes, a busboy came with broom and mop and Kassim resumed his seat opposite her.

"What language were you speaking?" Sallie asked. "Turkish?"

"Armenian." Kassim looked at her if expecting a reaction. "You don't seem surprised. Turks and Armenians are not known for friendliness to one another."

Sallie's knowledge of world history was linked to her study of literature. She couldn't think of any Armenian writers. Except maybe William Saroyan, and he was born in Fresno.

"Sorry. All I associate with the word Armenian is my grandmother's favorite harangue when I wouldn't clean my plate at supper. 'Think of the starving Armenians,' she'd tell me. I never could understand how eating sweet potatoes in Arkansas could help starving Armenians wherever in the world they were."

Kassim smiled gravely.

"I shall not be the one to explain. I'll simply ask you to remember, when you do read about that evil episode of history, that my family did what they could to help their Armenian neighbors."

Sallie was ready to hear anything Kassim wanted to tell her, but he looked at his watch and put a graceful end to the conversation by telling her how much he'd enjoyed their visit and asking her to meet him again later in the evening. Sallie walked with him as far as one of the stairways to the lower level and then retraced her steps to the lobby.

Not many people were about; the late afternoon sessions were still in progress. She glanced at the big clock behind the registration desk. Too early to meet Dave and Dani for supper, but too late for another go at sightseeing. Someone touched her on the shoulder.

"Say, Sallie. What do you say to having supper with me tonight?"

Harry Slocum stood there, smiling his Rockford smile. When he wasn't being a jerk, he certainly was attractive. For a moment she considered breaking her dinner date with the Kings to go with him but decided she'd better concentrate on one man at a time.

"Thanks, Harry, but I've already made plans for dinner. Another time, maybe."

A wave of exhaustion washed over Sallie as soon as she stepped off the elevator onto her floor. All she wanted to do was lie down. Back in her room, she kicked off her shoes, set her alarm for a quarter to seven, and fell onto the bed. As she shut her eyes, the exquisite strains of the Fourth Floor Flute playing the Pachebel Canon carried her into sleep.

When the alarm sounded, Sallie woke as if refreshed by a ten-hour sleep. "If I didn't know better," she said to the empty room, "I'd think there was something magical about the Fourth Floor Flute."

When Dani opened the door to Sallie's knock at seven, she was wearing heels. Sallie shook her head in disbelief. "How can you bear to wear those spikes after the way your feet hurt you at lunch?"

"It's the most amazing thing," Dani said. "When we got back to the room I literally collapsed. I thought I'd be lucky to be able to walk tomorrow, let alone tonight. But then I lay down and fell asleep to the sound of that flute someone keeps playing at all hours. When I woke, my feet were fine. Not a bit of pain. I feel absolutely marvelous and ready to go."

Dave propelled both women toward the elevator. "Come on, then. I'm starving."

As soon as they'd placed their orders in the Hunter's Den, Dave turned to Sallie. "By the way, what's become of your boyfriend?"

Sallie stared at him in bewilderment, wondering how he could possibly know about her coffee date with Kassim.

"The big football type I've seen you with," Dave said.

Sallie groaned. "You must mean Harry Slocum. I'd hardly call him my 'boyfriend.' We shared a seat on the plane from Dallas and we went to a pub yesterday evening with some other people. That's the extent of it."

Dani pulled the convention program from her purse. She opened it to the members' pages at the back and ran a finger down the pages. "I don't see a Slocum. Are you sure he's an IOFA member?"

Sallie was beginning to feel annoyed. "I assume so. He plays the flute for some orchestra in California. First flute."

"Did he mention the name of the orchestra? Or what city it's in?"

Sallie tried to remember. "I think he said San Francisco. The San Francisco Symphony Orchestra."

Dani frowned and looked at Dave.

"You'd think Pam would have told us if they'd got an orchestra in San Francisco." She took a swallow from her martini and turned back to Sallie. "We have several musical friends in California. Some in L.A., some in the San Francisco area."

"There's been some talk of starting a symphony in the Bay area," Dave said. "I heard that Barry Jekowsky may be trying to get one started."

"Could be," Dani said, "but so far, there's no symphony in San Francisco."

"I'm pretty sure he said California," Sallie said. "Wait!" The tape she'd bought that morning in the exhibit hall was still in her bag. She fished it out and handed it to Dani. "This might tell you something. I bought it this morning, mainly because Harry told me he played for the recording. It's conducted by Marcel Moyse." Dani took a brief look and passed the box to Dave.

"Mozart's *Gran Partita*." Dave frowned and looked up. "Slocum said he played in this? Played a flute part on it?"

Sallie nodded. "Second flute, he told me. Under Marcel Moyse. I thought that was pretty impressive."

"Extremely impressive," Dave said, handing it back.

"Is it a difficult part for flute?" Sallie asked, dropping the cassette back into her bag.

"I'd say so." Dave exchanged a glance with Dani

before fixing Sallie with an intense look. "You're sure he said he played flute on this recording."

Sallie was beginning to feel she was taking part in an interrogation rather than a conversation. "I told you, that's the reason I bought it." Thinking her tone of voice might have been a bit too sharp, she tried to make amends. "I thought it would be cool to be able to say that I'd met someone who'd made a recording with Marcel Moyse."

"I'm afraid you'll have to keep looking," Dave said. "Harry Slocum never played second or any other kind of flute part on this recording."

Sallie's face grew hot. "How can you know that?"

"Because," Dani said, "Mozart's K361—the *Gran Partita*—doesn't have a flute part."

"It's a serenade for thirteen winds." Dave said and proceeded to reel them off. "Two oboes, two clarinets, two basset horns, four horns, two bassoons, and one double bass."

"No flute?"

"No flute."

"Why would he lie about it?"

"Good question. Maybe he was just trying to impress you." For a moment a serious expression overlaid the flippant one Dave usually wore. "You say you didn't know Slocum before you met him on the plane?"

"You've asked me that more than once, Dave. I've told you, I never saw him before in my life."

Sallie had had enough. She grasped the strap of her bag and stood. "I'll be going now."

"Join us for the evening concert?" Dani asked.

"Thanks, but no. I'm meeting someone later for

coffee." There she went again. Offering more information than necessary to people who didn't need to know.

"Slocum?" Dave asked.

"No. Not Slocum. A flute salesman named Kassim. I met him in the exhibit hall." Damn. They didn't need to know that. The Kings exchanged another one of their eloquent, intimate glances.

"Be careful," Dani said. "You can always check out an IOFA member's credentials, but these exhibitors are another story."

Sallie left the restaurant in an icy frame of mind. Why were the Kings so interested in her acquaintance with Harry? And why had Harry lied about the Mozart tape? For all she knew, he'd lied about everything else he'd told her. She took the familiar path to the elevator. Might as well wait in her room until time to meet Kassim.

Kassim. Sallie smiled. She loved the sound of his name. Suddenly she realized that she didn't know if it was a first or last name. Whichever, it had a nicer sound than Slocum. She never thought Harry looked like a flute player. But he did know a lot about flutes and the artists who owned the most expensive ones. If he wasn't a musician, what was he?

Back in her room, Sallie considered changing into something more date-like and realized she still hadn't unpacked. She heaved one of the wheeled bags onto the bed and unzipped it, thinking with satisfaction of the cocktail dress and the gauzy negligee she'd brought. Knowing that Momma would probably snoop, she'd kept them in the car, waiting to pack them at the last minute. The dress would probably be wrinkled, but she'd brought a travel iron with an adapter for the British outlets.

She removed items from the first suitcase. Travel iron. More papers to grade. A chenille robe? She never packed that. Flannel pajamas? Where was fancy negligee? Where was the slinky black dress? They must be in the other bag.

First she hung the robe in the wardrobe and put the pajamas into a drawer. Then she opened the other bag. Hair dryer. Extra shoes. Five pairs of slacks. Five? She only packed two. She didn't remember putting in that thick woolen cardigan. No cocktail dress. No fancy nighty.

Momma.

Sallie thought back to the morning she left. Momma stood on the upstairs porch in her pink chenille bathrobe and fake leopard-skin slippers, watching as the airport shuttle driver loaded Sallie's bags.

"Whatever you do," Momma shouted down, oblivious to the fact that it was four-thirty in the morning and neighbors were trying to sleep, "whatever you do, dear, don't get involved in one of those shipboard romances like Joan Bennett did in *Trade Winds* or Joan Gardner in *Forget Me Not* or Joan Crawford in *Letty Lynton*. You don't know where one of those things will lead."

Momma's view of the world was shaped by old movies. She'd even named Sallie for her two favorite leading ladies of the Forties. "Sallie" was a nickname. As far as she was concerned, neither Myrna nor Greer was an option.

Sallie fingered the black slacks. So much for trying to dazzle Kassim with her femininity. Momma hadn't left her a single skirt. She had overlooked a white blouse with a frilly front that looked pretty good under a blazer. Doing the best she could with what she had, Sallie finished dressing and went downstairs to meet Kassim in the coffee shop.

He was already there.

Again the solicitous seating ritual.

"Did you enjoy your dinner?" he asked.

"Oh yes. I don't know why people make jokes about English cooking. So far I've liked everything. How about you? Sell many flutes today?"

He smiled.

"Flutes plural? If I sell one flute during the entire convention my employers will be pleased."

"How many did you sell at the conference last year?"

Kassim hesitated, choosing his words carefully. "I'm told that three sales at a conference is very good." He picked up the laminated menu. "If you have no preference, I recommend the Irish coffee."

The conversation quickly returned to the topic of their earlier meeting. Books. Discovering a mutual love of Samuel Johnson, they exchanged a volley of quotations.

"To him that lives well, every form of life is good." Kassim quoted.

"He that hath much to do will do something wrong," Sallie returned.

"The life of a solitary man will certainly be miserable, but not certainly devout."

"Human life is everywhere a state in which much is to be endured and little to be enjoyed."

"I am willing to love all mankind, except an

American."

Sallie laughed. "I don't take that one personally," she said. "Dr. Johnson loved the monarchy. To him Americans were rebels and convicts. And he hated slavery."

Kassim nodded and offered another of Johnson's epigrams. "How is it that we hear the loudest yelps for liberty among the drivers of negroes?"

The arrival of coffee put an end to the quotation competition.

Sallie was especially partial to whipped cream so she liked the Irish coffee. She didn't object when Kassim ordered seconds. They sat for a while in comfortable silence. When Kassim spoke again, it was with a total change of subject.

"Please don't think me impertinent, Sallie, but I have noticed you often in the company of a tall, broad-shouldered American gentleman. I do not know his name. Is he perhaps a friend with whom you have come to the convention?"

Sallie felt the blood rise. Not again.

"His name is Harry Slocum and I hardly know him. The first I ever saw him was when he sat down next to me on the plane in Dallas. We shared a taxi from Victoria Station. That's it."

Kassim smiled and brushed her hand with his fingers.

"I am glad to hear it." They sat a few more minutes in silence. When Kassim spoke again, Sallie expected anything but another question about Harry.

"Is Mr. Slocum a musician?"

"He says he is. My impression is that he's more interested in the price of a flute than in playing one."

"How so?"

"Every time a flutist's name comes up, he tells me what kind of flute he plays and what it's probably insured for."

Kassim frowned.

"Has he shown any interest in your flute?"

Sallie laughed. "He did, until I told him it was a low-end student's flute. He lost interest pretty fast."

"Did he perhaps say anything about being in Santa Monica last year?"

"He is from California. At least, that's what he told me. Supposedly he plays in an orchestra out there. I think he did say something about Santa Monica, but I don't remember exactly what. Something about somebody's expensive flute, probably."

"You say 'supposedly' plays. Do you doubt his word?"

Sallie shrugged. "I've discovered that people don't always tell the truth about themselves."

Kassim picked up a spoon and stirred his coffee. Looking at the frothy liquid, he quoted Dr. Johnson again. "All imposture weakens confidence and chills benevolence."

They finished drinking their coffee without further talk. When Kassim spoke again, it was to bring their second "date" to an end. "I regret to have to end our very pleasant interlude, Sallie. Unfortunately, I must rise very early in order to have my display set up by eight a.m."

He walked her back to the elevator.

"You must try to get away from the convention long enough to visit the Charing Cross Road, Sallie. It is famous for its bookstores. And it is not far from this hotel, just off Trafalgar Square. You can catch a Number Nine bus and be there in minutes."

When the elevator doors opened, he took her hand for a moment. "Come to my booth again tomorrow if you have the opportunity. I'll let you try out a $10,000 flute." He loosed her hand before the doors slid shut, but she continued to feel his touch all the way to the fourth floor.

The unknown flute player was still at it. Ordinarily Sallie would have felt annoyance that someone should be so inconsiderate as to play in a hotel at all hours, even at a music convention, but the sound of what she'd come to think of as "the Fourth Floor Flute" was never irritating. The music continued as she got into bed. The notes were like a gentle presence, soothing away the fatigue of travel and jet lag. Her last thought before drifting off into sleep was that five good days remained of the IOFA convention, time enough for the shipboard romance Momma warned her against.

Chapter Ten

Tuesday, 26 November 1985, Day Two of the

IOFA Convention

Sallie woke on the second day of the convention with a feeling of extreme well-being. Her first thoughts were of Kassim. She would definitely visit him again at his booth and try the $10,000 flute, but first she'd visit Charing Cross Road and browse the bookstores as he'd suggested.

Showering and dressing quickly, she made sure she had money and traveler's checks at the ready in the fanny pack. She was hoping to buy a few souvenirs, so she emptied everything from one of the shoulder bags onto the bed, repacking with only the most indispensable essentials such as the flashlight and a packet of disinfectant wipes. Her map of London went into the bag's outer pocket. Plenty of room in the interior compartment for souvenirs. She'd be looking for small, inexpensive things like pencils and key chains.

At the Kings' door she hesitated. They probably expected her to have breakfast with them. She raised her hand to knock, but then pulled it back. What did it matter what they expected? Wasn't it time she quit adjusting her plans to the expectations of others?

Lowering her hand, she headed for the elevator.

Harry Slocum, wearing the boxy red plaid overshirt that made him look like a lumberjack, was there before her. He carried a flute case that looked like the one she'd seen him take from the scary bald man in the Exhibit Hall.

"Morning, Sallie. Up and at 'em pretty early, aren't you?"

She fixed him with her classroom don't-even-think-of-messing-with-me look. "What's the idea?" she asked.

His cheerful expression clouded. "What's what idea?"

"What's the idea of telling me you played second flute on that Mozart recording? The one that doesn't have a flute part?"

Harry exploded in laughter and slapped Sallie so hard on the back that she staggered.

"I couldn't resist," he said. "I knew from the plane how little you know about flute players and flute music. It seemed like a good joke."

"It wasn't funny," Sallie said, stepping into the elevator and standing as far from him as she could.

"Aw, I'm sorry if I made you mad. Let me make it up to you by buying you breakfast."

Sallie knew she was being mercenary, but money not spent for breakfast could go for souvenirs. "All right."

The Armenian waiter was already at work, bussing tables and refilling coffee cups. Most of the guests in the breakfast line were teenagers, Amber among them.

"Good morning, Miss Dunbar!" Amber threaded her way through the line to stand next to her. "Are you going on the tour? It's mainly for the youth, but grownups can go too if they want."

Sallie avoided the kippers again and stocked her tray with her usual favorites: scrambled eggs, link sausages, strawberries, and melon. Grits would have been nice. "No, Amber. I have plans of my own. I want to browse the bookstores along Charing Cross Road."

When Sallie reached the cashier, she looked behind her, expecting to see Harry, but he was several places farther down the line, chatting with one of the youth players. She had to charge breakfast to her own room number after all.

By the time Harry joined her, Sallie had finished her eggs. She spoke without looking up. "Did you do it on purpose?"

"What's that?" Harry placed his tray on the table. He was still carrying the flute case and kept it on his lap when he sat down.

Sallie handed him the receipt for her breakfast.

"Oh, sorry. I'll take care of it right now." He put the flute case on the table. "Watch this for me," he said, and went back to the cashier's station.

Sallie glanced at the case. One of the latches was not completely shut, so she reached over to close it all the way. Suddenly she wanted to know what kind of flute Harry played. He was always going on about quality and price. On the plane he'd told her about Bernini's $70,000 platinum flute, and how some man at a conference had a $10,000 Maramatsu stolen from him while he was still paying for it. She looked over at the food line. Harry's back was to her as he waited for a chance to speak to the cashier. She pulled the case toward her. It wasn't new. It was a large case, one that could hold a C flute and a piccolo. A Ninja Turtles decal occupied almost a quarter of one side. Part of the decal had been torn away, taking the T with it, leaving URTLES. She opened the case.

The piccolo compartment was empty, but an instrument occupied the larger compartment. Sallie lifted out the head joint and made a scoffing sound when she read the manufacturer's name. Harry had described this particular make as "absolute rubbish, stiff-to-blow, out-of-tune, poorly fitted, needing repair every two months." Evidently he was in a position to know. She closed the lid and shoved the case back to the edge of the table.

Harry returned and waved the new receipt under her nose. "All taken care of," he said. "Your charge is now on my room." He took a sip of coffee. "Agg. Ice cold." He held up his cup and looked around for a waiter. The Armenian promptly answered the signal and replaced Harry's cold coffee with a fresh cup. Harry took a sip. "Ah, that's better. Cold eggs I can manage, but my coffee's gotta be hot. So, Sallie, what sessions will you be attending today?"

"Nothing this morning. Maybe something this afternoon. This morning I'm going to explore the Charing Cross Road." Resisting the idea that for politeness' sake she ought to stay until Harry finished, she stood to go. "Thanks for breakfast, Harry. And don't forget, no more jokes at my expense."

Harry grinned over the rim of his coffee cup. "Deal."

The lobby outside the Hunter's Den churned with new arrivals and a crowd of young people milling around a low table to the left of the revolving door. The teens were leafing through glossy brochures illustrated with London landmarks. A frazzled Alice Pinkerton sat by the table, gazing up at Amber's father, who was objecting to something.

"I want to know she'll be with an adult while I'm gone," he said. "I may not get back until late."

"Don't worry, Mr. Callahan, I won't let her out of my sight until you reclaim her."

Callahan looked dubious. "Are you sure? London is a big place with crowds everywhere. She could get separated from the group."

Miss Pinkerton flushed. "Mr. Callahan, I've been shepherding the IOFA youth for the past twelve years. I've yet to lose one of them."

Amber stroked her father's arm. "I'll stay close to Miz P, Daddy, I promise!" She stood tiptoe to kiss him. "You just stop worrying and enjoy your day trip to Oxford."

Callahan still hesitated, clearly reluctant to leave his daughter with strangers. His ornate silver belt buckle glinted in a flash of light from the street and Sallie again tried to make out the design. It wasn't an eagle or a flag or any kind of horned animal. It was taller than it was wide and narrower at the top than at the bottom, kind of like the Eiffel Tower.

"What on earth are you staring at?"

Sallie startled. Dani King stood beside her, trying to see what she was looking at.

"Nothing," Sallie said. "I was just, nothing." T-shirt reading was an acceptable vice, but staring at a man's belt buckle bordered on the impolite so she didn't try to explain.

Amber's father finally agreed to leave his daughter

in Alice's care and went to join his own excursion. Sallie turned her attention to Dani, who was carrying a large instrument case. "That can't be a flute."

Dani beamed. "Alto. There aren't very many of them around so I bring mine to improve my chances of getting into the Convention Choir. It always works. I'm on my way to practice now. Where's your flute?"

"In my room. I'm not going to embarrass myself by trying out for one of the choirs. I'm sorry I even brought it."

"Well, if you aren't going to keep it with you, it will be better off in Security than in your room."

"No one's going to want to steal my little student's flute, not with so many high-priced numbers around."

"Maybe not, but if it were mine, I wouldn't take the chance."

Sallie recalled finding the door to her room propped open by the cleaner's cart. "Maybe you're right. I'll take it to the security room when I get back. Right now, I'm on my way to have a look at London."

Dani moved off and Sallie turned toward the side door, passing Alice Pinkerton, who was now exercising her powers of persuasion on Max Paulson.

"Orlando needs a break, Mr. Paulson. Too much work and no play and all that. He'll be back in time for lunch."

"He needs to be rested for the final auditions."

"It's not rest he needs, it's relaxation. You've always got him at your side when he's not practicing or playing. He needs to spend some time with people his own age, for heavens' sake."

Out of earshot, Orlando stood near the side exit, talking earnestly to Benoît DeLille. The quality of their clothing contrasted starkly. Orlando wore an expensive black leather jacket with a fancy matching backpack slung over one shoulder. DeLille wore the scruffy duffle coat, its dreariness brightened by a fuzzy red scarf around his neck. Some kind of tension flowed between them. Orlando had a pleading look and seemed on the verge of tears. Benoît was frowning.

To avoid the drama, Sallie exited by way of the main entrance's revolving door instead of the side door as she'd intended. Outside, she came face to face with Alan Bernini.

"Miss Dunbar! I'm so glad to have run into you like this." Seizing her by the arm, Bernini drew her around the corner to the side entrance. He moved his right hand without any apparent pain. "I was hoping I might see you today. I'm afraid I must have been insufferable the other evening. I want to apologize for any rudeness on my part."

"You've nothing to apologize for. I'm glad I could help a little and that your hand wasn't badly injured. Looks like you will be able play the closing solo at Saturday's banquet."

"Oh yes. It would take more than a little sprain to stop me. But here, I want to return this." He reached inside his coat and brought out an outsized manila envelope. "Your bandage. Sorry for the enormous envelope. It's all I had."

Sallie felt herself redden. "You can keep it."

"Oh no! You never know when you might happen across another gentleman in distress!" Bernini laughed. Sallie took the envelope.

Bernini's lapel pin caught a gleam of sunlight. It was a tiny flute set with colored stones.

"What a beautiful lapel pin," Sallie said. "I've seen a lot of them since Sunday, but yours is the most unusual yet."

"It was custom-made," Bernini said, looking pleased. "Done by a jeweler in Switzerland. Actually, I had him make two of them. They're the only two like them in the world."

Sallie leaned in to get a better look. "The red ones must be garnet," she said, "but what are the lighter stones?"

"Sardonyx."

"Oh. Garnet for constancy and sardonyx for fidelity." Sallie had created a writing exercise based on birthstones and their symbolism.

Bernini's ruddy face flushed redder.

"Exactly. How clever of you to know the meanings."

Sallie felt herself blush. She loved it when someone thought she was smart. After shaking hands, Bernini entered the hotel by the side door and she smiled after him, speculating that he had a girlfriend somewhere who wore the matching pin. Orlando was still standing near the side entrance, looking directly at her with an expression she couldn't identify, but which was not pleasant. Even when she made eye contact, his expression didn't change. Behind him, Max Paulson came around the divider and touched his shoulder, startling him.

Sallie shrugged and turned away. She'd had enough of the strange comings and goings of the IOFA people. Max Paulson gave her the willies. And the expression she'd just seen in Orlando's eyes reminded her of the venomous look Max gave Benoît DeLille outside Truffaut's master class. She folded Bernini's envelope as small as it would go, slipped it into her bag, and went to find the first red bus going in the direction of Trafalgar Square and Charing Cross Road.

Boarding the bus, Sallie was glad to have bought a transportation pass at the airport. Not only was it cheaper than paying per bus ride, but it saved her from having to figure out exact change in English money.

Eager to see London from the top of the city's signature double-decker, she mounted the steps. At the top, she was engulfed by a thick cloud of cigarette smoke. Apparently the top level was the smoking section. Not wishing to inhale any of the yellowish-gray miasma, she descended and took a downstairs seat.

At Trafalgar Square the bus turned into Charing Cross Road, passing the little church of St. Martin-in-the-Fields and slowing to a snail's pace in the traffic that clogged the famous thoroughfare. As a tourist, Sallie was unbothered by traffic jams that probably infuriated the locals. For her, the slower the bus went, the better. She pressed her forehead eagerly against the window. Everything she saw thrilled the Anglophile in her, the blue and white tube sign for Leicester Square, the wide black and white stripes of the zebra crossings, a garbage truck painted with the City of London coat of arms, and a Bobby in his tall blue, almost black helmet weaving between the motor vehicles on a bicycle.

She descended at Oxford Street and breathed in the smell of London: traffic fumes, soot, food aromas of many cultures, and an unidentifiable olfactory patina of the ages. London! The Scottish poet Dunbar—presumably no relation—called it *the flower of cities alle*. And what did Dr. Johnson say? *When you're tired of London, you're tired of life.*

Across from the bus stop, an enormous billboard advertised the movie *Back to the Future*. Giant cutouts of Michael J. Fox and his time machine loomed above the scurrying London shoppers and commuters.

Crossing Oxford Street, Sallie went into a rather bare-looking café and joined a queue of morning tea-drinkers. Copying the other customers, she took a cup as big as one of her mother's soup mugs, filled it from a gigantic urn, fortified her tea with sugar and milk, and sat in a plastic chair at an unoccupied table. When the tea was cool enough to drink, she sipped and sighed. The decor might be vintage Trailways-waiting-room, but she had never in her life tasted such a perfect cup of hot tea. Now she understood why in so many English novels, at any crisis of nerves, somebody brings the protagonist "a nice cuppa." By the time she'd finished her cuppa, she felt ready for anything.

Outside, Sallie turned her back on Oxford Street with its fashionable department stores and boutiques and headed down Charing Cross Road. Kassim had not misled her. By far the dominant word on the signs along the famous road read, BOOKS.

Her first stop on the right was at Foyle's, a huge store with more than one entrance and occupying more than one building. As she pushed open one of the heavy front doors, the dry papery inky smell of books flooded her with a sense of happiness. Ever since childhood summer days hiding out from Aunt Ellie and Cousin Bertie at family gatherings, Sallie associated reading with clandestine pleasure. Family occasions always tried her resourcefulness. Just when she was ensconced in a hiding place where she could read in peace, Bertie would find her and sound the alarm: "Sallie's reading a book!" His tone was accusatory, as if he'd caught her filling the sugar bowls with salt. Sun-worshipping Aunt Ellie would come at once to shoo her out into the sunshine. For Sallie, reading had always been an act of civil disobedience.

In Foyle's, mesmerized by the smell and the sight of stacks and stacks of books, Sallie slipped into an altered mental state. All thoughts of her personal tribulations vanished as she responded to the riches around her. Two hours later, surfacing from a beautiful illustrated edition of Greek myths, she blinked and gazed around. For a moment or so, she wondered where she was and how she'd got there.

Sallie left without buying anything, not only because she was strapped for cash, but also because everything that tempted her was the size of a briefcase. She'd end up with suitcases too heavy to move, even on wheels. The store offered a mailing service for foreigners, but she could forget that. She had enough cash to buy the book on mythology, but not enough to cover postage. It was just as well she hadn't been able to obtain a credit card after Nick died.

Leaving Foyle's, Sallie glimpsed the reflection of a tall, cadaverous figure in the glass door. Whirling, she scanned the shoppers around her but didn't see anyone matching the reflection. It certainly looked like the Armenian waiter from the hotel. Surely he couldn't also have a job in the Charing Cross Road.

Next, Sallie crossed to the Oxford University Press bookshop opposite Foyle's. All the books published by the OUP in one place. Paradise. One bank of shelves was dedicated to the little blue-bound Oxford World

Classics. One or two of these wouldn't take up much space in her suitcase. She recalled what Kassim had told her about his reading habits, how he tried to read all the works of one author every year. Although a voracious reader, Sallie had never been a systematic one. She decided to emulate Kassim and choose a writer whose collected works she would read during the coming year.

Scanning the little Classics, she saw a two-volume set of Samuel Johnson's *Lives of the Poets*. She'd begin with Doctor Johnson. She'd learned to love him, American-hater that he was, through an abridgment of Boswell's *Life*. She'd read his tiny novel *Rasselas* at least ten times, underlining and memorizing the epigrams that stood out like jewels against the ponderous narrative. She'd read one or two of the *Lives of the Poets* in literature survey courses, but now she would read them all. After she paid and left the shop, she resolved to buy some souvenirs before spending any more money on herself.

In a novelty store, she bought several pencils and key chains decorated with Union Jacks. She'd give them to colleagues and students. In a tiny shop smelling of cloves, she bought tea in a fancy tin box for her mother, a box of marzipan for Uncle Curtis, and for herself, a University of Oxford sweatshirt.

By the time Trafalgar Square came into view, Sallie's feet, even in rubber-soled walking shoes, were beginning to hurt. Looking around for somewhere she could rest, she saw an unobtrusive brass plaque that identified the National Portrait Gallery. She opened the door to a steep flight of steps, climbed them, and sank onto the nearest bench.

She hadn't been sitting long when someone walked up and stood over her.

"May I join you?"

Sallie looked up to see Orlando Paulson. She recoiled a little, recalling the way he glared at her from the hotel window that morning, but now the beautiful face was lit by a dazzling smile. She moved her bag from the bench to the floor to give him room to sit.

"Hello, Orlando." A compliment about his kindness to the little girl in the park was on the tip of Sallie's tongue, but she thought better of it. No need to remind him of the unpleasantness that followed his kind gesture.

Orlando sat. "Too much walking?"

Sallie nodded, fascinated by the boy's chameleon qualities. She thought of Larry Lindsay, an over-achiever in last year's senior English class. Larry never failed to suck up to his teachers in his relentless quest of a four-point average and college letters of recommendation but entertained his fellow students by ridiculing those same teachers behind their backs. Being a teenager was complicated.

The warmth she'd felt toward Orlando in the park returned. "What happened to the rest of the youth tour?"

"They're upstairs, looking at the Tudor portraits. We came here from the National Gallery round the corner. I've had quite enough culture for today."

Sallie studied the boy's face. Close up, he was even more beautiful than at a distance. Exotic almond-shaped eyes beneath thick black eyebrows and eyelashes. An expensive smile that only American orthodontics could have produced.

"Your father is very proud of you." She regretted the remark as soon as she'd said it.

Orlando's smile fled. The dark eyes took on a distant look. "He often tells me so."

There was something inexpressibly sad about this boy. Another of Sallie's students came to mind. Kendra Washington. The child of a drug-addicted mother, Kendra had spent her young life bouncing from one foster home to another. She never smiled. Orlando's look was like hers. No telling what terrible experiences he'd suffered on the streets of Rio before being rescued and taken to Max's comfortable and protected home. The incident with Tacet suggested that he'd had to fight with animals for food.

"I'd like to hear you play," Sallie said. "I almost did yesterday but was kicked out of the master class with the rest of the audience."

The sad look passed and Orlando smiled. "Maestro Truffaut is very particular." After a few moments, he spoke again. "I saw you talking to Mr. Bernini this morning."

Sallie was surprised he would bring it up, considering the way he'd glared at her at the time. "Yes. Mr. Bernini is very accessible for such a famous man. Have you taken lessons with him?"

"No." Orlando studied her with his beautiful eyes. "Have you known Mr. Bernini long?"

Sallie's face grew hot. More questions. Why were these IOFA types so interested in how long she'd known people?

"I met Mr. Bernini for the first time on Sunday night," Sallie said, not so warmly.

"Really?" Orlando's surprise seemed genuine. "I

had thought the two of you must be well-acquainted. I saw him give you something."

Sallie laughed. "Oh, that!"

Before she could explain about the Ace bandage, the sound of pounding feet and laughter in the stairwell signaled the approach of the youth tour.

Alice Pinkerton emerged from the stairwell first. As soon as she saw Orlando, she marched over, her face a study in angry disapproval. Her manner with the son did not match the one she showed the father.

"Look here, Paulson, I'm responsible for you. How dare you go sloping off on your own without a word? Where have you been?"

"I'm awfully sorry, Miss Pinkerton." Orlando rose gracefully and assumed a look of contrition. "I was just one room ahead of you and the others. I prefer to look at paintings in solitude. Crowds can be so distracting, don't you think? I just this moment joined Miss Dunbar here. Please do forgive me for causing you any concern."

If she didn't know better, Sallie would have sworn he was telling the truth. Alice, pacified, permitted him to take her arm and escort her down the steep flight of steps that led to the outside. The others in the group had already swept out ahead of them.

Alone in the suddenly silent foyer, Sallie stood. She'd like to see the exhibits, but the pain in her feet convinced her that she didn't have much walking left in her. Instead of ascending the stairs to the galleries, she made a quick visit to the gift shop and browsed the postcards instead. She bought a few and left.

Sallie walked toward Trafalgar Square and the monument to Lord Nelson. Surrounded by a fluttering cloud of pigeons, Alice Pinkerton was trying to herd Amber and some of the other girls in the direction of the bus stop, but they broke away and ran to a birdseed vendor. Throwing up her hands in a helpless gesture, Alice sat down on the edge of the fountain in the shadow of one of the huge stone lions to wait while the girls fed the pigeons.

Sallie would have liked to spend more time in the Square, but her energy had reached a really low point. Too tired to care about anything but getting off her feet, she kept going, past the Square, to catch a bus back to the hotel.

Busses in DeSoto Springs were never so full that a passenger couldn't find a seat. London was a different matter. Not only were all the seats taken, the aisle was a crush of standing passengers. She could barely reach an overhead strap that did little to keep her on her feet as the vehicle lurched along the Strand. She had to exert all her strength to avoid swinging into the passenger sitting in one of the aisle seats. She couldn't see his face. She supposed it was a man. Like so many Londoners, he wore a jacket with the hood up. He was talking to the person sitting next to the window.

An especially vigorous bump caused the man's hood to slip back. Sallie recognized the peroxided rock star haircut. She swung away, but still heard what DeLille was saying to the other person. His voice was filled with tension. "You should have stayed with the group."

Sallie recognized the other passenger as well. It was Orlando Paulson.

"No one will notice I've gone. They're still feeding the pigeons in Trafalgar Square."

DeLille moved to get up. "I'm descending at the next stop. Do not follow me."

Sallie watched in disbelief as Orlando grasped both ends of DeLille's red scarf, pulled his face against his own, and kissed him full on the mouth. DeLille jerked away, leaving one end of his scarf in Orlando's hand, and plunged toward the rear exit. Sallie saw Orlando put the scarf to his lips for a moment before placing it around his own neck.

Chapter Eleven

After returning the Ace bandage to the American woman, Bernini went back inside the hotel. His request for an appointment with the Maestro after yesterday's master class had not been granted. He was not one to drop in on people unannounced, but it looked like that was his only recourse. Teddy had told him the Maestro's room number. He'd go to the room and knock until admitted.

He'd thought a lot about why Teddy would conceal the fact that he'd acquired the Fabergé Flute. The only possible reason was the belief it could heal his old teacher's disfigured face. Nonsense, of course, but the human mind can convince itself of anything. Bernini was reluctant to believe that Teddy attacked him to get it back, or, if he had, that he'd hurt him intentionally. Truffaut had to know something.

As he neared the Maestro's room, Bernini heard the haunting tones of DeBussy's *Syrinx*. The sound came from Truffaut's room.

Impossible. Ever since his stroke, Truffaut could play nothing.

Bernini tapped on the door. The music continued. He knocked louder, and the playing stopped. A few seconds passed before the lock clicked and the door opened on the chain.

"Who's there?" The Maestro peered through the

narrow opening.

"Alan Bernini, Maestro. I must talk to you. Please let me in." The door closed briefly as Truffaut disengaged the chain, then opened it again to allow Bernini to enter.

The room was furnished like all the others. A green armchair stood between bed and window, blocking what little view there was. A fringed shawl lay draped across the chair. Teddy's old Grundig tape recorder sat on the top of the dresser. That explained the music. The poor old man, huddled under the shawl for warmth, must have been listening to a recording of his former signature piece.

"I want to talk to you about something, Maestro."

Truffaut gestured toward the bed. "Sit."

Bernini sat. He expected Truffaut to resume his seat in the armchair, but the old man remained standing, the less disfigured side of his face toward him. "I heard you had injured your hand, Alan. How bad is it?"

Bernini smiled and flexed his fingers. "At the time, I thought I'd broken it, but today it's fine. Not a trace of pain or stiffness. I'll be able to play as scheduled at the banquet on Saturday."

Truffaut sat down on the bed beside Bernini. "For what have you come?"

"Something you told me many years ago, Maestro. I never quite believed what you once told me about a flute you played when you were a boy."

Truffaut glanced at the armchair and back at Bernini. "You were one of the few I ever told about it, Alan. I could tell you didn't believe me."

"I didn't believe in its healing powers, Maestro. I still don't. But I know now that the flute does exist."

Truffaut frowned. He could still frown on the good side of his face. "What made you change your mind?"

"I've seen it. I've seen the Fabergé Flute."

"*Pas possible*!"

"I have seen it," Bernini repeated. "I've held it in my hands. As soon as I saw it, I knew it must be the flute you told me about all those years ago."

Truffaut leapt to his feet, shaking with emotion. "*Menteur*! Liar!"

Bernini recoiled, astonished at the force of the old man's anger.

"Where is it, then?" Truffaut demanded. "If you held it, then tell me where it is?" The side of Truffaut's face turned to Bernini was contorted with fury. "Where is this flute?"

"I don't have it now. It was taken from me soon after I found it." Bernini held out his right hand. "That's how I hurt my hand. I thought my attacker would kill me for it."

The rage on Truffaut's face gave way to sorrow. "It begins again." For a moment he stood looking down on Bernini, as if pondering. Then, shrugging slightly, he moved to the chair and lifted the shawl.

For the second time, Bernini found himself looking at the Fabergé Flute. This time it was out of the case and assembled. He reached for it instantly, took it with both hands and instinctively nestled it beneath his lower lip.

Truffaut sighed deeply. "It was brought to me the first time on Sunday night. By whom, it is not necessary for you to know." He took it from Bernini and rolled it lovingly in his hands, creating shimmering kaleidoscopes in his spectacles. Then, in a fierce gesture of rejection, he thrust it back, as if the burnished gold had burned his flesh. "Take it. It is a beautiful evil. It turns good men bad. Take it. Sink it in the Thames. All it can ever be is a curse."

Bernini took the flute and let his eyes drink the rich pools of color from the gems embedded in the golden circles and rectangles of the keys. "You're wrong, Maestro. Nothing this beautiful can be evil." He sat on the green chair. "The desire to possess it to the exclusion of everyone else is the evil. It belongs in a museum where everyone can see it and no one can own it."

"It's dragon's gold. It belongs at the bottom of a river." Truffaut sat back down on the bed and cradled his head with both hands.

Bernini looked from the flute to the old man and back. "I don't understand how you can say that. It's so beautiful."

Truffaut breathed a deep, rasping sigh. "It is the beauty of a flower under which a serpent lies hidden. This cursed thing destroyed my family."

They sat a long while in silence. At last, Truffaut raised his head and looked at the flute where it lay across Bernini's knees. He reached for it, but Bernini pulled it away and held it to his chest.

Truffaut stared at him. "You feel it too. I see it in your eyes. So it was when Father took it out of its case the day he brought it home. My brother also played the flute, but I had the special gift. Like you, Alan. Like Benoît. Until then, it didn't matter that my brother Maurice did not have the gift. He played well enough, and we never felt any rivalry. But when that cursed thing came into our lives, everything changed. Father's gift was the sword that cleft the bond between my brother and me."

The old man's face flushed bright red. Fearing he might be on the brink of another stroke, Bernini half-stood, but Truffaut gestured him away.

"Our father must have fallen under the flute's evil spell the first time he saw it. Before, never had he made a difference between us. Always he brought each of us a present from his business trips. But that time, he brought only the Flute. And at once, both of us desired it."

Truffaut stared at the instrument where it lay across Bernini's knees. "It has a power, this thing. It demands to be held. It demands to be played, to be owned."

The words sent chills through Bernini. "Truly, Maestro. It's only a flute. A beautiful piece of art, but only an object like any other."

"Only a flute?" Truffaut laughed harshly. "Father would never tell us where or how he obtained it. He told us only that it was meant for one of us and that we must compete for it. In Marseilles, where we lived, tryouts for the Paris Conservatory were held every year. Dozens of young men auditioned, but only one per instrument could win. Maurice and I both registered for the flute auditions. The flute would belong to whichever of us succeeded in winning a place at the conservatory."

Again the color rose in the side of the maestro's face turned to Bernini. His words were bitter. "Our kind, loving father set us against each other. He locked the flute in his office safe and reminded us daily that it would belong to the winner. We were already in the habit of practicing three hours a day, but now we doubled our efforts, stealing hours from sleep in the hope of winning the beautiful flute. The thought of it locked in Father's safe drove us unmercifully. And then came the accident."

This time Truffaut paused so long that Bernini prodded him. "Accident?"

"Accident. Or Fate. One afternoon, on the way to school, I slipped while getting onto the trolley. A wheel ran over my foot. My screams brought people from blocks away. The doctor who tended me in the street said the foot was so mangled it would have to be amputated, but Father refused. He wouldn't permit me to be taken to hospital but brought me straight home and had a bed set up for me in his study. That is when the deception began."

This time the sorrow in the old man's voice gave way to open weeping. Bernini stared at the maestro's feet. He'd never noticed anything unusual or unnatural about the way the Maestro walked. No lameness. "But how, Maestro, if your foot was mangled, how…?"

Truffaut ignored the question. "My father's study became not only my bedroom, but my practice room. Papa unlocked the safe and gave me the wonderful flute to practice on. Maurice was not to know. I was to practice on it while he was at school. I protested that it wasn't fair. Papa ignored my objections. He assembled the flute and placed it in my hands. That was enough. Once I held the despicable thing, all thought of fairness to my brother vanished from my mind." He wiped his eyes and went on. "Playing it became a drug. The more I played it, the more I wished to play it. Then the inevitable happened."

Tears glazed the old man's eyes. "One day Maurice

came home early with toothache. I had just finished playing *Afternoon of a Faun*—fourteen years old and I had played it perfectly. Father was beside himself with joy. He'd omitted to lock the study door that day and neither of us heard the sound of its opening. I shall never forget his words, words that swelled my ego and fell on my brother's heart like hot coals. *Sylvan, Sylvan, my precious boy. You are the son I should have had. You are the son for whom I risked so much to obtain this wonderful flute!*"

In the grip of a terrible emotion, the old man strode toward the door, then whirled and lunged toward Bernini. The younger man raised the flute protectively above his head, but Truffaut was reaching for something else, something under the armchair.

"Here," Truffaut said. "It was brought to me in this." Bernini recognized the battered case with the repaired handle. Truffaut snatched the flute from Bernini's grasp and disassembled it, placing the pieces in the case.

Bernini hated to upset him further but had to ask. "What of your brother, Maestro? What became of your brother Maurice?"

Truffaut's back stiffened. "I do not know." He sighed from an abyss of grief. "On that terrible day when he heard our father disown him, Maurice rushed from the room without a word to either of us. Next morning the office safe was smashed and the flute gone. So was Maurice. Father raged so wildly he fell into convulsions and died. I won a place at the Conservatory and went to live in Paris. As I was legally adopted, I inherited everything but sold none of it. The house is still there, waiting for Maurice. He was the true-born son, I the foundling." A sob escaped the old man's throat. "Despite my best efforts, I have never learned what became of him." He clicked the case shut and backed away from it as from a venomous animal. "Do with it what you will. I wish never to see it again."

Bernini took the flute case. His heart was racing, but he kept his voice steady. "I'll see that it's taken care of, Maestro. I'll take it to the British Museum straightaway."

Truffaut preceded Bernini to the door, opened it, and stood aside. He'd managed to keep the bad side of his face turned away from Bernini for the entire visit. With a rush of feeling, Bernini wished that the flute did possess healing powers, that it could restore the poor ruined facial muscles. He wished that Truffaut could play his signature piece once more before he died. Impulsively he embraced the frail old man, holding him for several moments. If he could feel such rush of love and compassion for the broken old musician, no wonder that Teddy—believing as he did in the power of the flute—had been willing to deceive him. There are many kinds of love, and love is a powerful thing.

Bernini hurried to the elevator, holding the flute case with both hands. He was struck by the feeling that something had been wrong about his interview with the Maestro, something odd and unsettling.

He stepped inside the elevator, shaking his head, trying to order his thoughts. The safety of the flute must be his chief priority. He'd grab the first taxi that passed and take his precious cargo to the British Museum before anything else could happen to him or to it. Only then would he go back to the hospital and tell Duby that he'd found it.

****

Sallie tried to understand what she'd seen on the bus. If anyone had asked her, she'd have said there was a budding romance between Orlando and Amber. Call her sheltered, but she'd never seen two men kiss. She followed Orlando off the bus, careful to stay behind him as they walked to the hotel. His newly acquired red scarf made him easy to follow as he threaded his way through the crowd ahead of her.

Midday traffic clogged the street and sidewalk. Adding to the sidewalk congestion, a tour bus in the hotel's loading alcove had just disgorged a horde of weary passengers. They staggered about like dazed insects whose rock had been disturbed, bumping into passers-by and against one another, impeding access to both the front and side entrances to the lobby.

Traffic brushed so close to the loading zone that the bus's panels shook. An elderly couple in matching T-shirts teetered dangerously close to the edge of the curb and Sallie instinctively put out a hand to steady them. The bus driver, a huge man with Popeye arms protruding from short sleeves despite the cool November weather, pulled bags from the compartments under the bus. Cut off from the side entrance by the press of people, Sallie headed for the revolving door. She looked around for Orlando, but if he was still on the sidewalk, she didn't see him. She did, however, see DeLille approaching from the direction of Trafalgar Square.

****

Thoughts in turmoil, Bernini stepped out of the elevator. He realized too late that he'd got off on the mezzanine. Rather than wait for the elevator to return, he decided to take the moving stairs. As it made its slow descent, he gazed idly at the reception area. It was teeming with new arrivals, but he hardly noticed, his mind still on his interview with Truffaut. The details of the great man's troubled childhood had occupied his attention fully at the time, but now that he was out of the room, he realized that something had been different. The old man's speech. Bernini had been able to understand every word he'd said. He gasped as he realized the enormity of the fact. What if it hadn't been a recording he'd heard on his way to Truffaut's room? What if it had been Truffaut playing *Syrinx* on the Fabergé Flute?

Impossible! But what if it were true? What if the Fabergé Flute could heal? How else explain the ease with which Bernini had understood the old man's speech? Bernini's legs turned to water. Incredibly, the flute had healed the burned, stroke-damaged face. An even more stupefying thought struck him. The mangled foot! Truffaut never explained how he could have suffered a mangled foot in childhood and retain no evidence of it. All those years ago, the Flute must have restored his ruined foot.

The escalator reached the lobby floor, but Bernini had changed his mind about taking the flute directly to the British Museum. He must take it back to the Maestro to finish its work.

Heart pounding and breath coming short, Bernini stepped off the escalator and tried to turn back toward the elevator. The crowd was too dense. He was caught up in a stream of people moving toward the main entrance. Blast all these people. Blast his own blind disbelief. Why had he doubted? Teddy's instinct was always to be trusted. The Flute must be permitted to do its work. Afterward, when the Maestro was completely healed, they would take the wretched thing to the authorities together.

Despite his efforts, the flow of the crowd carried Bernini against his will into a compartment in the revolving door.

****

Sallie stepped into the revolving door from the sidewalk. Through the glass, she saw Alan Bernini enter the door from the lobby. He was carrying the same battered flute case she'd seen him stuff into the canvas conference bag two nights ago. His left hand gripped the handle, and his right arm held it against his chest. She could see his jeweled lapel pin between his right fist and his left wrist. Wanting to be sure of what she was seeing, Sallie stayed in the door for a complete revolution. No doubt about it. The same case all right, wired handle and all.

****

Through the glass, Bernini saw the American woman enter the revolving door from the street. She was looking at him with a strange expression. Curious woman. A veritable fountain of helpfulness and miscellaneous information. He wondered why she was staring at him like that.

****

After a complete circle in the revolving door, Sallie found herself back on the sidewalk, again in the midst of a human maelstrom that was pushing her toward the street. The bus driver was having difficulty removing a bag from an under-compartment. Caught on something, it resisted his efforts and then came loose, knocking him off balance and against one of the passengers, who bumped into the person next to him, and fell into the next person in a domino effect. Brakes screeched and a woman screamed.

A taxi stopped at a crazy angle and the cabbie, a dark man in a blue turban, scrambled out and rushed to a fallen figure in the street. Sallie gasped. Alan Bernini, his right arm flung out, and the other bent beneath his body, lay on the asphalt. The distraught taxi driver, kneeling beside him, looked up at the people crowding around him. "Someone, please, call an ambulance."

Sallie moved closer and knelt at the other side of the fallen flutist. She didn't have the nerve to feel for a pulse, but simply stared at Bernini's pale face, willing him to be all right. The taxi driver, eyes closed, rocked back and forth, muttering something repetitious in a low moan. Sallie looked for the flute case that had been in Bernini's grasp as he exited the hotel. He must be lying on it. Certain that the tidy little man would hate being seen in disarray, Sallie reached out to straighten a twisted lapel. Her fingers felt something metallic. It was the back of a lapel pin, the part that holds it on. She looked around for the little jeweled flute. Could the impact have been enough to detach the pin?

The sound of klaxons announced the approach of emergency vehicles. Police arrived first, dispersing spectators and sending Sallie back to the sidewalk. She lingered at the curb, unwilling to leave, hoping to see some sign of life in the little flutist. As ambulance attendants lifted him onto a gurney, the arm that had been concealed under his body dangled over the side; the clenched fist opened, dropping something black onto the pavement. Sallie knew at once what it was.

The handle of the battered flute case had finally come loose. She scanned the street where Bernini had been lying. Nothing. Only the handle remained. The flute case was gone.

Chapter Twelve

The sight of Bernini's lifeless arm dangling from the gurney was too much for Sallie. Her stomach churned and bile invaded her throat. She knew she couldn't hope to reach her own room in time, so she pushed her way toward the public restroom off the lobby. Peripherally, she was aware of Harry Slocum, Max Paulson, and the Kings among the guests pressing toward the windows to watch the scene outside.

The Armenian waiter, a stained canvas bag slung over one shoulder, crossed in front of Sallie, forcing her to pause by the escalator, where she glimpsed a black leather jacket and red scarf worn by someone taking the steps two at a time. Another stomach spasm caused her to break into a run.

When it was over, Sallie mopped her face with a wet paper towel and stared at herself in the lavatory mirror. Her face was what Huckleberry Finn would call fish-belly white. She leaned against the basin, shaking all over. As soon as she felt that nothing else was coming up, she left the restroom and went to the elevator. The doors opened and Benoît DeLille stepped out, quickly averting his eyes. She watched him slope off toward the side street door, wrapping a red scarf around his neck as he went. She wondered vaguely if he kept a supply of them. Anticipating the soothing strains of the Fourth Floor Flute, Sallie pushed the button marked 4. But when she got off the elevator, the fourth floor lay in silence. And the door to her room was standing open again.

She shouted "Hello," but this time no smiling maid appeared. So she dragged the cart into the corridor. Her flute case still lay on top of the chest of drawers, in full view of anyone who might pass the open door. Dani was right. Leaving her flute in the room was not a good idea. Her little student model might not be worth thousands, but even at three hundred dollars, she wouldn't be able to replace it any time soon. She'd better cough up the five pounds security deposit. But first she had to get the sour taste out of her mouth.

She brushed her teeth. The face looking back at her from the mirror this time had a bit more color. Her hands were still shaking. Suddenly she wanted the crowded lobby. She needed to be around people. First, she'd take her flute to the security room. Then, she'd immerse herself in the crowd.

From habit, she hoisted her Needments bag to her shoulder, but when she felt the weight of the morning's accumulation of purchases, brochures, and book catalogues, she let it slide off onto the bed. All she really needed was her fanny pack. Snatching the flute case from the dresser, she locked her door and retraced her steps down the silent corridor to the elevator. The Fourth Floor Flute remained silent.

Getting off on the mezzanine, Sallie went straight to the security room. Harry Slocum was there checking in an instrument. He closed his hand around an identification chit and slid it into his pocket. "Hi, Sallie. Finally putting your flute where it'll be safe?"

Not in a bantering mood, Sallie simply nodded,

laid her case on the counter, handed the attendant a five-pound note, and signed her name and room number in the log. The burly woman took the money, attached a tag to the handle, and slapped a chit with the matching number onto the counter. Sallie watched her place the case in an open compartment against the back wall. It would have cost the same five pounds if she'd checked it the day of arrival. She regretted having waited. The parable of the workers in the vineyard flitted through her mind. She'd always identified with the laborers who had started work early.

Sallie slid the plastic ID tag into a pocket of her slacks and stepped onto the DOWN escalator to return to the lobby. Unencumbered by her bag of Needments, she felt an unaccustomed and welcome sense of freedom. She recognized Harry's broad back and red plaid overshirt in front of her. That's odd. He's carrying a flute case. She'd just seen him check a case into the security room, but he was carrying the one with the URTLES decal. How many instruments did he have, anyway?

Her inattention caused her to stagger a little as she reached the bottom. A hand closed on her elbow. Instinctively, she jerked away before she saw who it was. Kassim. A warm feeling of security replaced the instant of fear. He steered her to the coffee shop. The only available table was in a high traffic area. He seated her before taking the other chair.

"Have you heard about Alan Bernini?"

Sallie nodded. "I was on the sidewalk when it happened."

Kassim's voice was tense. "Did you see anything in his hand? Anything on the ground near him?"

Sallie tried not to think of the body on the gurney, the dangling hand. She breathed deeply. "Before it happened, I saw him coming through the revolving door. He was carrying a flute case then."

"What did it look like?"

Sallie frowned. The intensity of his questions made her uncomfortable. "An ordinary C-flute case. Black." Something prevented her from being more specific. She didn't want to admit that she'd seen the case before. "Later, when I saw him lying in the street, it was gone. His arm was twisted underneath his body, so at first I figured the flute case was just hidden. But then, when the medics lifted him, I could see that the case wasn't there."

They sat in silence for a while. Sallie took the plastic chit from the security room from her pocket and slid it round and round on the marble tabletop. The table jiggled and she looked up to see Max and Orlando looking down at her.

"Miss Dunbar," Max said. "Such dreadful news. You have our sympathy in your loss."

Sallie glanced at Kassim, who was looking at her with a surprised expression. She turned back to Max, unable to keep the sharpness from her voice. "If you're referring to Mr. Bernini's accident, it is dreadful, but his death is no more my loss than yours, as far as I know."

Max looked questioningly at Orlando and then back at Sallie. "Oh? I thought...I was given to understand...well. In any case, his death is a sad loss to us all." He seized Orlando's elbow and moved off without further comment.

"What was that about?" Kassim asked. "I thought

you said you never met Bernini before Sunday."

Sallie's face grew hot. "I hadn't. Sunday was the first time I'd ever laid eyes on him. This morning, I talked to him for about five minutes outside on the sidewalk. That's the extent of my acquaintance with Alan Bernini."

"Then why…"

"Orlando, that's why. He saw me chatting with Bernini this morning. Later, when I ran into Orlando at the National Portrait Gallery, he had the idea that I was great friends with Bernini. I told him what I've told you. Could be he didn't pass the information on to Poppa."

Kassim's eyes searched her face. Leaning forward, he placed a hand over hers. "You would tell me, wouldn't you Sallie? You would tell me if the Fabergé Flute was in the case that Bernini was carrying at the time of his accident?"

Sallie's jaw dropped. What was wrong with these people? Could everyone she talked to be confusing her with some other Sallie Dunbar? What did they think she knew, anyway?

"Was the Fabergé Flute in that case?" Kassim squeezed her hand, but this time Sallie didn't feel a thrill of excitement. She pulled away. The security room chit was still on the table. She returned it to her pocket. A knot of people moving past the table prevented her from standing at once.

Kassim grew more insistent. "Forgive me, Sallie, but I must ask. Aram thinks you know who has the Fabergé Flute."

"Aram? Who the heck is Aram?"

"The waiter who dropped the cups near our table

the other day. All I intended was to help him with the tray. I spoke a few words to him in Armenian because of the word he used when he dropped the tray. He was so amazed that a Turk would bother to help an Armenian that he sought me out later. He has told me facts about the Fabergé Flute that I didn't know before. He's convinced that you know something about it. He saw Bernini give you something this morning. He…"

The heat in Sallie's face was from anger this time and not embarrassment. She almost upset the tiny table in her angry rush to stand. "You've been talking to a waiter about me? A waiter who's been spying on me?" It hadn't been her imagination after all. The reflection in the glass door at Foyle's had belonged to the waiter. Following her. She cast a disillusioned look at Kassim. When would she learn?

He called her name, but she turned her back on him and walked away. Tears of anger and disappointment threatened to break out before she could reach the shelter of her room, so for the second time that day, she bee-lined it for the lobby restroom. She was able to gain the privacy of a stall before the emotional dam burst.

Sallie stayed in the stall until she'd recovered her composure. She washed her face with a wet paper towel and did her best to ignore the curious glances of the other women. Heart pounding, she went back into the lobby, uncertain what to do next. How could she have been so stupid? All Kassim had ever been interested in was finding out what she knew about that wretched flute.

She paused at the restaurant entrance. She'd missed lunch, but the thought of food did not appeal to her. She didn't want to go back to her room. A small notice flapping in the gust from an air vent caught her attention and she went over to take a look.

The Convention Flute Choir had been split into Intermediate and Advanced sections. Sallie was seized with a terrific urge to play her flute. She thought of the peace of weekly band practice at home and decided she would try to join the intermediate section. According to the flyer, practice began at four p.m. If she hurried, she could retrieve her flute from the security room and get to the practice room in time.

Back on the mezzanine, Sallie burst breathless into the security room, expecting to see the dour woman in blue gabardine presiding behind the counter. The attendant would wonder why she'd returned for her flute so soon after checking it in, but Sallie noted with some satisfaction that she didn't care what the woman thought.

The chair behind the counter was empty.

"Hello? Anyone here?" No answer. She could see her flute case in cubicle twenty-two, but, law-abiding creature that she was, she hesitated to go behind the counter and take it for herself. Sallie wouldn't even cross an empty street if the "Don't Walk" sign was blinking.

She called again, louder. "Anyone here?" Still no response. She waited a full five minutes. Still no attendant. "What the hell!" she said aloud. "It's my flute, after all."

Lifting a hinged section of the counter, Sallie slipped behind it. Two enormous instrument cases, too big for any cubicle, obstructed the way to the farther shelves. Bass flutes. She'd seen one in the exhibit hall and could hardly believe the monstrous size of it.

Sallie's case was on the next-to-highest shelf. She stood on the attendant's chair to get it down. Her name was on top of the case, emblazoned in large gold letter decals, S DUNBAR. She'd put them there with great pride the week she bought it. Then Sallie remembered with a sinking feeling the dent she'd put in the head joint when she knocked it against the lamp. How noticeable was it, anyway? What would the other players think? Maybe it wasn't as bad as she remembered. She set the case on the counter. Unsnapping the clasps, she lifted the lid, looked in, and gasped.

She slammed the lid shut to double-check the name on top. There it was. S DUNBAR. She opened it again and stared. It was her case, but it was not her flute. A riot of color gleamed against the blue velvet. The golden tubing had a pinkish cast and the keys were dazzling pools of color under the incandescent light. She reached for the head joint to get a better look at the intricate inlaid design.

"OW!" Something struck Sallie behind the knees. Her legs buckled and she fell. On the way down, her chin struck the counter and hands shoved her roughly to the floor. Something hard and heavy fell on top of her, pinning her, facedown, against the cold concrete. Fingers worked their way under the weight and grasped her wrist. They pulled at it, dragging her arm out from under the large object that was holding her down.

She yelled. "Help! Somebody! Anybody! Help!"

A man's deep voice responded. "Hang on, we're coming."

The groping fingers released her wrist. Sallie felt something scratch her arm, a jagged fingernail maybe.

Near her, footsteps receded toward the back of the security room while from the front, farther away, but approaching rapidly, heavy footsteps pounded toward her. And then she felt the weight being lifted from her back.

Sallie tried to rise, but someone pushed her back down.

"Lie still, miss. That was a heavy instrument case on your back. Could be, something's broken."

Sallie struggled to a sitting position. "Let me up. I think I'd know if something were broken."

Her rescuer, a uniformed policeman, helped Sallie to her feet. He pulled the attendant's chair to the other side of the counter and seated her on it before going back. More men crowded into the small space. The officer who had gone behind the counter called out. "The attendant is back here. Unconscious. We'll need an ambulance."

Dani King rushed into the cloakroom, Dave close behind. "Sallie! What's happened? Are you hurt?"

Sallie rubbed her chin where it had struck the counter on her way down. "I came to get my flute, but the attendant wasn't here. I called a couple of times, waited awhile, then went behind the counter to get it myself." Her mind's eye filled with the piercing colors that had gleamed briefly from inside her case. She looked at the counter. "Where's my case? My case was there on the counter just a minute ago."

The policeman came out from behind the counter. "This was on the floor back here. Is it yours?"

Sallie saw the gold letters on top and nodded. Dave took it from her. He held it by the handle, allowing both sides to fall open. Empty. Had she been dreaming?

"You checked an empty case into the security room?" Dave asked.

Sallie didn't like his tone. "It wasn't empty when I checked it."

"Strange that anyone would steal a flute and leave the case," he said, looking at her closely.

Sallie didn't like his expression either. She returned his stare. "Strange indeed."

By now conference-goers were jostling one another outside the doorway, trying to see what was going on, Harry, Max, and Orlando among them. Sallie knew she ought to tell the police what she saw in her flute case before the attack but didn't think it would be a good idea to do it with so many people around to hear.

"Coming through, please. Make room for the gurney. Coming through."

The police cleared the area of spectators, including Dani, but allowed Dave to remain.

Two ambulance attendants maneuvered their way behind the counter and brought out the motionless body of the cloakroom attendant. She didn't seem so large lying on the gurney. They wheeled her out.

A third ambulance attendant, who looked as young as one of her eighth-graders, stayed to check out Sallie. "Now then, Love. Where do you hurt?"

"The back of my knees. Somebody whacked me behind the knees and I fell. My chin hit the counter on the way down." The young man pressed his fingers gently along her jawbone. "How's that feel?"

"It doesn't feel good."

"Best come have it X-rayed."

Sallie pulled away. She had barely enough money for five more days of meals. She didn't need to pay for an X-ray. She knew that the Brits had universal health care but didn't believe it would cover an American tourist. "Even if it's broken," she said, "what will they do? Put it in a cast? No thanks. I'm not going with you."

The attendant grunted. "As you like, Love, but you'll need to sign a form saying that you refused to go with the ambulance." He produced a form and a pen. Sallie signed and he left.

Two more uniforms and a man in a rumpled brown suit pushed through the crowd of gawkers.

"How'd the police get here so fast?" Sallie asked of no one in particular. "As soon as I shouted, they answered."

"British efficiency, miss." The man in the brown suit introduced himself as Chief Inspector Garrett. "Actually," he said, "my men and I were on the premises regarding another matter and were on our way here."

He dropped a black and white plastic tag onto the counter. "This was in Bernini's pocket," he told the uniform behind the counter. "See what it goes with." Taking the chit, the officer returned almost immediately, depositing a square, expensive-looking black leather case in front of the inspector. A brass identification tag hung from the handle.

Garrett produced a key but had trouble with the tiny lock.

Dave King came forward "Here," he said, "let me help you."

Garrett stood aside. Dave opened the square case, revealing two smaller cases of kidskin, one for a piccolo and the other for a C-flute. He removed the flute from its covering. The overhead light danced and flashed on the brilliantly polished metal of the three sections. Dave hefted the head joint. "Too heavy to be silver. Definitely platinum."

Garrett barked an order. "Check every case in here for one that's missing its handle." He stroked the platinum flute with a forefinger. "If this is the famous $70,000 flute, what was in the case Bernini was holding when he died?"

Sallie left the security room feeling more energetic than shaken. She no longer felt like an observer but a player in the strange business of the Fabergé Flute. She wanted to tell someone what she had seen in her case, but she no longer trusted anyone. Not only had she lost her flute, the police had taken her case. She was beginning to think that her impulsive trip to London had been a very bad idea. The tedium of DeSoto Springs was beginning to look good.

Dani was waiting in the corridor. "Let's go get something to eat, Sallie. I know it's early, but food would be a comfort after all the excitement."

Dave joined them. "Good idea. Come on, Sallie. I'll even buy you a drink."

Sallie hesitated. She didn't like the way Dave had questioned her about the empty flute case. Still, she craved human company after all that had happened. His expression and tone were back to their previous friendly registers. Their company was better than none. She started to touch her face when she noticed the dirt on her hands. "Yuk. Look at that. The floor behind the counter hasn't been swept in a month or so. I'll go back to my room for a few minutes and meet you in the dining room."

When Sallie joined Dani in the Hunter's Den, she was sitting alone.

"Where's Dave?"

"He went to walk the dog, but he should be back by now."

When the waiter came for their order, they asked for gin and tonics and said they'd order when the rest of their party got there.

Still reluctant to mention the Fabergé Flute, Sallie made small talk. She told Dani about her visit to the Charing Cross Road, beginning with the plain-looking shop with the wonderful tea. "I could live here for the tea alone. And the bookstores. DeSoto Springs has a hundred churches and about as many antique stores, but not one bookstore."

"I don't think I could live in a small town," Dani said. "I can't imagine a town without a bookstore."

"We used to have a bookstore. Collins Books. I bought my first Modern Library edition there, *Plutarch's Lives*. Every time I saved enough money, I'd buy another Modern Library book. By the time I was a high school senior, I'd made a pretty good start on a collection of hardbound classics. But then the government passed the free textbook law and Mr. Collins went out of business."

Dani frowned. "I don't see how the textbook law could put a bookstore out of business."

"Before the law, parents had to buy textbooks for their children. Mr. Collins sold textbooks. He needed the school trade in order to survive."

"Well," Dani said, "that was too bad for your Mr. Collins, but a good thing for parents and students, wouldn't you say?"

Sallie made a scoffing sound. "No, I wouldn't. Before that law, because parents paid for schoolbooks, they made sure that their children took care of them. Students knew they'd be in trouble if they didn't. They covered them and kept them clean so they could sell them back at the end of the school year. Now, thanks to the free-textbook law, textbooks are left all over the place, to be rained on or run over."

Dave still hadn't appeared when they finished their drinks, so they ordered seconds. Sallie found it harder and harder not to tell Dani about what she'd seen in the security room. She returned to the subject of her morning outing. "I stopped at the National Portrait Gallery before coming back to the hotel." She retrieved the packet of postcards she'd bought. "Here are some reproductions of my favorite paintings." She let Dani assume that she'd seen the originals. "Alice Pinkerton and the youth tour were there." She described the pigeon-feeding in Trafalgar Square but omitted seeing Orlando kiss DeLille on the bus.

As Sallie's narration reached the terrible moment when Alan Bernini fell to his death in front of the taxi, she lapsed into silence.

"I can't imagine what's keeping Dave," Dani said. "He's had time to walk the dog to Buckingham Palace and back by now."

At the restaurant entrance, people were waiting for tables. The waiter came again and asked if they were ready to order.

Dani had run out of patience. "Yes," she said. She ordered for Dave as well as for herself. "I dare him to complain."

The waiter had been gone perhaps five minutes

173

when Dave finally joined them.

"Where've you been?" Dani demanded.

"Very long story."

"Let's hear it."

"Don't you want to order first?"

"We've ordered."

"What did I order?"

"Wait and see."

Dave sighed and rolled his eyes.

"Well?" Dani prodded. "What took you so long?"

"Obviously you've never tried to bathe a Jack Russell."

"You've been washing the dog?" Dani shook her head. "I'll be glad when you've found a home for that creature. What happened that he needed a bath?"

"I took him out right after we left the security room planning to go as far as the Savoy and straight back. Which we did, but when we got back to the hotel, Tacet showed a great interest in going down the alley at the side. There's an entrance by the kitchen dumpster, so I decided to humor him and come in that way."

"You never worry about humoring me," Dani said.

"Just as I was close enough to read the 'Employees Only' sign, somebody ran out of the service door, tossed something into the dumpster, and pelted past us toward the Strand. Tacet went absolutely bananas, barking his head off and leaping this way and that until he'd jerked the leash out of my hand and tore off. Whoever it was must have gotten into a cab or hopped a bus or something because before I got very far in pursuit, the dog was back, sniffing and barking around the dumpster like a lunatic."

"Nothing new in that," Dani said.

"Have you ever seen a Jack Russell jump, Sallie? They're like helicopters. They can take off vertically. That's what Tacet did. He leapt straight up and into the dumpster.

"I guess that explains the bath," Sallie said.

"I got the kitchen staff to call maintenance. A poor flunky very low on the employee totem pole went in after the dog. By now Tacet had been thrashing about in the garbage and smelled pretty ripe."

"Whatever would possess him to jump into the dumpster," Dani said.

"Maybe he was hungry," Sallie suggested.

Dani shook her head. "I fed him at noon. With real dog food. He couldn't have been ravenous enough for a display like that."

"He wasn't after food," Dave said. "He was after whatever the person who ran past us tossed in."

"What was it?" Dani asked.

"Don't know. It can't have been very large because it didn't make much of a thunk when it hit the garbage. And it was small enough and light enough to sift down through the refuse when Tacet churned everything up. I climbed the flunky's ladder for a look, but didn't see anything but lettuce leaves, fish bones, bloody plastic wrap, and other delightful kitchen leavings."

Dani shrugged. "So much for that, then. We'll never know."

"Not so, my love. The hotel staff gave up, but London's finest arrived and took over. When I took the hound and left, a very unhappy looking constable was on his way up the ladder to search the dumpster."

"Did you recognize the person who ran past you?" Sallie asked.

Dave laughed. "You bet I did. There's no mistaking that Billy Idol hairdo."

Chapter Thirteen

After dinner, the Kings invited Sallie to go with them to the evening Baroque concert, but she declined.

"I'm about done in," she said. "I think I'll calm my nerves by reading a little Dr. Johnson and try to get to sleep early."

"That would put me to sleep, all right," Dave said. "Sleep tight."

The fatigue was genuine. Not every day was Sallie knocked down, buried by a bass flute, and stepped on. She was glad to gain the privacy of her room. She sat in the armchair and closed her eyes. Almost at once, the image of Bernini lying in the street appeared behind her shut lids, causing all her muscles to tense. But then the Fourth Floor Flute, silent earlier that day, began to play. The rich tones entered at her ears and diffused throughout her body, relaxing every muscle and soothing away the day's trauma. She almost missed hearing the tap at the door.

Sallie walked over to the door and listened. The tap came again. She looked through the peephole. Kassim. A thrill of pleasure followed by the recollection of their last parting. The fact that he knew the Armenian waiter was spying on her and hadn't told her.

"Sallie."

Kassim's voice saying her name carried through the door. "Please, Sallie. Permit me to apologize. I would never do anything to put you in danger. Believe me, please."

Sallie opened the door. The look of delight on his face was enough. She was ready to give him another chance, but with reservations. "Well?" she said. "How can I be sure your friend Aram isn't lurking around the corner?"

Kassim smiled ruefully. "You have my word that he is not." They stood looking at each other, he in the hallway and she in the room. Sallie wasn't about to ask him in. He read her mind.

"Come," Kassim said, "let me buy you an Irish coffee."

They said little on the way downstairs, but once they were seated in the coffee bar, Kassim asked her if she felt any ill effects from the attack in the security room.

"The backs of my knees are a little sore, and I've a scratch on my arm, but otherwise no ill effects."

"Let me see the scratch."

Sallie held out her arm.

Kassim looked closely at the raised white mark. "I believe this scratch was caused by a hypodermic needle grazing your arm. I think that because the security room attendant had an injection mark on her arm. She died in hospital of a lethal dose of insulin."

Bile rose to her mouth. "How do you know that?"

"I overheard the police talking. In the Exhibit Hall. They interviewed all the vendors, questioning us about a flute case without a handle. They are searching the hotel for it." Kassim stroked the backs of her hands with his long dark fingers. "Is there anything you didn't tell the police, Sallie?"

Sallie hesitated. She wanted to trust him. At one level, she still feared that he was using her. But her instinct was to trust him. She might regret it but decided to go with her instincts. "I didn't tell them that the Fabergé Flute was in my case."

Kassim stared. Sallie grabbed his hands where they lay on the table between them. "Oh, Kassim, it was beautiful. Rose-tinted gold and brilliant colors. I felt like Dorothea Brooke looking at the jewels with her sister in *Middlemarch*. The colors were as penetrating as scent. The gems and enamel on the keys gleamed like fragments of heaven, feeding my eyes." She stopped. Her stomach sank. Kassim was staring at her with an unreadable expression in his eyes. She shouldn't have told him. She waited for him to say something. After seeming minutes, he spoke.

"Before then, Sallie, when did you last open your flute case?"

"Monday. In my room. Before lunch. I was going to play it." She didn't mention bashing it against the lamp. "But then I decided not to. I put it back into the case and laid the case on top of the dresser. I didn't touch it again until today when I took it to the security room. After Bernini's accident."

"What time was that?"

"Not very long after Bernini was struck by the taxi. I stayed downstairs for a while before going up to my room. Fifteen or twenty minutes perhaps." She didn't mention the puking. "I didn't stay long in my room. I was too agitated to settle. I wanted to be around people. I took the case and went out again. I'd no reason to open it."

Kassim frowned.

179

"What made you decide to check your flute into the security room?"

Sallie detected a note of suspicion in his tone. "For one thing, my door was standing wide open when I got there. The case was in plain sight, asking to be taken by anyone passing in the hall. And another thing, Dani King has been urging me to check my flute into the security room ever since I got here."

Kassim looked at her blankly.

Sallie repeated the name. "Dani King. She and her husband Dave have the room next to mine. You've probably seen them around. They have a little white dog with them."

Kassim gave no indication he recognized the names. "Tell me exactly what you saw in the security room."

"When I didn't see the attendant, I called. I thought she was probably in the back. After about five minutes, when no one came to help, I went behind the counter and got down my flute. I laid the case on the counter and opened it, expecting to see my silver flute."

"Why open it? Why not just take it and go?"

Sallie felt the blood rise to her face. "I, I wanted to be sure that it was all right. I'd dropped it earlier."

"Go on."

Sallie couldn't tell if he believed her or not. "I expected to see my silver flute. Instead, I saw what I'm sure was the Fabergé Flute. The lip plate was engraved with some kind of intricate design. I'd just picked it up for a closer look when something that felt like a pipe hit me behind my knees and I fell. Whoever hit me made sure I'd stay down by knocking a bass flute case on top of me. I couldn't see anything, not even shoes. When the police came, my case was on the floor, empty."

Kassim frowned without speaking.

Sallie knew her story sounded suspicious. Her body tensed as she anticipated more disagreeable questions.

Kassim fixed her with the steady gaze she found both disconcerting and exciting. "Why did you not tell the police about the golden flute?"

"For one thing, there were too many people standing around to hear."

"And for another?"

Sallie looked into his eyes and felt the tension ebb. Whatever she saw there, it wasn't threatening. "I wanted to tell you first."

Kassim smiled. "Thank you, Sallie Dunbar."

"You're welcome, Kassim…" She laughed. "Kassim what? I don't know your last name."

Kassim stood, grasped Sallie's hands, and drew her to her feet.

"I will tell you that and many other things about me as well. Only not here in this dreary little coffee shop. Come, Sallie Dunbar. I will tell you as we walk about London by night."

Sallie and Kassim began their walk by strolling up the Strand to Somerset House. The enormous eighteenth-century façade was lighted like a fairy tale palace.

"It's where they keep all the birth, marriage, and death records," Kassim said.

They walked round to the back, which overlooked the river, and descended a steep flight of steps to the lower level. "Before the Embankment was built, the Thames came up close to the South Wing and boats and barges could tie up within the building."

"How do you know so much about London?"

Kassim shrugged. "Anyone who bothers to read a tourist guide can be an authority on London. Come, I'll show you Cleopatra's knitting needle."

Walking beside Kassim felt comfortable and right. Sallie wished the time remaining before the end of the conference was something tangible that she could take in her hands and force to move more slowly. She didn't want it to end. She wanted to be with Kassim forever.

"Did you ever find a pair of flute earrings that pleased you?" he asked.

"No. They all look like little sticks. I've decided that I'd rather have something bigger than earrings, something big enough to be recognizable as a flute. A pendant maybe. Or a brooch. Mr. Bernini had a beautiful little jeweled lapel pin. I'd like something like that. Only bigger."

As they came to the bottom of the steps, Kassim steadied her by holding her elbow. The Embankment was transformed from its daylight appearance. Dancing lights from one of London's many bridges reflected on the water.

"Which bridge is that?" Sallie asked.

"Waterloo. Boatmen call it the Ladies' Bridge."

"Why?"

"Because it was built mostly by women construction workers. During World War II, when so many men were away in the armed services, about 25,000 women worked in construction in England."

Not far from the bridge rose a gigantic Egyptian obelisk flanked by sphinxes facing it. "Cleopatra's knitting needle," Kassim said. "Six men drowned bringing it from Alexandria so that it could stand here to be eroded by English weather and traffic pollution."

"You think they should have left it in Egypt?"

"Of course. Every nation has a right to its historical treasures."

"Did the English steal it?"

"No. They bought it. Just as Lord Elgin bought the Parthenon frieze that is displayed in the British Museum. But the men who sold these things had no right to do it. Ancient objects that have survived the ages in their places of origin should not be sold away by a handful of greedy inheritors or conquerors."

"So, if Cleopatra had sold it to the English, it would have been all right?"

Kassim laughed. "Yes, if it had belonged to Cleopatra originally, she would have had the right to sell it to whomever she pleased."

"Why do you say *if*?"

Baby spots illuminated the obelisk. Incised hieroglyphics on its sides showed black and mysterious. Kassim looked up at them.

"This monument was more than a thousand years old when Cleopatra was born, Sallie. It's one of a pair made by a much earlier pharaoh for a temple in Heliopolis. The ancestors of the Englishmen who brought it here were still painting themselves blue when the Roman Emperor Augustus took both obelisks to Alexandria to embellish one of his projects there."

Sallie didn't like to hear her beloved England put in the wrong, so she tried to find something positive to say. "You said this is one of a pair. At least the Egyptians have one left."

Kassim laughed again, took Sallie's hand, tucked it

under his arm, and resumed walking along the Embankment.

"I'm afraid not, Sallie. The twin to this obelisk was also taken away from Egypt. Taken by a nation that didn't exist in the days of Augustus when Englishmen painted themselves blue."

Sallie laughed. "I give up. What greedy country stole the other one? Where's the twin to London's Cleopatra's needle?" She expected him to name some other European capital.

"New York City. In Central Park."

"You're kidding."

"Both obelisks were taken from Alexandria in 1877. One traveled here and the other to New York. Paris also has such a needle, but it comes from a different site, and its twin still is in Egypt."

They walked in silence for a time. The night air was growing cooler, but Sallie didn't mind. She could walk forever with her hand in Kassim's. When they reached Westminster Bridge, she caught her breath. The lighted Houses of Parliament and the clock tower containing the bell called Big Ben were a picture postcard come to life. She really was in London. And with a gorgeous man, apparently as drawn to her as she was to him. She tried to remember if she'd ever felt such a perfect sense of well-being and contentment. She couldn't think of anything.

Kassim broke the silence. "It's twenty-five minutes before the hour. Would you like to wait for Big Ben to strike?"

"Oh yes! Please."

They sat on a bench.

Sallie had never given much thought to where

countries got their monuments or the museum furnishings they put on display. "Do you think the obelisks should be returned to Egypt?"

"Not even I would go so far as to suggest that," he said. "It cost the English $200,000 to bring Cleopatra's needle here in the nineteenth century. I tremble to think what it would cost to send it back at today's prices. No, not the obelisks. Too big. The Elgin Marbles in the British Museum? Maybe. There's a valid argument to restore them to the Greeks. But there is the conflicting argument that if Lord Elgin hadn't bought them from my own ancestors during their occupation of Greece, it's doubtful the marbles would still exist. The Ottoman riflemen are said to have used them for target practice."

Sallie sighed, regretting the depths of her ignorance. Kassim knew as much as she did about literature, but he knew so much more than literature. She wanted to visit the British Museum. If only she had more time in London. Like a year, maybe.

Kassim lifted Sallie's hand and brushed it against his cheek. "The question of repatriating national treasures puts me in mind of the fable of the mice and the cat. You know the one. The mice all agree that putting a bell on the cat is an excellent idea, but no mouse is willing to make the first move. I have heard many Frenchmen demand that the English return the Elgin marbles to Greece, yet the Louvre is filled with treasures looted from Egypt by Napoleon."

"Are you saying that all the museums in the world should send their exhibits back to the countries of origin?" Sallie's head teemed with the vision of an army of middlemen descending upon the world's museums, making fortunes from the business of relocating precious artifacts, many of which would certainly be damaged or stolen in the process.

"Perhaps. At least those that are smaller than an obelisk."

Sallie laughed.

"I'm not joking," Kassim said. "I accept the impracticality of repatriating things the size of an Egyptian obelisk, but I think that when the size of the artifact permits, the civilized thing among governments would be to return the historical heritage of other countries to their places of origin. You don't agree?"

Sallie considered. On the rare occasions Nick asked her opinion about anything, he always expected it to coincide with his own. She usually complied, afraid to infuriate him.

"Well," she ventured, "I think that a wholesale effort to return museum holdings to their places of origin would be a misguided effort to change history."

In the yellow light of an old-fashioned lamppost with a cast iron dolphin base, Kassim's expression conveyed genuine surprise. "Really? In your opinion, it is not possible to make amends for the injustices of the past?"

"No, it isn't. It's a nice idea. Good-hearted people read about the bad things their ancestors did a hundred years or so ago. Or had done to them. And they get all emotional and want to make things right. But people have been doing bad things to other people since the dawn of time. They're still doing them. I think it makes more sense to concern ourselves about the people who are alive now and suffering than to worry about what was done to individuals who no longer exist."

"So, I'm foolish to think that national treasures

belong in their countries of origin?"

"Not at all. I don't think there's anything wrong with having laws to keep valuable historical artifacts from leaving their countries of origin—from now on. I just don't see the sense of trying to change the past by looting the museums of the world to return what was acquired in less politically correct times."

"I see."

Sallie's heart pounded. Kassim was actually considering her point of view. Encouraged, she elaborated. "Having things scattered about the world could even be a good thing. Suppose, for example, that an earthquake destroyed the Parthenon. The Greeks would lose their temple, but some of their heritage would be preserved in other countries."

"A point to consider."

They sat in silence. The minute hand on the clock tower clicked its inevitable way toward the hour. Sallie wished she could make it stop where it was, freezing the moment.

"Enough of my hobby horse," Kassim said. "You asked me a question before we left the hotel and I have not answered it."

Sallie tried to remember what she'd asked.

"You asked to know my surname. Surnames are a, what do you say, a big deal to the Turks. My people acquired surnames only recently."

"Europeans too," Sallie said. "It wasn't until the Middle Ages that people in England started using surnames." To Sallie, who had driven her mother to distraction by drawing Egyptian hieroglyphics on the walls of her closet in the fourth grade, the Middle Ages ranked relatively recent.

Kassim laughed. "More recently than that. We Turks waited until the twentieth century to start using surnames. Have you heard of Ataturk?"

"Father of modern Turkey," Sallie rapped out.

"And they say that Americans know nothing of other cultures."

Sallie felt like a fraud. All she knew about Ataturk was his name and epithet. She remembered the name because it sounded so much like "Atta Boy." Before she could confess her ignorance, Kassim went on.

"Kemal Ataturk passed a law requiring all Turkish families to choose a surname. That was in the 1930s."

"I'll have to admit that's more recent than the thirteenth century. How did families decide on a name?"

"Some chose to identify themselves by profession. They chose Turkish words equivalent to Advocate, Doctor, Teacher, Soldier, Carpenter. Others chose names for attributes they believed—or wished—they had, like *Courageous, Generous, Wise*. My grandfather chose the name *Aydinlisoy*."

"What does it mean?"

"I'm embarrassed to tell you. It will sound pretentious." Kassim kept his eyes fixed on the Gothic tracery of the Parliament buildings. Sallie looked at the clock. Fifteen minutes before the hour. Kassim leaned closer. "Do you remember, Sallie, that I told you that my family has a tradition of helping Armenians when we can?"

"Yes."

He took a deep breath, as if to fortify himself to tell a painful story. "My grandfather grew up in the town of Sivas. He was quite young during that dreadful time, but old enough to remember the horrors. When orders came in to rid the town of its Armenian inhabitants, Grandfather refused to obey. He hid his Armenian neighbors in the loft of a barn. A farm family of seven. Another neighbor informed on him. The family were found. My grandfather and his family were forced to watch them slaughtered. First the soldiers raped the women, including a ten-year-old girl."

A strangled cry escaped Sallie's throat.

Kassim put an arm around her. "I'm sorry, Sallie. It's something that doesn't bear telling, but I want you to understand my interest in Aram. I want you to understand that my sense of duty toward Armenians is more than a whim."

Sallie expelled a deep sigh that took any remaining resentment she might have felt regarding the Armenian waiter. "Please, go on, Kassim."

"My grandfather made a vow. He said that if he, a poor sinner, could be so horrified and sickened by what he had seen, then a merciful and compassionate God would surely be offended by it. He thanked God for opening his eyes. He vowed that he would never kill or approve of killing any unarmed non-combatant. He bound his children to the same vow. When time came to choose a surname, he took the name Aydinlisoy. It means *enlightened family*."

A sudden breeze swept up from the river and Sallie shivered. Kassim enclosed her with both arms.

"You're cold. Would you like to go back to the hotel?"

"Not until we've heard the chimes."

Warmed by each other's body heat, Sallie and Kassim sat close together, gazing at the illuminated buildings and the reflections of the light glinting on the surface of the Thames. As if Kassim's painful story had opened the way to intimacy, recollections and ideas tumbled out of both of them, like water from broken dams.

Kassim told her about his childhood, his travels, studies, dreams. Sallie told him about life in the United States, her work, family—even something of her disappointing marriage. Never in her adult life had she felt so completely unthreatened, and Kassim seemed to feel the same. There was no logical reason for such rapport after such brief acquaintance, but it was undeniable. They were like long-separated friends who had been reunited and had much to catch up on.

As the first deep BONG of the eight most famous notes in the world sounded, they stood to give the bell tower their full attention. The tenth stroke was still vibrating when Kassim turned Sallie's face to his and gently, tenderly, placed his lips on hers. Any thoughts of a convention fling, a "shipboard romance," fled. Sallie wanted this to be for keeps.

Chapter Fourteen

Wednesday, 27 November 1985, Day Three of

IOFA Convention

Sallie and Kassim said goodnight at the elevator. The walk back to the hotel had been mostly silent, emotion taking the place of words.

Sallie went straight to her room and bed, but her mind was too agitated for sleep. Even the soothing notes of the Fourth Floor Flute couldn't calm her. She lay awake for a long time, reliving the walk along the Embankment and Kassim's kiss. When she finally did drift off, she dreamed.

She was in Central Park, looking at the other obelisk, when a thick fog descended. Turning from the obelisk, she glimpsed the back of a man she was certain was Kassim and ran after him. Every time she was close enough to put out her hand to touch his shoulder, the fog drifted between them and she couldn't see him. She could hear his footsteps, and then, the barking of a dog. The barking grew louder. Then she heard knocking and someone calling her name. She woke to realize that someone was pounding on the door of her hotel room. Scrambling out of bed, she put on Momma's chenille robe and looked through the peephole. The Kings.

"We're on our way to breakfast," Dani said when

Sallie opened the door. "Want to join us?" Dani was wearing another stunning pantsuit—brocaded taffeta in shades of crimson and gold. Dave stood behind her, yanking on Tacet's leash with no effect. The terrier jumped and barked madly, lunging at the open doorway. With a sudden spurt of energy, he pulled away and hurtled into the room, bee-lining to the bed, sniffing and snarling along the bottom edge. Dave recaptured the leash and dragged him back into the corridor.

"If I couldn't see for myself how close the bed stands to the floor," Dave said, "I'd think Tacet smelled a man hiding under there."

Sallie laughed and felt herself blush. "Not today." Realizing how the words might be construed, she blushed again. "I mean, no breakfast today. I'm not dressed. Besides, I don't feel like having another big breakfast. I'm not used to such a spread every morning. I'll grab a croissant in the coffee shop."

As soon as she shut the door on the Kings, Sallie looked at the bed, wondering what had sparked the dog's interest. As Dave had observed, the bed was too low to the ground for a person to hide under, but Tacet had been barking at something. She got the flashlight from her Needments bag, lay flat on her stomach, and peered underneath.

Something was there all right, shining silver in the beam of the flashlight. Sallie reached under and pulled out the three pieces of her missing flute.

Sallie's flute case was still in police custody, so she wrapped the three sections of her instrument in a T-shirt and placed the bundle in one of the wheeled bags. She'd tell Kassim about this when they met at noon.

They'd arranged the night before to have lunch together. He promised to take her anywhere she wanted to go. She'd seen in a brochure that a pub associated with Dr. Johnson was still in operation. The Cheshire Cheese. She couldn't be sure if Kassim knew its whereabouts so she went to the registration desk to ask directions.

A pretty dark-haired woman was on duty. "The Cheshire Cheese? I'm sorry, miss. The concierge isn't here yet, and I'm afraid that I can't help you. There is a travel agency just across the road. They'd be able to tell you how to find it, I'm sure."

Sallie thanked her and decided to go directly to the travel agency. She could grab coffee and a croissant later. Thinking more about Kassim and Dr. Johnson than she was about where she was going, Sallie walked up behind some pedestrians she thought were waiting at a crosswalk, only to discover when she got to the curb that they were waiting for a bus. She gasped as a red double decker hurtled to a stop within inches of the commuters. She went in search of a crosswalk, wondering how often someone was hit in the scramble to be first to board.

The travel agency wasn't open yet. The coffee shop next to it, however, was. Sallie looked over the variety of baked goods and fancy desserts in the window and decided she'd treat herself to one of their whipped cream concoctions while waiting for the agency to open. Her eyes traveled from the pastries into the shop beyond, in which early morning business types with furled umbrellas shared small tables with strangers. Most of them studiously ignored each other, reading folded newspapers over their steaming cups of tea or coffee. At one table, however, two men were deep in conversation. This was no inconsequential sharing of remarks about the weather, but an earnest exchange of information. Sallie stared in disbelief. One of the men was Kassim. The other was Dave King.

The Cheshire Cheese forgotten, Sallie retraced her steps to the zebra crossing. What was going on? She'd mentioned Kassim to Dave and Dani at least twice. As for Kassim, the time she'd mentioned the Kings to him, he'd waited for her to explain who they were. If the Kings and Kassim knew each other, why pretend they didn't?

Thoughts whirling, Sallie took her place with a group of people she thought were waiting for the light to change, but as they surged forward, she realized that she was at a bus stop. As the huge red hulk of a Number Nine hurtled toward the curb, she felt the pressure of a hand at the small of her back and found herself being propelled forward into the street. For the first time, she noticed that red London buses have black fenders and that one of them was inches from her face.

As the black fender rushed toward her, Sallie's main emotion was one of chagrin, knowing that if she were killed, Mother would say she'd told her so. But before her face collided with the approaching metal, strong fingers clamped onto her shoulders and yanked her back. She was still alive, breathing the exhaust of the departing bus.

"You are OK, yes?"

The gloomy, angular face of Aram the Armenian waiter studied her gravely.

"Someone pushed me. Did you see? Did you see who pushed me?"

Aram shook his head. "I saw only you were falling toward that bus. Many people."

Sallie scanned the area. Whoever shoved her in front of the bus was gone, merged with the crowds of commuters.

"Come," Aram said, taking her arm. "I walk with you back to that hotel."

Legs shaking, Sallie permitted Aram to steer her back across the street to the hotel. What if he was the one who pushed her? Then had second thoughts and pulled her back. Kassim said the waiter had been following her. He'd followed her that morning. Otherwise, why would he have been at the bus stop?

Back at the hotel, Aram steered Sallie through a door marked "Employees Only" into a room with a few tables and a counter furnished with coffee- and tea-making paraphernalia. He seated her solicitously at one of the tables and brought her a cup of tea.

"You OK?" he asked again and sat down opposite her.

For the first time Sallie took a good look at the man who had been stalking her since her first night in London. Sad hooded eyes, large nose, and little Hitler mustache gave him the look of an old-timey silent movie star, not quite Charlie Chaplin—laughable but for the genuine concern in the eyes looking back at her.

Sallie bit back an angry accusation and reached across the table to touch his hand. "Thank you. I really thought that was it."

They drank their tea in silence. Sallie wanted to know more but didn't know exactly how to ask. Aram saved her the trouble.

"I meant no harm to you," he said. "I thought you

knew where to find this Flute. I thought you would lead me to it. Kassim tells me you know nothing."

"Why is it so important to you? Do you want it so you can sell it?"

The thick eyebrows arched. "Sell? Never. This flute belongs to Armenian people."

"I don't understand, Aram. It's a flute. It's beautiful, but in the end, it's just a flute."

Aram told his story in broken English, but it entered Sallie's mind in complete sentences.

"The flute is made from gold and jewels stolen from the Armenian church. Before Constantine had his vision of the cross and before Theodosius closed the pagan temples, the nation of Armenia was converted to Christianity by Gregory the Illuminator. For centuries, through all the invasions and take-overs, three precious reliquaries and the saint's own chalice were preserved in a shrine tended by Armenian monks. My grandfather worked for the monks. One day in 1918, he was at work behind a curtain in the shrine. He saw a man kill a monk and steal the holy objects. The murderer was an American, like you."

For a moment, Sallie felt the sickening humiliation of being unfairly lumped with the worst members of a group with which she shared an identity.

Aram's hands trembled and his eyes were dark with emotion. "Ever since that day—my grandfather, my father, and now me—my family searches for the saint's holy things. Grandfather followed the murderer to Russia. He could not stop him from having the treasures melted down, but he learned what became of them. The shape is changed, but the holiness remains. The Fabergé Flute is still Saint Gregory's chalice. And it belongs to the Armenian people."

Goosebumps crawled along Sallie's arms. She recalled the way the music of the Fourth Floor Flute made her feel, how the sound coursed through her body, soothing and relaxing every muscle. Was the Fourth Floor Flute the Fabergé Flute? Did that explain why she woke refreshed after so little sleep? How Dani's aching feet recovered in such a short time after the picnic?

Before she could ask Aram for more details, the maitre d' entered the little lounge and told him he was needed in the dining room. Aram left, but the maitre d' remained standing in the doorway, glaring at her disapprovingly. Sallie took the hint and left the break room by way of the door to the lobby.

Outside the break room Sallie stood thinking about what Aram had told her. In just a few minutes, a man she'd regarded as a threat had been transformed into a patriot deserving of her sympathies. Or maybe not. How could anyone be sure of anything? Dave and Dani had pretended not to know Kassim. Bernini insisted he hadn't had a flute with him in the pub. DeLille lied about being at the pub on Sunday night. And Kassim. Her beloved Kassim had implied he didn't know the Kings and then she saw him in deep conversation with Dave. What was it Hamlet said? *One may smile, and smile, and be a villain.*

Her plans in ruins and the joy of the previous night's idyll with Kassim tarnished, Sallie sat on a bench that gave her a view of the revolving door, half-hoping, half-dreading to see Kassim come through. What she would do if he did? She wanted desperately not to think ill of him. Or the Kings. Dave and Dani seemed so nice, so open. They had a dog, for heaven's sake.

People came and went. Max Paulson stopped briefly to ask her if she'd seen Orlando. Big Daddy and Amber passed, their features set respectively in pained and sulky mode. Harry Slocum walked by in the direction of the escalator. Sallie was certain he saw her, but he looked away. She checked her watch. She'd been sitting there for twenty minutes or so. Still no sign of Kassim or Dave. Maybe they weren't coming back to the hotel from their assignation at the coffee shop. Maybe they'd found the Fabergé Flute and were planning their getaway. Or maybe they'd used another entrance.

Sallie vacillated between feelings of betrayal and denial. She couldn't be that wrong about Kassim. Not after last night. There had to be an explanation. Too restless to sit any longer, she got to her feet. Walking might help her think.

With no destination in mind, Sallie took the escalator to the mezzanine. The IOFA registration tables were gone. She moved to the railing and looked down at the almost deserted lobby. The dark-haired woman at the check-in desk, having no guests waiting to check in, was sorting through papers.

Sallie turned away from the railing and walked down the corridor in the direction of the security room. As she passed, she looked in. No one was waiting to check instruments in or out, but someone wearing street clothes and not the blue hotel uniform was moving around behind the counter.

Still without a plan, Sallie continued to the end of the corridor and stopped between facing restroom doors. Might as well stop in as long as she was there. As she entered the Ladies, a man in a hotel uniform exited the Gents.

Sallie stood overlong at the lavatory, washing her hands and staring at her reflection in the mirror. Everything seemed unreal, even her own features. Who was she anyway? What was she doing with her life? Thirty-three years old and living in her mother's basement. She washed her hands a second time, dried them, and wandered back into the hallway. This time, when she passed the security room on her way back toward the escalator, the uniformed man she'd seen leaving the restroom occupied the chair behind the counter, reading a magazine.

Again Sallie checked the time. She'd been moping around for two hours. Enough of this dithering! She wasn't going to waste the rest of her trip wallowing in doubts and hurt feelings. And she wasn't going to pretend nothing had happened and hope that everything would be all right. She strode purposefully to the escalator. No more of this passive aggressive shit. She'd confront Kassim at his booth in the Exhibit Hall. If he wasn't there yet, she'd wait for him to come back. She'd tell him that she'd seen him talking with Dave and ask him what was going on. Last night had been magic. She wasn't going to throw that away without a fight.

Disoriented when she entered the Exhibit Hall from a different entrance, Sallie wasn't sure which way to go to find Kassim's booth. Some of her newfound energy already at an ebb, she strolled unhurriedly past the displays. She saw nothing to compare with the flute-playing gnome that had made her laugh in Kassim's hearing. Two days ago. It seemed so much longer.

She paused at a booth dedicated to pet supplies. The little red sweater with the appliqué of a dog playing a flute would be perfect for Tacet. But no! How could she even think of making a friendly gesture to the Kings? They lied to her. Dani had actually warned her not to have anything to do with "an unknown flute salesman." They'd been so friendly to her, funny and helpful. How could she have been so wrong? Who were they really? What were they up to?

A white mug printed with a green octopus playing a flute caught her attention. It appealed to her sense of whimsy and didn't cost much, so she bought it and put it in her shoulder bag. A glint of silver moving above the heads of the crowd caused her to do a double-take. It was an assembled flute. She moved to where she could see who was carrying it. Aram. Had he snatched it from one of the tables? But if he was stealing it, wouldn't he make an effort to conceal it? Or was he just nuts? Maybe he had pushed her in front of the bus. Crazy people do crazy things. She turned into the next aisle. Let the IOFA people worry about Aram. As long as he quit following her, he was not her problem.

A lattice partition told Sallie she'd found the right aisle. Kassim was at his booth, talking to a customer. She wasn't going to lurk out of sight while she waited for him to be free. She'd walk right up to where he could see her. Feeling aggressive, she went up to the blue plush-covered display table and looked over the assembled flutes. She picked up a gold one, cleaned the mouthpiece with a disinfectant wipe, and raised it to her lips.

First, she played a slow, careful chromatic scale.

Low C came out full and fruity. Low D, E, and so up the scale, each note coming out without the effort they required on her $300 flute. An expensive instrument really did make a difference. She glanced toward Kassim.

He'd finished with one customer, but another was waiting at his elbow. As he turned, he noticed Sallie. The smile that lit his face seemed genuine and spontaneous. He lifted his chin in a gesture of greeting. Sallie felt a warm glow, glad beyond measure that she'd decided to give him a chance to explain.

She ran another scale and decided to play something. What did it matter that she couldn't dash off arpeggios from Debussy? She knew how to play "Greensleeves." She fingered middle octave C and blew. Instead of the expected note, she heard a sharp pop and felt a puff of air near her cheek.

Fearing irrationally that she'd done something to the flute, Sallie cast a panicky, apologetic look in Kassim's direction. The customer he'd been serving no longer stood next to him. Kassim, with the grace that accompanied all his movements, was in the act of falling forward. Frozen, Sallie watched as his body struck the floor with a little bounce. He landed on his left side. He lay there motionless. On the right side of his head, at the temple, a bright red flower blossomed.

Someone shouted. "My God, he's been shot! Get down, everybody. Somebody has a gun!"

A cacophony of screaming, shouting, and thudding erupted as people ran for the exits or dived for cover. With great care, Sallie placed the golden flute back onto the table. Only when the flute was out of her hands did she succumb to the waves of nausea kneading her stomach. Her gut heaved so violently that she fell to her knees and was sick all over herself and the floor. She never quite lost consciousness but had a surreal awareness of what was happening. She learned the details later.

A medical doctor attending the convention with his wife rushed to see if he could help. As soon as he'd determined that Kassim was beyond assistance, he turned his attention to Sallie. With the help of two hotel employees, he took her to her room and put her to bed. At some point Dani King joined them. Sallie heard Dani tell the doctor that she had medical training and knew what to do. The doctor wrote out a prescription and told her to call him if necessary.

When everyone had left the room, Dani came back, carrying an attaché case. "You're going to be just fine, Sallie. The doctor prescribed Valium. I have some samples so you don't have to wait while I go looking for the British equivalent of a drugstore." She laid the attaché case on the bed and opened it, releasing a faintly pharmaceutical smell. Something fell out onto the bed. While Dani opened a packet, Sallie groped at the object that had fallen from the case. Her fingers told her it was long and wrapped in cellophane.

"Here, sit up and take this," Dani said. "It will help you relax and sleep. Dave and I won't let anyone disturb you. When you wake up, phone the desk. They'll page me."

The Fourth Floor Flute started playing something by Brahms. Dani picked up the slender object under Sallie's fingers and put it back into the case. As the medicine and music took effect and she drifted into healing sleep, Sallie recognized the slender object and wondered briefly why Dani would have a hypodermic needle in her bag.

Chapter Fifteen

The travel alarm showed six p.m. when Sallie woke. She tried to stand up, but a dizzy spell hit her, so she sat on the side of the bed. She felt nauseated, probably from the medication. She hated taking medicine. Never could understand the concept of "recreational" drugs. She stood. The dizziness did not return, but the memory did. Kassim lying on the floor of the exhibit hall, the red blossom spreading at the side of his head. She fell back onto the bed and sobbed until she slept again.

Next time she woke, the room was dark, and the mysterious flute was playing "Dance of the Blessed Spirits." Sallie lay listening to the music until a tentative knock on the door penetrated her consciousness. She stumbled out of bed, turned the knob without bothering to look through the peephole, and stumbled back to the bed.

Tacet hurtled in and headed straight to the bed, sniffed a bit, and lost interest. The dog's owners followed, shutting the door behind them.

"You really ought to use the peephole," Dave said. "You don't know who might have been out there."

"You've got that right," Sallie said, in the surliest tone she could manage. She recalled the hypodermic needle Dani had in her bag. Feelings of suspicion and hostility clawed at her throat as she looked at the friends-turned-enemies.

"How do you feel?" Dani asked.

"I'll live." Sallie glared at the couple and at their little dog too. She placed a forearm over her eyes to shut out the glare of the overhead light. "Do they know who shot him?" Her tone was cold and rude, but she didn't care. Death is like a rock thrown at the window of social conventions. Before time repairs the window, we're able to say anything we want.

"The police are investigating," Dave said. "They want to talk to you because you were there when it happened."

"They'll have to come looking for me, then. I didn't come to a flute convention to end up spending half the time being grilled by the police about things I know nothing about."

Sallie's aggressive side had definitely taken over from her passive.

Dani touched the arm shielding Sallie's eyes. "Come have supper with us."

Sallie moved her arm and glared at them openly. "Do you still want to pretend you didn't know Kassim?"

The Kings exchanged uncomfortable glances.

"You know what I'm talking about. The flute salesman I should be careful about meeting for coffee."

Dani opened her mouth to speak, but Dave gave her a warning look. "We're really sorry about Kassim, Sallie," he said. "We'll talk when you're feeling better."

They left, closing the door gently behind them.

Sallie stood. Her head felt fragile and heavy, her stomach queasy from the sedative. The flute music, unnoticed while the Kings were there, followed her into the bathroom. Her face in the mirror was as white as Alice Pinkerton's powdered flapper face. The flute picked up Mozart's "Turkish March," a piece that never failed to get her moving. By the time she was ready to go downstairs, she felt better. Physically, at any rate. She even felt peckish, as the Brits would say. She'd had nothing to eat all day.

In the lobby, Sallie scanned the faces of the other guests. Any one of them could be Kassim's killer. Habit led her to the entrance of the Hunter's Den, but unable to face another meal in the surroundings she'd shared so often with the Kings, she turned away. She'd hail a taxi and let the driver recommend an inexpensive restaurant.

The planter partition between the front and side exits had been removed following Bernini's death and replaced with tables where everyone leaving the hotel was required to show identification and open any bags large enough to conceal a flute case. Sallie showed her passport to one of the two uniformed London policemen at the table by the main entrance. He checked her name against a list. Frowning, he looked from the passport to the list several times and then up at her. "Miss Dunbar?"

"Yes."

"Are you registered for the music convention, miss?"

"Yes."

The officer again looked from the passport to the list. "There is a Dunbar on the list, but the Christian names don't match."

Sallie laughed humorlessly. "The names on the

passport are the ones on my birth certificate. I go by *Sallie*."

"Ah." His fingers closed on the passport and he stood.

"In that case, Miss Dunbar, you'll have to come with me."

The officer led Sallie to the escalator. "Chief Inspector Garrett wants to speak with you in the incident room on the mezzanine." He stood aside to let Sallie step onto the moving stairs ahead of him. *So I can't make a break for it.*

The inspector who had come to her rescue in the security room stood in the open doorway dismissing a small woman in a maid's uniform with a "thank-you-here's-my-card-call-if-you-think-of-anything." Nodding at Sallie, he ushered her into a small conference room almost completely filled with a long table.

"Hello again, Miss Dunbar. I'm afraid you're not having a very pleasant holiday."

"People do seem to be dying in my vicinity."

Garrett pulled out a chair for her and then sat beside her. Their knees were close enough to touch. He glanced at his notes. "I understand that there was some sort of relationship between you and the salesperson who was killed yesterday."

Sallie was still feeling the effects of social liberation. "And what would make you understand that, Inspector?"

"Was there none?" He watched her closely, no doubt looking for a guilty reaction.

"I met Kassim on Monday. We had coffee together a couple of times. Last night we took a walk on the Embankment. We were planning to have lunch together today. We didn't."

Garrett consulted his notes. "You were with him at the time of his death."

"I was trying out one of his flutes. He was a flute salesman, remember?"

"You were taken from the scene in an extreme state of shock." Again, the searching gaze.

Sallie felt the anger rise. What was he implying? "I expect I wasn't the only one in shock, Inspector. Your experience with violence is no doubt different from mine. In my world, it isn't every day that someone has his brains blown out three feet from where I'm standing."

The detective remained silent, his gaze never wavering. Sallie stared back defiantly. She was too grieved and angry to be intimidated. Death liberates the living, at least for a little while, by making lesser fears inconsequential.

Garrett stood and opened the door. "You can come in now."

Sallie stared as Dave King walked in.

Garrett indicated a chair, but instead of sitting in it, Dave pulled it out, and perched on the edge of the table with his feet on the seat.

Garrett cast Sallie an apologetic look. "I can appreciate your feelings, Miss Dunbar, your feelings about being…" He searched for the right words. "if not lied to, at least not kept informed of matters that might affect you." He looked at Dave and back at her. "I'm in a similar case myself. I've only just learned that Mr. Adi…Adis…that Kassim was an Interpol agent. Mr. King here was assisting him in his investigation."

Sallie whirled on Dave. "You told me you were an

oboe player."

"I am, but I'm also retired Chicago police, detective division. Kassim and I met a few years ago when he was in Chicago tracking a stolen Stradivarius. When he saw I was registered for this convention, he phoned and asked if I'd help him look for whoever's been stealing flutes at these big gatherings." Now the apologetic expression was on Dave's face. "I'm really sorry, Sallie. Dani and I had to pretend not to know him."

The door opened and a policeman leaned in. "We've found the murder weapon, Sir." He held out an object on a towel.

Sallie frowned. "It looks like a flute."

Dave slid off the table and fingered the discolored tubing. "It is a flute. A flute that shoots .22 caliber bullets."

The flute on the towel may have been silver at one time. Now it had a dark patina swirled with rainbow patches, like oil on water. Some of the keys were altogether black.

The policeman laid the flute on the table and Dave leaned over it. "It's a spy flute. That's what Duby calls it. He has one in his collection." He sat down next to Sallie. "Morris Duby is an instrument maker and repairman. I lived with him for a couple of months about a year ago." He tapped his knee. "Injury in the line of duty. I had to take disability retirement and take up something less strenuous than police work. With my musical sideline, I figured instrument repair would be a good fit. Duby has a reputation as one of the best. He's a misanthrope, but with the help of a little reverse psychology, I talked him into taking me on. During my time with him, I became acquainted with his instrument collection. It's the only thing in the world he cares about."

Dave gestured toward the flute lying on the table. "Duby has a flute like this. He let me take it out and fire it." He looked more closely. "This could even be the one from his collection." He glanced at Garrett for permission. Garrett nodded and Dave picked up the flute. He showed them the mechanism and explained how it worked.

Garrett made a scoffing sound. "I realize there are flutes all over the place during a convention like this, but don't people usually carry them round in cases? Wouldn't a person carrying something like this through a crowd be noticed? We can't find anyone who saw the killer approach Kassim's booth with the weapon in hand."

"Assembled flutes are all over the place in the Exhibit Hall," Dave said. "They're laid out like that for people to try. Although," he added, "people don't usually walk away from the tables with them."

"Oh."

Both men looked at Sallie.

Garrett spoke. "You saw something?"

Despite her own mixed feelings about him, Sallie hated to cast police suspicion on Aram. He had, after all, saved her life at the bus stop. Still, this was a murder investigation. She had to say something. "Not long before it happened, I saw someone weaving through one of the aisles holding an assembled flute above his head."

"Did you recognize him?" Dave asked.

Sallie nodded. "It was one of the waiters here at the

hotel." As briefly as she could, she told them about the Armenian waiter, Kassim's interest in him, and how he'd come to her assistance at the bus stop. "He's the last person I'd suspect of wanting to kill Kassim."

Garrett sent an officer to fetch the waiter. Then he asked Dave to go downstairs where crime scene investigators were working out trajectories. "Since you've actually fired this thing or one like it, you may be able to provide useful information."

Dave left with another officer, and within a few minutes, Aram arrived, wearing his waiter's uniform and a nervous expression. He sat obediently in the chair Garrett indicated.

Sallie stood to go, but Aram half-rose with a beseeching expression. He looked at the inspector. "Please, may the lady stay?"

The fact that Aram regarded her as a friendly presence made Sallie feel guiltier than ever for telling on him.

Garrett didn't object, so Sallie resumed her seat.

"Please state your name," Garrett said.

"Aram Selkos."

"Mr. Selkos, you were seen carrying a flute in the exhibit hall earlier today. Can you tell me why you didn't have it in a case?"

"My boss, he give it me that way. Say take it back to exhibit room. I take it back."

"What was your boss doing with a flute?"

Aram shrugged. "Ask boss."

Garrett sent an officer to talk to the restaurant manager and turned back to Aram. "Just a few questions while we verify your story, Mr. Selkos. Did you know the man who was killed in the exhibit hall?"

Aram nodded.

"I believe he was a Turk," Garrett said.

Aram looked at him as if to say, "So?"

"You, Mr. Selkos, are an Armenian, are you not?"

"An Armenian, yes. True Hayastantsi, born there."

"From what I understand, Mr. Selkos, there is little love between Armenians and Turks. I don't suppose you're particularly sorry to hear of the death of a Turk."

Aram stared at Garrett as if working out what he'd said. His eyes widened as the meaning became clear. "What you say is pretty stupid, Mr. Police Officer."

Garrett reddened, but his voice remained calm. "Please explain, Mr. Selkos."

"Kassim was Turk, yes. But he was good Turk. In the bad times, in 1915 when Turkish government ordered the slaughter of my people, not all Turks obeyed. Would I be sitting here talking to you if all Turks killed Armenian neighbors? Good Turks hid my mother and I am here. What lunatic hates whole race for wickedness some do?"

The officer returned from questioning the restaurant manager.

"This man's story checks out, sir. A convention presenter named Melisande Truffaut brought a flute up from the exhibit hall to the restaurant and didn't want to walk it back down. The maitre d' sent this gentleman to take it back. I checked with the flute seller and he says that it was returned."

Garrett thanked Aram and told him he could go.

Dave rejoined them as the waiter left. "We worked out the trajectories. I remember from the time I shot it that it pulls to the left. It took me several tries before I could hit what I was aiming at." He turned a grave look on Sallie. "The other person who was on duty with Kassim this morning was able to tell us exactly where you were standing when she heard the shot. She said she was keeping an eye on the gold flute you were trying out." He paused, as if reluctant to continue.

"Well?" Sallie prodded. "Why do you keep looking at me like that?"

"I'm pretty certain that Kassim wasn't the target, Sallie. You were."

The bullet was meant for her. Sallie's stomach kneaded as the nausea returned. Again she heard the popping sound and felt the whiff of air against her cheek. Only this time, the mental picture was that of her own head oozing blood onto the floor of the Exhibit Hall.

"What haven't you told us?" Garrett barked.

"What do you mean?" Sallie asked, her voice up a register. "I don't know any more than you do. Why would anyone want to shoot me?" Why had she ever come on this miserable trip? Even Momma couldn't have anticipated this much mayhem.

Garrett softened his tone. "I'm not accusing you of anything. I just want to know what you know about the so-called Fabergé Flute. Someone may think you know where it is."

"Kassim was convinced that you didn't know anything," Dave said. "He tried to convince me, but I thought you had to be up to no good because of your friendship with Slocum."

"Slocum?" Sallie had forgotten the man. "What does Slocum have to do with anything?"

"Slocum has been on the scene of the theft of expensive instruments in the States and in Europe. His specialty is flutes. He attends music conventions masquerading as a musician. It's not too great a leap to believe he might be after the Fabergé Flute as well."

Sallie actually sputtered in renewed annoyance. "I never so much as heard of Harry Slocum before he sat down next to me on the plane in Dallas." Her response was beginning to sound like a mantra.

"I believe you," Dave said. "Now. And now I also believe you had no more than a passing acquaintance with Alan Bernini. But Bernini was known to be looking for the Fabergé Flute and you were seen more than once in conversation with him."

Dave's expression was a mixture of apology and self-justification. "You can't really blame me for thinking you might know something when you were seen with both Slocum and Bernini on your first night in London."

Coincidence. Sheer coincidence, but enough to get her killed.

"Whoever tried to kill you today is likely to try again," Garrett said. "You may wish to leave the convention and return to the States immediately."

Fear mingled with desperation made Sallie's mouth go dry. Lack of money trumped any danger she might be in. "I can't go home before Sunday. I don't have the kind of ticket that can be changed. And I don't have enough money to go to another hotel."

"You needn't worry about that, Miss Dunbar," Garrett said. "In the circumstances, the airline can be persuaded to change your ticket."

Sallie's hands and legs began to shake. She'd been the target of the bullet that had killed Kassim. Beautiful, gentle Kassim was dead because someone wanted to kill her. "Do you think it was Slocum?"

Dave shook his head. "Not his style. Slocum's a thief of opportunity. Nothing in his profile suggests he would kill to get what he's after. If he can't steal one flute, he'll steal another. The killer is a different animal altogether. He wants the Fabergé Flute. He killed Bernini to get the flute. He killed the security attendant to get at the flute that he'd concealed in your case."

"But why did he put it in my case to begin with?"

"It's only a working theory," Dave said, "but here's what I think happened. Whoever shoved Bernini in front of the taxi and snatched the flute case from him ran inside the hotel to hide. Finding your door open was simply fortuitous. He had no way of knowing whose room it was. He probably guessed that the police would be looking for a flute case without a handle. Your unattended case in an open room was a stroke of luck."

Garrett interrupted. "What did he do with Miss Dunbar's flute?"

Dave frowned. "That puzzles me too. I suppose he must have taken it away and dumped it somewhere your men overlooked in their search of the hotel."

"Their search was thorough," Garrett snapped. "If Miss Dunbar's flute was anywhere other than in one of the wheelie bins, they would have found it. They're still filtering the bins in the service area."

"He didn't take my flute anywhere," Sallie said. "He threw it under the bed. I found it after Dave and Dani left my room this morning." This morning. She marveled at the crazy tricks time was playing at this convention. She'd arrived on Sunday and today was only Wednesday. Yet she felt she'd lived at least a year during that time.

"What do you mean, he didn't take your flute?"

Sallie could tell both men were annoyed with her. In another lifetime, she would have offered an apology. "It was under my bed." To Dave, she said, "I wanted to see if I could tell why Tacet barked at the bed. As soon as you and Dani left, I looked under it and found my flute. My question is, why didn't he take my case once it had the Fabergé Flute in it? Why did he leave it in the security room?"

Dave shrugged. "I haven't figured that out yet."

"And what about the hypodermic needle? My attacker had the flute. All he had to do was take it and run. Why did he try to kill me?"

Dave started to speak, but Garrett interrupted him. "If you don't mind, Mr. King, I'll take over now." He turned to Sallie. "I can't be sure, Miss Dunbar, but I think it's possible that this person believes you saw him push Bernini into the street. You were nearby when it happened. If he thinks you know his identity, that would explain the attempts on your life."

Sallie shuddered. "I want to go home. Now."

Garrett began to speak, but Dave prevented him.

"No one could blame you for leaving, Sallie." he said.

"But?"

"If you stay, you could help us flush out Kassim's killer."

Sallie's muscles tensed. Why should she risk being killed for someone she'd known for barely three days? Yet three days had been enough to make her want to spend the rest of her life with him. Three days filled with memories. The impulsive way he'd gone to the aid of the embarrassed waiter. Their shared enthusiasm for books. The way he made her feel that her opinions mattered. As if she mattered.

And there was Bernini. Sallie had barely known him, but the hateful injustice of his death grieved her to the core. The monster who'd killed him was still out there. She thought of the courage of Kassim's grandfather who risked his life to save his Armenian neighbors. Was she going to turn tail and run the first time she was being asked to stand up for justice? She took a deep breath.

"What do you want me to do?"

Chapter Sixteen

Inspector Garrett tried to dissuade her, but Sallie insisted it was what she wanted to do. She would stay until the end of the convention and attempt to draw the killer into the open.

Once Garrett was persuaded, he assigned two plainclothes detectives, a man and a woman, to stay within ten feet of Sallie whenever she left her room.

Dave stayed to talk some more to Garrett while Sallie's guardians escorted her from the mezzanine to her room on the fourth floor. They stood close as she put her key into the lock.

Sallie tried to make light of the situation. "I hope you don't plan to move in with me."

The male detective responded in all seriousness. "No, miss, we'll see you into your room and then keep an eye on things from out here." With his rosy cheeks and rumpled hair, he didn't look old enough to be out of high school, let alone have completed police training.

The door next to Sallie's opened and Dani King peered out. "Still mad at us?"

"Not mad exactly, but I do have a few questions. Like, what were you doing with a hypodermic needle in your bag?"

Dave King joined them and, with Dani, followed Sallie into her room. Dani kicked off her shoes, plumped up a pillow, and made herself comfortable on the bed. "Hope you don't mind, Sallie. My feet are killing me again."

"I'll join you." Sallie took the other side of the bed. Tacet jumped up and claimed a spot between them.

Dave drew the desk chair close to Dani's side. "The hypo in your sample kit had Sallie worried," he said.

"Sorry about that, Sallie. I should have explained, but at the time you needed sleep more than explanations."

"Dani's a pharmaceutical representative," Dave said.

"Here we go again," Sallie said. "She told me she was a flute teacher."

"She is," Dave said, "but she's also a sales rep. And before that she was an Army nurse. And now, thanks to her Aunt Rose, may she rest in peace, she's independently wealthy. My Dani's a woman of many talents."

Sallie wasn't convinced. "Even if she's a pharmaceutical rep," she said, "why bring hypodermic needles to a six-day flute convention? Are you diabetic?"

"No, just afraid of getting sick in a strange place and not being able to find medicine. I was packing motion sickness medicine when it occurred to me that we might catch cold or eat something that disagreed with us or be unable to sleep. I decided to take along the whole sample case and be ready for anything. The hypo is just part of the standard contents." She leaned forward and rubbed her feet, moaning a little before continuing.

"We had our suspicions about you too," She said.

"For one thing, I couldn't figure out why you were so reluctant to check your flute into the security room. I suspected that you had something to hide."

Sallie laughed. "I was just too cheap to spend the five pounds."

"So," Dave said, "now that we know that none of us is a master criminal, let's pool our information and try to figure out who pushed Bernini in front of the taxi, killed the security attendant, and shot Kassim while aiming at Sallie."

Sallie's chest contracted painfully and tears flooded her eyes at the mention of Kassim. Here she was talking and laughing as if he hadn't been killed. The unknown flute player came to her rescue, sending exquisite arpeggios of sound into her grief, soothing it, dulling the pain. Dani stopped rubbing her feet and leaned back against the pillow. Sallie's need to sob subsided.

"Before we go any further with any of this," Sallie said, "I want you to tell me what you know about the Fabergé Flute. How long have you two known about it?"

Dave nodded. "Morris Duby told me about it. The summer I stayed with him. I thought it was just another manifestation of his craziness. Mind you, he's great at what he does, but I'll be the first to admit that his elevator doesn't go all the way to the top. I've been to see him in the hospital. The nurses hate to go near him. Still, I like him, and when Dani persuaded me to sign up for the IOFA convention, I phoned him to say we'd be in London and that I'd like to visit him."

"I persuaded you?"

Dave grinned and went on. "Talking to Duby is

usually like trying to pry the first olive out of a jar, but when I phoned from Chicago, he seemed unusually jovial and expansive, almost manic. He told me he'd heard some very interesting news. At first he only hinted, but I kept at him until he told me that the Fabergé Flute had surfaced in London. He was talking so fast that I couldn't catch everything he said, but I think he may have said he had the flute. Then he clammed up. I had the feeling that he knew more than he was telling me."

"We came over a few days early," Dani said. "I wanted to look up some Baroque music in the Rowe Collection at Cambridge."

"And I needed to meet with Kassim," Dave said, "to work out details. He was looking for the thief or thieves who have been making off with super-expensive flutes at international flute conferences."

"Tacet! No! Bad dog!" Dani and Sallie shouted at the same time as the dog attacked their feet, growling and barking.

Dave laughed. "That's what you get for moving your feet in time to the music."

Sallie hadn't been aware of it, but she and Dani had been beating time to the Fourth Floor Flute with their feet.

"Tacet is Duby's dog," Dave said. "I gave a few oboe lessons while I was staying with Duby. That's when I learned that Tacet cannot abide to see students keep time by tapping their feet."

Dani and Sallie stopped moving their feet and the dog settled down between them.

"Very sensible of you, Tacet," Dave said, scratching the dog's head. "Musicians should be able to count in their heads." He went on with his story. "I dropped Dani in Cambridge and came into London to see Duby on Saturday. When I arrived at the house, Tacet was holding off a crew of ambulance attendants. I went in to subdue the dog for them. Duby isn't the tidiest of men, but it looked to me as if the place had been tossed. An empty flute case was face down on the floor and papers everywhere."

Dave leaned across Dani and rested his face against Tacet's head. "You wouldn't let the ambulance attendants in, but you didn't do much to keep out the burglars, did you?" The dog rewarded Dave's attentions with slobbery kisses.

"Yuck!" Dave pulled away and Tacet leapt over Dani and pranced around Dave's chair. "Adagio, Tacet, adagio!" The dog stopped and curled up under the desk. Dave laughed. "Other dogs learn commands like *Down* and *Settle*. Tacet's words for 'calm down' and 'lie down' are *Adagio* and *Dolce*." He pulled a small, clear plastic bag out of a jacket pocket. "I want to see if you can help me with these, Sallie. I found them under Duby's workbench.

The bag contained two objects, what looked like a torn business card and something cylindrical. Dave dumped them onto the bed. He picked up the latter and held it out to Sallie on the palm of his hand. "I've no idea what this is."

Sallie took it. Bell-shaped rather than cylindrical, it was a dirty piece of leather that might have been cream-colored once. She rolled it between her fingers. "I've seen something like this recently. It's a tassel, the kind you see on loafers." She shut her eyes and the memory rose behind them. Benoît DeLille leaning back on a chair, his feet propped on a low table. "Benoît DeLille was wearing tasseled loafers the day Dani went to the master class."

"Monday," Dani said. "That was Monday."

"I noticed that one of the tassels was missing because he had his feet up on a table. I remember thinking how hard-up for money he must be to wear such dirty, worn-out shoes. I couldn't understand why he would provoke Max Paulson and risk losing the money he was getting for Orlando's flute lessons."

"DeLille," Dave said. "He could have motive. Mrs. Pinkerton says he'll play the *Syrinx* in Bernini's place at the closing banquet."

"He played in Bernini's place at the opening session," Dani said.

They sat in silence for a while, the only sound that of the Fourth Floor Flute. Now it was playing the Habanera from *Carmen*. Sallie had a hard time keeping her feet still.

Dave returned the tassel to the plastic bag.

"There's something else," Sallie said. "DeLille saw me looking at him and we exchanged a few words. I mentioned that I'd seen him in the pub on Sunday. He denied being there, but I saw him. He came in and sat at the bar just minutes after Bernini left the table to go out the back way."

"How long did he stay at the bar?" Dani asked.

"Not long. He stayed long enough to look around and then left. He would have had time to catch Bernini at the alley entrance."

"Not really," Dave said. "If DeLille didn't go out until after Bernini left the table, Bernini would have been long gone."

"No," Sallie said. "He wouldn't. Bernini told me he'd stopped to use the restroom on his way out. And something else. I think the reason Bernini left when he did is because he saw DeLille before he came in."

"How?" Dani asked.

"There's a little stained-glass window next to the front door of the pub. I looked through it before going in. It was dirty, but I could see how crowded the place was. If DeLille looked before going in, Bernini could have seen his face at the window. That could explain why he left in such a hurry."

"You may have something there, Sallie," Dave said. "If Bernini knew DeLille was after him, he would want to avoid him."

"But," Sallie said, wanting to be fair, "Harry Slocum and Max Paulson also left the pub soon after Bernini did. Either of them could have gone around back and snatched the flute case."

"But there are other reasons to suspect DeLille," Dani said. "Tacet doesn't like him. Remember how he ran at DeLille in the lobby, snapping at his shoes?"

"Yes," Sallie said, "but DeLille and the students with him were looking at sheet music. They may have been beating time with their feet. That would have been enough to set Tacet off."

"What about the tassel?" Dave said. "The tassel puts DeLille in Duby's workshop. DeLille could have been there the day the old man had his stroke. Tacet might have thought DeLille was hurting him. In fact, DeLille may have lost the tassel because the dog attacked him there."

"Maybe," Dani said. "Or, as Sallie said, Tacet may have just been reacting to foot-tapping. I have noticed that Orlando and Amber are both foot-tappers."

"OK," Dave said, "but what about the fit Tacet threw at the dumpster? There's definitely bad blood between the dog and DeLille."

"I just thought of something else," Sallie said. "Do you remember how Tacet barked and snarled at my bed this morning?" Was it only this morning? "He could have been barking at my flute, which was under there. If DeLille had handled my flute, Tacet could have been reacting to his scent."

Dave pursed his lips. "Not likely. Metal doesn't hold much of a scent. Still, show me your flute."

Sallie retrieved the flute. "Inspector Garrett still has my case, so I wrapped it in a T-shirt."

Dave unwrapped the pieces, sighting down each piece as if it were a gun barrel. "Did you polish the pieces before you wrapped them?"

"No. Just pulled them out from under the bed and put them away."

"Except for the places you would have touched it bringing it out from under the bed, it's without prints or smudges of any kind." He picked at one of the keys with a fingernail. "What's this? Looks like a thread. Do you use a red polishing cloth?"

"No. Yellow. And it doesn't leave threads."

"Whoever took your flute out of your case could have handled it with some type of red cloth, so as not to leave prints, and then pulled the cloth away when the pieces were under the bed, snagging a thread."

"DeLille has a red scarf." Sallie thought back to her sightings of DeLille and his scarf on the day Bernini died. He was wearing it in the lobby before the youth tour left, but Orlando took it from him on the bus.

Orlando still had the scarf when Max paused to offer his condolences to her regarding Bernini. Not long afterward, though, after she'd thrown up in the downstairs restroom, she saw DeLille wearing what looked like the same red scarf.

Dave rolled the thread between a thumb and forefinger. "Appears to be wool, a very fine wool. It's possible Tacet was able to detect DeLille's scent on it."

"Looks like the evidence is piling up," Dani said. "The shoe tassel at Duby's workshop. At the pub the night Bernini was mugged and denying he was there. The valuable exposure he gets from replacing Bernini as soloist."

Dave reached for the telephone. "Good enough for me. I think it's time to phone Chief Inspector Garrett."

"Wait." Sallie pointed to the other object from the evidence bag. "Don't call yet. There's still this torn business card you found in the workshop. Couldn't it point to someone besides DeLille?"

Dave held out the paper fragment. "Not much on it. No text, just a bit of what looks like part of a logo."

Sallie took the scrap. "I've seen something like this." She studied the triangular shape, wide at the bottom and narrowing toward the top. "Got it! Big Daddy's belt buckle."

Dave and Dani looked at her blankly. "Big Daddy?" they both said.

"Amber's father. Before I knew their names, I called him 'Big Daddy' and her 'the Princess.'" Sallie shrugged. "Whenever I'm stuck waiting, I make up stories about the people around me and give them names." Sallie smiled at their expressions. Let them think what they will. "Mr. Callahan, Amber's father, has a Western belt with a huge buckle with this image on it. It's an oil derrick."

Dave put the fragment back with the tassel. "What would his card be doing in Duby's workshop, I wonder."

Sallie slid off the bed and went to pick up the telephone. "Let's ask him. I'll see if he's in his room."

Amber answered and Sallie asked to speak to her father. "I'm sorry to bother you so late, Mr. Callahan…"

Mr. Callahan did not allow her to finish her sentence. His voice came through the receiver loud enough for Dave and Dani to hear. "Odean," came the friendly Oklahoma drawl. "Call me Odean. We're just settin' here, so come on down. That's to say, come on up. It's Room 735."

The sound of the Fourth Floor Flute followed them only to the fifth floor. The Callahan suite on the seventh floor was redolent with the smell of cooked food. A food cart stood next to a table.

"Sorry, Mr. Callahan," Sallie said. "We didn't intend to interrupt your dinner."

"Not at all, not at all, Miss Dunbar. It just got here and is all covered up fancy. It'll stay hot awhile yet. Say, can I order something for you all?"

"No, thank you," Dave said. "We'll just ask a couple of questions and get out of your way."

Odean was a talker. And he wasn't shy about providing personal information. He was from Miniver, Oklahoma, not far from Ardmore, which city he informed them had more millionaires per capita than any other town in the United States.

Sallie interrupted his monologue long enough to

compliment his daughter on her playing. "That was quite an accomplishment for Amber to qualify for Monsieur Truffaut's master class."

The object of her praise burst into tears. "And I was awful, just awful. I just can't get any kind of tone out of that flute."

"Now Amber, honey, I told you to try out them high-priced flutes in the basement and find you one that you like better than the one you have. Maybe you need one of them platinum jobs."

"I know a man who makes flutes," Dave said. "Maybe what Amber needs is a flute made to order. Ever hear of an instrument-maker named Morris Duby?"

Sallie watched Callahan, looking for a guilty reaction. He surprised her.

"Sure have. I've been looking into these things for some time now, ever since I knew how much my girl has her heart set on being a professional musician."

Sallie didn't miss the grimace that passed over Amber's face.

"Got her a silver flute when she was unhappy with the one the school started her on in eighth grade," Callahan said. "Then, when she went into high school band, I got her a gold job. Set me back plenty, let me tell you." He turned a doting face to his daughter. "That's what she has now." The look of pride on his broad red face changed to bewilderment. "Seems like it ought to work well enough."

"It's no good for low D, Daddy."

Callahan shrugged. "Found out about that Duby fellow and came over to London a few days early so's I could look him up." He took a bread stick from a basket on the food cart and commenced eating it like a piece of celery.

"Did you go to his house?" Dave asked.

"Sure did. Amber and me got to London last Friday. On Saturday, I left Amber with Miz Pinkerton and went to talk to Mr. Duby. Funny sort of man if you ask me. Course, I'd never met him before so I don't know if that's how he usually acts."

"How's that?"

"I don't know, sort of jumpy, somehow, and excited. The door was open when I got there so I walked straight in. He was sitting behind a table with a flute case open in front of him, looking at what was in it. He slammed down the lid as soon as he saw me. Anyway, I told him I'd heard his flutes was top of the line and asked if he had any to sell. Well, his eyes were all glittery and he talked kind of goofy, like he might be drunk, but I didn't smell liquor on him. He asked me what kind of flute I was looking for and I told him I wanted something really good, something that would give my daughter an edge. In that contest, you know, the one all the youngsters are trying out for. When I said that, he started, well, giggling, that's the only word for it. He said, 'An edge? An edge? Why man, I have a flute that can make a dead man play!' "

Dave leaned forward. "Did he by any chance show you this wonderful flute?"

"He sure did. Opened up the case and showed me. It was a dandy, all right. The tube part was mostly gold, and the keys were different colors. It was real pretty and I offered to buy it from him. I figured a flute that pretty might do something for my girl's self-confidence if nothing else."

"Well?" Dave urged. "What did he say? What did he say when you offered to buy the flute?"

"He slammed the case shut and started in again with that crazy giggling. Said that I probably couldn't afford it—which I bet I could—but that it was already sold and he was expecting the buyer along at any minute."

"Did you see anyone? Did the buyer come while you were there?"

Callahan cast a longing look at the covered dishes on the food cart.

"I don't know if I saw the buyer or not. I gave the old man my card and told him to get in touch with me if the sale fell through. He almost pushed me out the door and locked it behind me. I figured he was nuts and went back to the hotel."

Dave frowned. "Is that all? Did you notice anything unusual, anyone in the street?"

Callahan nodded and reached for another bread stick. "I did see a peculiar-looking fellow coming up the steps as I left." He laughed, spraying crumbs. "If the old coot didn't think I could afford his fancy flute, I'm durned if that fellow was the buyer."

"How do you know?"

"The way he was dressed. He had on raggedy blue jeans and a raggedy coat with a hood. And with those spooky bug eyes and crazy hair he couldn't have been in any kind of money-making business I can think of."

"Crazy hair?"

"His hood slipped back and I could see some of it." Odean winked. "Bottled blonde. Like Marilyn *Mon*roe."

As the elevator took them back to their floor, the

sound of the Fourth Floor Flute playing again came through as they passed the fifth floor. Back in her room, Dave was jubilant. "DeLille again! I'd say it's time to phone the chief inspector."

Sallie and Dani listened to one side of the conversation as Dave told Garrett about his suspicions. "Really? Well, that clinches it, doesn't it?" Dave hung up, grinning.

"Well?" Dani demanded. "Don't just sit there smirking. What did he say?"

"Garrett's men finished sifting the contents of the dumpster." Dave ruffled Tacet's ears. "Good work, Tacet." To his human companions, he said, "They found a flute case without a handle."

Dani slapped her hands together. "That settles it. DeLille must be the thief and the killer. He stole the Fabergé Flute from Mr. Duby's house. Somehow Bernini got hold of it. DeLille mugged him to get it back. He put the flute into your case after the accident because the police were looking for a case without a handle. It all fits."

Sallie wasn't convinced. "Why did he leave it in my room? Why didn't he take it with him?"

Dave shrugged. "I don't know. Maybe he planned to go back for it after he tossed the other one into the dumpster."

"How could he be sure he could get it back before I opened my case and saw it?"

Dave huffed in exasperation. "Garrett will get it out of him," he said. "He's having him picked up even as we speak."

Sallie wasn't convinced. It was too easy. Despite all the circumstantial evidence, Sallie felt that DeLille was no murderer. His devotion to his old teacher. The way he'd defied Max outside the closed master class. The way he behaved with Orlando on the bus, as if he were reluctant to hurt the boy but didn't want to encourage him. Ordinarily, Sallie wouldn't dream of contradicting someone like Dave on a professional matter, but Kassim had given her confidence in her opinions. Her perception of DeLille was as valid as Dave's.

"I find it hard to picture DeLille as a murderer," she said.

Dave raised an eyebrow. "Everything points to him, Sallie. He was at Duby's house and could have taken the flute before the ambulance got there. Tacet has some reason to dislike him. And you can tell by the way he dresses that he needs money."

Dani got off the bed and went to the door. "Let the professionals worry about it, Sallie. Tomorrow's Thanksgiving. I'd like to see a show while we're here. We're in the theater district." She turned to her husband. "What do you say we take in a matinee tomorrow?"

"Great idea. How about it, Sallie? Join us? My treat."

"Don't you think I'd better stay out of crowds until we're sure DeLille really is the killer?"

"Don't worry," Dave said. "Dani and I won't let anyone push you in front of a bus. Besides, I'm sure DeLille's our man, and so is Garrett. He's confident enough that he's pulling your protection detail."

Sallie was tempted by the prospect of seeing a London production. "I suppose you're right." All the same, she couldn't quell the feeling that DeLille was not their murderer.

Chapter Seventeen

Sallie shut the door on the Kings and got ready for bed, anticipating the flute lullaby she'd come to expect. But now, the Fourth Floor Flute was silent and Sallie fell into a troubled sleep, waking intermittently to thoughts of Kassim, weeping uncontrollably for a time, and then falling back into a fitful doze.

Toward morning, the ethereal flute began to play and, like magic, brought solace and rest. When Sallie finally woke at eleven, she had to scramble. She and the Kings had arranged to leave the hotel at one.

Dave had obtained the tickets from the hotel concierge and wouldn't tell Sallie what play they were for.

Sallie was in a high state of excitement at the prospect of seeing a West End play. "Is it *Les Miz*?"

"Maybe," Dave said maddeningly. "You'll see when we get there. Come on, the theatre is just around the corner from here, so we can walk."

Sallie's spirits drooped. She knew then that it could not be *Les Misérables*. That and the other show she'd like to see, *Cats*, were at theaters in the Charing Cross Road. She'd noticed the signs the day she explored the bookstores. Oh well. It didn't matter, really. Anything in the West End was bound to be good. She felt her enthusiasm return. As long as it wasn't one of those silly slapstick comedies that run forever because they're so corny.

On the way to the theatre, they had to navigate a narrow wooden passageway bordering a construction site.

"Watch your step," Dave called out. Just in time.

Her mind on the upcoming play, Sallie almost stepped into a gap between two boards, dislodging a piece of wood that fell several seconds before hitting bottom. She kept her eyes on her feet the rest of the way and was glad when the temporary walkway came to an end a few yards from the theater entrance. Here, a length of red plastic the width of police crime scene tape was all that separated pedestrians from an open trench.

"Let's be sure to walk back on the other side of the street," Sallie said.

Dave still hadn't told them what play they were going to see, so Sallie continued to fantasize. Maybe it would be a Shakespeare play. She'd like any one of them.

Her fantasy crashed as soon as she saw the theatre marquee. *A Funny Thing Happened on the Way to the Forum.*

"It's really funny," Dave said. "The desk clerk promised we'll love it."

The posters outside showed dumpy men in togas cavorting with shapely, scantily clad women. Sallie forced a smile. Inside, the red and gold foyer raised her spirits. How bad could a play in a West End theater be? She felt a thrill of excitement. She was in London. Their tickets took them to good seats on the front row of the second level.

When the house lights lowered, Sallie watched for

the curtain to rise, but it didn't. Instead, an actor came out from behind it and proceeded to sing a Welcome song that he accompanied with vulgar gestures of sexual innuendo. The song was an apt prelude to the action. The play was a mindless romp filled with sophomoric scatological humor. The audience loved it. Even Sallie laughed at some of the physical jokes. High drama it wasn't, but simply being in a London theater was exciting.

At intermission Sallie and the Kings edged through the crowd to the bar. Then, drinks in hand, they moved to a spot close to the wall where they could observe without being crushed. Odean Callahan, holding a beer in one hand and grasping Amber's elbow with the other, joined them. "Say, isn't this the funniest thing you ever saw?" Amber was looking away, scanning the crowd for more interesting company. The scent of Juicy Fruit emanated from her busily working jaws.

"I never expected to like it," Odean said. "I figured anything in London would be too egg-headed for me. But this one's sure a dandy."

Sallie murmured something that might be taken as agreement. Following Amber's gaze, she saw Max Paulson moving toward them. Sallie began to suspect that the hotel concierge must get a generous cut of ticket sales.

"Where's Orlando?" Amber asked as soon as Max was close enough to shake hands with Dave.

"At the bar," Max said. "I hope the intermission is long enough for everyone to be served."

"I doubt the bell will ring before everyone has a chance to order and pay," Dani said. "The theatre probably makes more money from the drinks than from the tickets."

Orlando joined them and handed a glass and a napkin to Max, who thanked him courteously. Sallie wondered at their relationship. Outside the master class, Max had referred to Orlando as *protégé* and not *son*. The formality between them was unlike anything Sallie had ever seen between parent and child, even when the child was adopted.

Max placed a proprietary hand on Orlando's shoulder. "Orlando has proved to be a real credit to me at this conference."

Maybe it was the unaccustomed wine, but Sallie couldn't resist saying what was on her mind. "Would you say he's more a son or a protégé?"

Max looked at her expressionlessly. "I think of him as both protégé and son. He came to me with a wonderful musical gift. I do all that I can to nurture and advance it."

Orlando, his face showing neither pleasure nor any other emotion, nodded politely to the adults and excused himself to go talk to Amber. Max watched him walk away with an expression of pride and affection, yet Sallie felt a shudder of distaste as she recalled the scene he'd created when Orlando rescued the balloon for the little girl in the park. She watched Orlando, who, with Amber, was completely transformed.

Sallie found it difficult to reconcile the vivacious youngster chatting and joking with Amber with the intense youth who planted a kiss on Benoît DeLille's mouth on the bus. She wondered what Max would say if he suspected that his beloved protégé and adopted son was interested in men. On the other hand, as she watched Orlando with Amber, Sallie began to doubt the significance of what she'd seen on the bus.

She tuned back in on the conversation. Max was still holding forth on Orlando. She hated it when adults talked about children as if they weren't there. She tried to think of something to say to change the subject. Her glance fell on Max's polished walking stick gleaming under the overhead lights. "That's a beautiful cane you have there, Mr. Paulson. Mahogany?"

Max smiled and held it out to Sallie. It was heavier than she'd anticipated. He laughed as the unexpected weight forced her hand down. The wooden shaft was topped with some light-colored material "Is the handle ivory?"

"Jade. And the wood is Brazilian rosewood. Note the grain."

Sallie examined the elaborate design carved on the jade handle. At first she thought it was just an interlocking abstract, but then she realized what she was looking at. Two naked male bodies entwined. Max laughed again as she thrust the cane back as if it had become hot in her hands.

Max handed Sallie his wine glass to hold. "I'll need two hands to show you this." There he went again, treating her like his servant. He held the wooden part of the cane with one hand and pressed something on the jade handle, then drew back his arm, pulling out a slim, shining blade.

Before he could do more, the warning chimes sounded. The drinkers quickly disposed of their cups before moving back to the auditorium. Orlando came swiftly to Max's side, the expression on his face again neutral. Sallie handed him Max's cup to dispose of. Max slid the sword back into the cane and they parted to their separate seats.

The second half of the play was shorter than the first, and before long the audience was making its slow shuffling exit, so packed together that shoulders touched as they descended the stairway. On a landing where the staircase turned, Sallie could see that the shoulder pressing her on the right belonged to Orlando. She studied the beautiful brown face. It held no hint of the boyish vivacity that lighted it when he spoke to Amber. Without thinking, only wishing to make conversation, Sallie commented on the oppressive crowding. "This is kind of like the bus from Trafalgar Square, isn't it?" She couldn't see his expression, but their bodies were touching and she felt him pull away.

By then, they had reached the foyer and were moving out onto the sidewalk. Sallie had space to look around. Orlando had vanished. Dave and Dani were nowhere to be seen. Caught up in the movement of the crowd, Sallie felt herself being edged toward the wooden walkway and the gap beside it. She felt the pressure of a hand, squarely between her shoulder blades. "Dave?" She tried to turn. The pressure on her back increased. For the second time in two days she was being pushed where she didn't want to go. She felt her foot slide off the edge of the wooden walk and dangle in air.

"Whoa there!" Another hand grabbed her by the forearm and yanked her back with a painful twist and scrape.

"Sorry if I hurt you, miss," said a red-faced man in a bowler. "You were falling into that hole there."

"Sallie!" Dave and Dani pushed through the crowd of pedestrians.

"Are you all right?" Dani asked. "We were looking for you on the other side of the entrance. You said you didn't want to go back on this side."

They returned to the theater entrance.

"What happened?" Dave asked.

"The same thing that happened the morning I saw you talking to Kassim in the coffee shop. Somebody deliberately pushed me. Ow. Damn, it hurts!" She held onto Dave's arm, put her weight on the injured foot, and yanked it back up. "It hurts when I step on it."

Dani stooped to feel Sallie's ankle. "It could be broken."

"I don't think so." Sallie pressed down on it again. "I can stand on it if I have to. Doesn't feel too good, but I can walk on it."

"No, you don't," Dave said. "Everybody stay where you are." Moving to the curb, he flagged a taxi. After a long negotiation, Dave opened the back door and helped Sallie in. "I had to promise the driver a huge tip to get him to take us such a short distance."

Sallie settled gratefully onto the backseat and Dani got in next to her.

"OK, Mr. Detective," Sallie said, "if Benoît DeLille is our killer, who just tried to push me down the construction hole?"

By the time they reached the hotel, Sallie's ankle had doubled in size and was hurting worse. The Kings helped her hobble to a chair near the coffee shop and went to locate a wheelchair. She saw Harry Slocum passing. This time he didn't avoid looking at her.

"Sallie! Just the person I want to see." He dropped his flute case, the one with the URTLES sticker, onto her lap. "Hold this for me a minute, will you?"

"I'm not going to be here very long, Harry."

"Just be a minute. Right back. Word of honor." He walked over to a knot of youth players sitting at a table and joined their conversation.

Sallie played idly with the clasps on the case in her lap, opening and shutting them. Why hadn't Harry taken it with him? Maybe he was afraid one of the students would ask to see his flute and was ashamed to see him with a…what was the make of that crummy flute? She couldn't remember. She glanced over where Harry was schmoozing with the students. His back was to her. She opened the flute case.

"What the heck?" Sallie didn't have to read the name on the head joint to know this wasn't the flute she'd seen the morning Harry bought her breakfast. That one had been a cheap off-brand silver flute. The one occupying the URTLES case this time was a gold Muramatsu.

Dani and Dave returned in short order. Sallie shut the case.

"Whose flute?" Dani asked, nodding at the case.

Transferring from lobby chair to wheelchair made her ankle hurt so much, all Sallie could manage in reply was to point and say, "Harry." The gold flute went clean out of her mind.

Thanksgiving Day ended with a whimper. Sallie was ready to go home. Her life in DeSoto Springs might be tedious, but at least it was safe.

Back in her room, Sallie soaked her ankle in Epsom salts from Dani's medicine hoard and propped up her foot for the rest of the day.

Around seven, Dani brought her a sandwich. "Dave and I are on our way to a Bach concert, but if you want me to stay, I will."

"No, I'll be fine. Inspector Garrett has restored my security detachment. They're out in the hallway."

Sallie took her throbbing ankle to bed early. As she lay there, the Fourth Floor Flute commenced a melody she didn't recognize. As she drifted off, the throbbing stopped and her injured ankle lay wrapped in a soothing warmth.

Chapter Eighteen

Friday, 29 November, Day Five of
IOFA Convention

The jarring brill of the telephone woke Sallie on
Friday. Dani King was on the line. "Chief Inspector
Garrett wants us in the incident room."

"Did you tell him I can barely walk?"

"That was yesterday, Sallie. Have you tried to walk
on it this morning?"

Sallie put down the receiver and scooted out of
bed. Tentatively, expecting renewed agony, she put
weight on the injured foot. No pain.

She walked across the room and back. No problem.

She picked up the phone. "Good as ever."

"Thought so," Dani said. "It's been like that with
my feet all week. I'll go to bed ready to scream with
pain, certain I'll never walk again, and next day my feet
are just fine. It's just a bit of mind over matter."

"It's the flute."

"What flute?"

"The Fourth Floor Flute. The one we hear playing
at all hours of the day and night. That is what has been
healing all our aches and pains."

"Rubbish. We'll meet you in the hall."

On the way to the elevator, Dave warned Sallie that
Garrett was in a foul mood. "He's more than a little

peeved with me. Turns out that DeLille has an air-tight alibi."

Sallie resisted the urge to say, "told you so."

Dave punched the button for the mezzanine. "The hotel clerk on duty at the time of Bernini's accident says she saw DeLille come through the front entrance, pass the registration counter, and go into the stairwell before the commotion started outside. She noticed because a woman sitting on a bench in the lobby jumped up and went after him, as if she'd been waiting for him."

"All that proves is that he's not the one who pushed Bernini," Dani said. "He could still be the one who stole the Fabergé Flute and the spy flute from Duby's workshop. He could be working with someone."

The elevator, not as convenient to the incident room as the escalator, opened at the far end of the mezzanine, requiring them to walk farther.

"DeLille has alibis for everything," Dave said.

Dani scoffed. "If he's so innocent, why does Tacet react the way he does? DeLille did something at Duby's house. We know he was there the day the flutes were stolen.

"A lot of people were at Duby's house that day," Sallie said. "Any one of them could have taken the flutes—including Dave." She made a face at him, a reminder that he had suspected her of skullduggery.

"Touché," Dave said.

"DeLille was at the pub the night Bernini was mugged," Dani said. "And he lied about being there."

Garrett was waiting for them at the door of the incident room. "Please come in."

The much-discussed DeLille was in room. Sallie had to look twice to recognize him. Instead of his usual scruffy ensemble of jeans, dirty loafers, and hoodie, he was dressed in an expensive suit and shod with gleaming Oxford wingtips. A jeweled flute pin identical to the one Bernini had worn gleamed on his left lapel. Perhaps the greatest difference was that he was not slouching but stood next to the police inspector with an erect posture that lent him dignity and authority. His eyes were red-rimmed. A flute case lay on the long table.

"Mr. DeLille has lodged a complaint," Garrett said. "Regarding this instrument." He opened the case. "This is Mr. Bernini's case, but Mr. DeLille says that this is not Mr. Bernini's flute."

DeLille touched the case with a contemptuous gesture. "This is not Alan's flute. And it is certainly not platinum."

"Have another look at it, Mr. King," Garrett said. "This is the case we had you look at the day Mr. Bernini died. It's been locked up in the security room since then."

Dave fingered the brass tag. "It's the same case."

DeLille made an impatient sound. "It is Alan's case. *C'est vrai*. But it is not his flute. My flute now." His voice broke.

"Mr. DeLille has shown me papers," Garrett said. "He co-signed the loan with which Bernini's flute was purchased. The serial number on this flute does not match the number on the papers."

Dave hefted the head joint. "He's right. This is not platinum." He ran his fingernail along the ring where the silvering turned to base metal at the join. "It's not even high-quality silver." Dave put the tube back into the case. "This is not the flute that I looked at on Tuesday."

"Could you have been mistaken when you looked at it then?"

Dave's indignant expression did not require a spoken response.

Garrett shrugged. "I had my man put the case back into its cubby hole, as good a place as any for it. The hotel manager swears that the security room has not been left unattended since then."

"And yet Alan's flute has been taken," DeLille said. "I must have that flute. It's all I have left."

Sallie saw tears in the red-rimmed eyes.

"We shall do all that we can to recover it," Garrett said. "Please, won't you sit down?"

DeLille sat, propped his elbows on the conference table and held his head in his hands. Sallie and the others sat too, uncertain what to say in the face of the man's grief. Finally, Garrett broke the silence.

"I'm sorry for your loss," he said. "And I hate to trouble you at a time like this, but you might have information that could help us."

DeLille lifted his face from his hands and looked at them with a tear-stained face.

"What kind of information?"

"We've been told that Mr. Bernini was overheard on several occasions talking on the phone with someone named 'Teddy,' with whom he seemed to be on intimate terms. Are you acquainted with such a person?"

DeLille uttered a sound that was a cross between a laugh and a sob.

"*C'est moi.* I am 'Teddy.' It was Alan's pet name for me. I was his 'Teddy Boy-Teddy Bear.' Because of my hair, you see. He thought the sideburns made me look like a Teddy Boy." He stood. "We were life partners, Inspector. If I'd wanted anything belonging to Alan, all I'd had to do was ask."

When DeLille had gone, Garrett scowled at Dave.

"Turns out this impoverished flute player is the only son of a French concrete baron. The only way Bernini, even with his reputation, could buy that $70,000 flute was by getting DeLille to co-sign for him."

Sallie had been certain that DeLille was an impoverished musician. When would she stop judging people by appearances?

"What are you going to do about finding Bernini's flute?" Dave asked.

"I'm going to step up the searches in the lobby. From now until Sunday morning, no one comes in or goes out without a serial number check."

"How you know Bernini's flute hasn't already left the hotel?" Dani asked.

"I don't," Garrett said, "but even if Bernini's flute is gone, we've a list of serial numbers belonging to other stolen instruments. We may as well see if any of those turn up. Thank God this wretched convention is nearly at an end."

Dani frowned. "If the security room was never left unattended, Bernini's flute must have been stolen by one of the attendants."

"So it would seem," Garrett said, "but we've questioned all of them and searched their lodgings without results."

247

Sallie frowned as something teased her memory. Something to do with the security room, but what it was eluded her.

Chapter Nineteen

The insistent ringing of a telephone greeted Sallie and the Kings as they returned to their rooms.

"It's ours," Dave said, scrambling to open the door.

Sallie opened her own door but remained standing in the hallway while Dave answered. He said a few words she couldn't make out and hung up.

"It was the hospital," Dave said. "Mr. Duby is being moved to a nursing home."

"Uh-oh," Dani said. "What about the dog?"

"Don't know," Dave said. "Duby's bound to know someone who can take him. Meanwhile, I'd like you look after Tacet while I go see what I can do to help with the move. Hopefully, it won't take all day."

He kissed Dani and turned back toward the elevator.

"What are your plans for the day, Sallie?" Dani asked.

Sallie could see her security detail farther down the hall. "Considering that Inspector Garrett thinks someone is still out to kill me, I think I'll just stay in."

"If you want me to, I'll stay and keep you company."

"No. Really, all I want to do is kick back, write a few postcards, and grade some papers. You can leave Tacet with me, but you'll have to come back to walk him. Let me know when Dave gets back from his errand of mercy and we can do something then. Maybe with you, Dave, and my police detail to guard me, we can take a break from the Hunter's Den and have supper in a real restaurant."

No sooner had Sallie settled down to grade the papers she'd brought when a knock sounded on her door. It was Amber.

"Are you sick?" the girl asked.

"No. Come on in. I'm just trying to catch up on some grading so I won't have it to do when I get back home. What's up?"

Amber threw herself into the armchair, and Tacet launched himself onto her lap. "It's Daddy," Amber said. "Why can't grown-ups ever listen?"

"What is it now?"

"The same thing. I don't want a professional music career and he thinks I do. I'll be glad when they announce the winner of the Youth Award so he'll stop going on about how he's sure it's going to be me."

Sallie looked at the girl sprawled on the armchair, absently scratching the dog around the ears and chin. Amber was quite beautiful, with the added loveliness of not being aware of it. Even the distorting scowl could not conceal the exotic planes of the face, the legacy of an American Indian ancestor.

"Have you told him how you feel?"

"*Yes*. Millions of times."

Sallie smiled. "Sometimes we think we're telling someone what we mean when in fact we're talking around it. Have you ever straight out said, 'I don't want to be a professional flutist'?"

Amber frowned. Then she sighed. "You know, I don't think I ever have. When he goes on about how good I am, I just mumble something." She looked beseechingly at Sallie. "It's so hard. I know he thinks he's making me happy and I can't bear to hurt him."

"How do you think he'd feel if he knew he was hurting you by insisting on a musical career?"

Amber's eyes glistened. "Oh dear! I never thought of that. He'd hate it. But I just don't know how to tell him, Miss Dunbar. I just don't."

"Why not write him a letter?"

Amber made a moue of objection. "That would be mean!"

"Not if you sit by him while he reads it. It will open the conversation you've been finding so hard to initiate. Just tell him that you want to have a talk but that you'd like for him to read something first."

Amber jumped up, dumping Tacet on the floor and subjecting Sallie to a crushing hug. "That's a wonderful idea. Then, when he's read it, I can tell him what I really want to do."

"What do you want to do with your life, Amber?"

"I want to get married and have lots and lots of children, at least six, but first I want to be a kindergarten teacher. That way I'll learn all about how children develop and then I'll teach for about five years so that by the time I have my own children, I'll know what I'm doing."

Sallie laughed. "I see. You'll practice on other people's children."

Amber frowned. "Why not? Anything important takes practice. I'd never walk onto the stage at a recital without having practiced the piece I'm going to play. Why would I want to take chances with messing up my own children?"

"You have a point."

"Besides, I wouldn't be messing up somebody else's children. I'd be observing what their parents had already done to them." She moved around the room, gesturing enthusiastically, Tacet nipping at her heels. "My Aunt Nona teaches first grade. She says some children come to school ready to learn, but that some act like no one ever taught them anything at home. I want to get to know a lot of different kinds of parents and learn which ones not to be like."

"Have you come up with a check list for your children's father?"

Amber blushed and sat back down on the edge of the chair. "Kind of."

"How does Orlando fit the job description?"

The girl's blush darkened. "It's hard to tell about him. Sometimes he does something really nice, like helping that little girl in the park. But other times—I don't know. He gets a scary look in his eye, like he's thinking about something really awful."

"He had a hard life before being adopted by Mr. Paulson."

Amber grimaced and shuddered. "Him."

"I take it you don't like Mr. Paulson."

"I don't want to say anything against somebody's father, but Mr. Paulson doesn't treat Orlando like a son. He acts like he's something he owns. He gives him expensive things and praises him about his playing and brags about him to other people, but you saw how he was in the park. Sometimes he talks to Orlando just awful, calling him 'stupid' and such. I don't care if it isn't nice of me to say so. I don't like him a bit."

Sallie shared Amber's feelings about Max but

thought the wisest thing would be to change the subject. "Do you and your father plan to stay for the banquet tomorrow night?"

Amber giggled. "That's exactly what Mr. Slocum asked me coming up in the elevator." She blushed again. "Is Mr. Slocum your boyfriend?"

It was Sallie's turn to turn red. Where were people getting the impression that she and Harry were an item? "Of course not. What gave you that idea?"

"I saw you having breakfast with him. And he talks about you a lot."

"Talks about me? How? When? Why would you be spending time with Mr. Slocum anyway? Does he have something to do with looking after the youth players?"

"No, he just seems to like us. He treats us to Cokes and stuff."

"What do you talk about besides me?"

"Oh, things like what kind of flutes we play, where we're from, if we're going to stay for the whole conference or will be leaving early. That kind of thing. He's really nice and funny."

Sallie frowned. Slocum didn't seem to be the generous type. What could he be up to, buddying up with the youth contingent, treating them to snacks? Come to think of it, Sallie had seen him in the coffee bar in the company of teen players more than once. His manner was avuncular, patting shoulders, adjusting jackets on chair backs, laughing appreciatively. "What has he said about me?"

"Nothing bad. Just that you're a teacher and you came over on the plane together. I didn't mean to make you mad."

"You didn't." Sallie took a deep breath and

managed a smile. To change the subject, she asked, "Are you looking forward to the banquet?"

"I sure am. In fact, Daddy wanted to leave today as soon as the youth winner is announced, but I begged him to stay another night." The blush reappeared. "I'm hoping we can sit at the same table as Orlando. I just wish Mr. Paulson wouldn't be there. Maybe he'll have one of his spells and have to stay in his room."

"What kind of spells?"

"He's diabetic. Orlando says sometimes he won't take his shots and then he has a spell. If I'm lucky, he'll have a spell tomorrow night." She blushed and shook her head. "That was an awful thing to say. I'm sorry, but, really, he's not very nice to be around."

Amber fell silent and this time Sallie stood up and moved to the door. Amber took the hint. "I guess I'll go write that letter to my daddy," she said. Then she jumped up and treated Sallie to another rib-crushing hug. "Thanks heaps for the idea, Miz Dunbar."

Instead of getting back to grading papers, Sallie let her mind fill with memories of Kassim. Not the hideous images of the shooting, but the conversations and the magical walk along the Embankment. She put away the school papers and got out the first volume of Samuel Johnson's *Lives of the Poets*. Kassim had read it. Kassim's eyes had traveled across every page. Sallie curled up in the armchair to commune with her lost love by reading words that he had read, opening her mind to thoughts that he had thought.

Sometime later, an insistent knocking roused Sallie from her connection with Kassim and she went to open the door.

"He's here." Dani King shoved her husband into

the room ahead of her. "Finally. Mr. Duby is safely ensconced in his new home."

Dave sank onto the edge of the bed. "I'm starving."

"So are we," Dani said. "It's already nearly eight. Let's go. And to a real restaurant. I've had enough of the Hunter's Den."

Dave groaned and fell backward. "I've made so many three-way trips between the hospital, Duby's house, and the nursing home that I have no strength left for walking. I beg you, ladies. have mercy on me. What do you say we order in room service?"

Sighing a deep, disapproving sigh, Dani snatched the menu from the writing desk. "Have it your way, Mr. King, but be warned. I'm ordering the most expensive dish they have. You too, Sallie. Get whatever you want. He's paying."

Sallie took Dani at her word. She ordered coq au vin and bananas Foster, neither of which she'd ever had. While they waited for their order, Dave told them about his day,

"Poor old Duby doesn't have a living soul to care what happens to him. He's completely at the mercy of the British social services. And guess what! He's not even English!"

"You're kidding," Dani said. "He certainly sounds English. He talks like a Cockney."

"That's because he's lived in the East End since 1922. He was still in his teens when he immigrated."

"What kind of name is Duby?" Dani asked.

Dave laughed.

"A mispronounced one, apparently. I saw his birth certificate and it didn't say 'Morris Duby.' He said he could never get the English to pronounce his real name properly, so he just went ahead and started spelling it the way they said it."

A knock on the door interrupted Dave's anecdote. Expecting room service, they were surprised to see a tearful Amber Callahan standing in the hall.

Dani took her by the hand and drew her into the room. "Come in, dear. What's the matter?"

To the accompaniment of much sniffling, Amber poured out her misery, pointing to no fewer than five zits on her face, two on her forehead, two on either cheek, and one especially angry-looking one in the middle of her chin.

"I can't possibly go to the banquet like this! I look like I have smallpox! Orlando will think I'm disgusting!"

Sallie and Dani comforted her as well as they could. Dani went next door and came back with a little green tube. "It's a medicated cream formulated especially for acne."

"Will it make the pimples go away in time for the banquet?"

Dani patted the girl's hand. "I'm afraid I can't guarantee that."

Amber burst into a new round of weeping. Dave shifted uncomfortably. "Say, Amber, how'd you like to have a job tomorrow night? I mean, if you decide not to go to the banquet."

The unexpected question stopped the waterfall.

"A job?"

"Yes, just in case, you know, in case that stuff doesn't work fast enough and you decide not to attend. I could use your help."

Amber stared questioningly.

"It's Tacet. I don't like to leave him by himself for too long at a time. It'd be a big help to us if you could sit with him while we're at the banquet. There wouldn't be much to it. Just being with him will keep him happy. You can watch TV, order room service, anything you like. And I'll give you twenty bucks besides."

Amber's lower lip quivered. "I'd rather go to the banquet."

"Of course you would, dear," Dani said. "And we hope that you'll be able to. But just keep in mind that if the pimples don't…if you decide you can't go, you can have your own private banquet here with Tacet."

At length Amber was calm enough to leave. She paused at the door. "If I do have to come here instead of going to the banquet, I might like to take Tacet for a walk. Would that be OK?"

Dave shook his head emphatically. "No! Not even on a leash! He may be small, but he's hard to control. You must keep him in the room. I'll give him a good long walk before the banquet and he'll be fine until we get back. Remember, keep him in the room."

The food order arrived as Amber left. For the next twenty minutes, conversation took second place to dining. Sallie wasn't too taken by the appearance of the coq au vin swimming in brown liquid, but it tasted good. And the bananas Foster was a treat, with the whipped cream and pecans. Dave torched it for her when she was ready.

At last, the food was gone and yawns became more plentiful than words. Dani got off the bed. "I'm glad we didn't go out. I'm so sleepy now that it's a relief to know my bed is only a few steps away."

As the couple moved into the hall, Sallie

remembered that Dave never finished what he was telling them earlier about Morris Duby. "Wait a minute, Dave. You never told us what you found out about Mr. Duby. What is he, if he's not English?"

"French. He was born in Marseilles. The name on the birth certificate is *Maurice Dubuis*."

The name meant nothing to Sallie, but Dani squealed. "Really? *Dubuis*?" "Don't you remember, Sallie? When I told you about Maestro Truffaut, how he was adopted by a wealthy French merchant?"

Sallie recalled the conversation on the way to the master class. "Yes, of course. How as a boy Truffaut replaced an organ-grinder's monkey and then went to live with a rich merchant and his son." She managed to say it without laughing.

"That's right. Well, the merchant's name was Marcel Dubuis and his son's name was Maurice. If Morris Duby is Maurice Dubuis. He is the lost brother Sylvan Truffaut has been looking for all these years."

Chapter Twenty

Morris Duby lay on the narrow bed in his new accommodations, staring at the ceiling. This kind of bed in a hospital was one thing, but what kind of bed was it for a place where he might have to spend the rest of his life?

If Morris had been a man given to tears, he would have wept. But the tears had dried up long ago. All he could do was stare at the dingy ceiling in the Tower Hamlets nursing home and try to see pictures in the water stains. Damned if that long thick one didn't look like a bass flute.

Flutes. What would become of his flutes now? Bernini promised they'd have a home in the British Museum. But that was before the Fabergé Flute went missing from his workshop. The American said the flute had turned up again, briefly, but that now it was gone again. Bernini dead. The flute gone. Something like tears moistened the corners of Morris's eyes.

****

Saturday morning. The last day of the convention. Sallie's first thought when she woke was to wonder how dangerous it might be to have breakfast in the Hunters Den. As tired as she was of the hotel dining room, she was even sicker of being confined to the stuffy hotel room. The smell of last night's entrees lingered. Once she was dressed, she cautiously opened the door to the corridor.

"Everything all right, miss?" Her guards were on duty.

"Everything's just fine. Only I would really like to go downstairs for breakfast. What do you think?"

The officers exchanged glances and shrugged. "Very well, miss," the male officer said. "We'll stay close."

The first person Sallie noticed as they got out of the elevator in the main lobby was the scary bald-headed man she'd seen with Harry. The Godfather. He was walking toward the stairs that led down to the Exhibit Hall. Sallie did a double-take as she recognized what he was carrying. Surely there couldn't be more than one flute case branded with the word URTLES. She looked around for Harry but didn't see him.

The police detail accompanied Sallie through the breakfast line and picked up coffee for themselves but wouldn't sit with her. She would have liked to chat with them, but they insisted upon sitting separately at tables to either side of hers. She ate her eggs and sausage without much enjoyment and left the restaurant, closely followed by her escort. Traversing the lobby, she saw Harry coming up the stairs from the Exhibit Hall, the URTLES case back in his possession. He was up to something, and it had something to do with the Godfather.

Amber was waiting outside Sallie's door. The chin zit was larger and had turned an alarming shade of maroon. Her eyes were red from crying. "Nothing helps. Whatever I try only makes it worse. I can't go to the banquet."

Sallie invited her in and tried her best to comfort her. "I know you're disappointed, Amber, but look on the bright side. Sitting with Orlando would mean sitting with Mr. Paulson. You wouldn't be able to talk easily the way you do when it's just the two of you. You'll have a much better time staying up here with Tacet. You can order anything from room service. Mr. King is paying, so you can live it up."

Amber smiled wanly. "That's what Mr. Slocum said when he bought me breakfast this morning. He saw me hesitate by the yogurt after I'd already put several things on my tray. He said, 'Don't be shy, Amber. I'm paying, so go ahead and live it up!' "

Sallie felt a warning vibe. "Mr. Slocum? How did Mr. Slocum happen to be buying your breakfast?"

"We walked up to the buffet line at the same time and he just offered. I told him all I had to do was put it on Daddy's bill, but he insisted. And then we shared a table and talked."

Understanding began to stir in Sallie's mind. "Did he ask you any questions?"

Amber directed her eyes to the ceiling in remembering mode. "He asked me if I'd packed my flute and was ready to go."

"What did you tell him?"

"I said I was going to leave my flute in the security room until the last minute. That was one of the first things Mrs. Pinkerton told us when we got here. 'Only check out your flute when you need to play it.'"

"Did he ask you anything else?"

Amber considered. "He asked if I had anything

scheduled for today. You know, to play for. I told him I was finished with all my auditions and performances. I expect to leave my flute in the security room until just before we're ready to check out."

"Did he leave the table at any time while you were having breakfast?"

"Let me think. Yes. I'd just started eating my grapefruit. He said he saw someone by the door he needed to talk to for a minute. I didn't look up to see who. I really have to concentrate when I eat grapefruit to keep from squirting myself in the eye."

"Did he come right back?"

Amber frowned. "No. He was gone a pretty long time. I'd finished the grapefruit and my eggs and was almost through with the yogurt when he came back. He laughed and said something about some people being real talkers. Then he helped me on with my jacket and we left the restaurant."

"Think very hard, Amber. Did he have an instrument case with him?"

Amber squeezed her face in earnest thought. "When we came in, he did. But when we said goodbye in the lobby, he wasn't carrying anything. I remember because he put both his hands on my elbows for a second. Maybe he gave the flute to the talkative person."

Sallie nodded decisively. "He gave it to someone, all right. Do you have your security room chit with you?"

Amber patted her green youth blazer. "Here it is." She pulled the piece of plastic out of the right pocket.

Sallie opened the door to the corridor. "Come with me, Amber. We're going to investigate something."

The penny had finally dropped and Sallie knew what Slocum and the Godfather were up to. She told her police detail what she was thinking and they phoned Inspector Garrett, who met them at the security room.

Amber presented her identification tag and the attendant laid her case on the counter.

"Open it, Amber," Sallie said.

The girl opened it. An inexpensive silver flute lay in the expensive flute case. A stricken look contorted Amber's face. "That's not my flute!"

Sallie turned to Inspector Garrett. "I know how he's doing it. He's in it with that bald-headed flute dealer. Harry targets players with expensive flutes. The youth players are especially easy marks. They usually carry their security room IDs in one of the big pockets in their youth blazers. Slocum makes friends with them, notices which pocket they keep their ID in, and palms the tag while he's schmoozing with them. He checks out a case, takes it somewhere private, like a toilet stall, and swaps the expensive flute with the cheap one he has in his own case. Then he checks the other person's case back in and takes the URTLES case to the Godfather."

"The what kind of case?" Garrett asked.

"Harry's case has a Ninja Turtles decal on the side. Only, the first T is missing on the word TURTLES. His partner looks like a mobster, so I call him 'the Godfather.' He takes out the stolen flute, replaces it with another cheap one, and returns the case to Harry for the next swap."

"Wouldn't the security room attendants get suspicious? The same person checking out different instruments?"

"Probably not," Amber said. "A lot of players ask

someone else to pick up their cases for them. The attendants are only interested in whether or not you have the right tag."

Feeling a little like Judas, Sallie accompanied Garrett to identify Harry and his confederate so they could be arrested. The stab of remorse she felt as she watched an officer put Harry's wrists in handcuffs did not last long. Her erstwhile seat-companion favored her with a look of amazement.

"I sure never thought you'd be smart enough to figure it out, Sallie."

Chapter Twenty-One

Saturday evening finally arrived, the night of the banquet that would bring the six-day convention to its end. Sallie marveled at the protean nature of time, the way it can expand and contract, changing shape according to events. Had it been only seven days since she boarded the plane for London? It seemed a year at least.

The anticipated tap signaled the arrival of Dave and Dani and the police escort to walk Sallie to the banquet hall. She wasn't prepared for the sight that greeted her when she opened the door.

A bewigged eighteenth-century gentleman in black velvet knee britches, and a lady in a low-cut crimson gown and elaborate hairdo stood before her.

Sallie stepped backward in astonishment. "Wherever did you get those costumes?"

"We brought them with us," Dani said. "We belong to a Baroque ensemble. This is what we wear for performances."

Kassim would have enjoyed the incongruous sight of Sallie in a red polyester pants suit flanked by the Kings in eighteenth-century costume, followed by solemn police guards dressed in the black slacks and white shirts worn by hotel wait staff. The ill-assorted company processed to the elevator and made their way to the same room where the opening session had been held.

The room had been transformed. The scene might have come out of a DeMille film. A classical motif picked up on the gold and ivory decor, with papier-mâché caryatids along the walls and cupids on the lamp sconces. Niches made of fluted columns and plants which, if not real, appeared to be, marked the periphery of the area that enclosed long banquet tables covered with white cloths and gleaming cutlery and china. Ready for the performers who would take turns playing during the meal, each niche contained a white music stand.

Most of the guests wore contemporary dress, but here and there among the tables strolled ladies and gentlemen who could have stepped out of an illustrated guide to historic dress.

Sallie's bodyguards escorted her and the Kings to a table not far from a door that connected with the kitchen. Their clothing permitted them to blend in with the genuine wait staff, but a careful observer would notice that they never strayed more than a few feet from Sallie's table.

Dave and Sallie took their seats, but Dani had fallen behind. At the moment, she was chatting with a Persian belly dancer.

"Dani seems to know a lot of people here," Sallie said.

Dave nodded. "These conventions get to be like family reunions. Go to enough of them and pretty soon you keep running into the same people."

Sallie picked up a blue sheet of paper beside her place setting. It was a correction to the program that was printed in the catalog, announcing that Benoît

DeLille would perform the piece that Bernini had been scheduled to play, DeBussy's *Syrinx*.

A middle-aged man dressed like Goethe's Werther, in a blue frock coat and fawn trousers, sat down at Dave's right and engaged him in conversation.

Sallie felt suddenly alone and exposed. Showing herself at the banquet didn't seem like such a good idea after all. If her unknown attacker really wanted to kill her, this would present a great opportunity. She looked around for places that might conceal an assassin.

A temporary partition separated the food preparation area from the rest of the room. A broad-shouldered waiter bumped the partition, causing the whole wall to shake. Having directed more than one school play, Sallie knew something about erecting flats and partitions and she had misgivings about this one. It was secured with concrete blocks along the bottom, presumably paired with others, like matching bookends, on the opposite side. The main support was a large sideboard set midway along the partition.

"Are these seats taken?"

Sallie looked up at the calm, beautiful face of Orlando Paulson and smiled a welcome. Her smile faltered, however, when she saw Max Paulson behind him, making his slow way with the help of the fancy swordstick he'd shown them at the theater. Tempted to lie, she hesitated, but Dave stood and answered for her.

"Orlando. Max. Come join us. No one's sitting there." He indicated the places opposite him and Sallie.

Orlando seated his foster father and placed the cane under the table.

"Good evening, Miss Dunbar," Max said. "I hope you don't mind sharing our company."

"Not at all," Sallie lied. What was it about this man that so repelled her? Not his looks. He was good-looking, well dressed, and well spoken. Dani and Dave liked him. Why couldn't she share their admiration of the man for having salvaged a child from the slums of Rio?

Because when she looked at Orlando, she sensed that something was not quite right in this fairy tale. Orlando's beautiful face rarely showed a smile and when it did, only the mouth smiled. The eyes retained their habitual expression of, what, sadness? Whatever it was, it was not joy or contentment or gratitude. It was a look that she had seen in certain high school students, the ones who resisted all her efforts to communicate with them. Mary Thrower. That's who he reminded her of. It was the eyes. Mary Thrower, a pretty tenth-grader who, with five older and younger brothers, lived with an addicted mother and a succession of "uncles."

"Miss Dunbar."

Max's voice penetrated Sallie's musings. The tone suggested that he had been trying to get her attention for a while.

"You seem to be fascinated by my son."

"Oh. Was I staring? Sorry. I was thinking of something. Even all this way across the Atlantic I find myself thinking of my students. Orlando reminds me of one of them and I was off on a train of thought."

Dani joined them. "Max! How nice that you and Orlando are sharing our table."

"Where is your charming Jack Russell this evening?" Max inquired. "It's a pity that the English aren't as tolerant about dogs in restaurants as the French. On my last trip to Paris, I dined out with friends who took their poodle, a perfectly behaved animal, to the restaurant with us. The dog stayed under the table the whole time and no one seemed to mind."

"Tacet is in our room, but he has company," Dave said.

Sallie thought of Amber, sorrowfully dog-sitting Tacet because her zits had failed to clear up. Her zits hadn't gone away! They'd even become worse.

She pondered the fact that her own ailments and afflictions had come and gone overnight. First, there was the jet lag. Then the overwhelming shock of Kassim's death. Her injured ankle. And what about Dani's feet? The image of Alan Bernini standing in the alley, his arm hanging limply at his side flashed into her mind. Not a trace of his injury remained next day. Crazy or not, Sallie couldn't help associating the rapid healings with the haunting, mostly nocturnal, music of the Fourth Floor Flute.

So why had Amber's zits persisted? Sallie thought back to the night she and the Kings rode up to the seventh floor to interview Amber's father. Of course. The sound of the Fourth Floor Flute hadn't carried beyond the fifth floor. Amber had been too far away to benefit. The Callahans' suite was out of healing range.

The sound of metal tapping against glass interrupted Sallie's musings and quieted conversation in the banquet hall. Alice Pinkerton stood at the speaker's daïs, banging a spoon against her water glass.

"Welcome, all," she said. "On behalf of the International Oboe and Flute Association, I want to welcome you to our closing banquet. Except for committee meetings tomorrow morning, the banquet marks the end of the 1985 IOFA convention. While you enjoy your meal, you will be hearing some of the finest flute and oboe players in the world. They will play in the niches that you see surrounding the area. Their names and the names of the pieces that they will be performing are on page eighty-six of your programs." She paused. "Tragically, the final piece, Debussy's *Syrinx* will not be played by Alan Bernini."

A hushed murmur went around the room. Sallie felt her throat contract. Poor Bernini. What a loss.

Alice gestured at a table occupied by two men in identical costumes of the time of Frederick the Great. Between them sat Melisande Truffaut. One of the costumed men was Benoît DeLille. Sallie presumed that the other man was Sylvan Truffaut. His chin was buried in a ruffled shirt and the upper part of his face was barely visible under a wig too big for his head. Maybe he'd deliberately chosen to conceal his facial deformity. On the other hand, DeLille's wig didn't seem to fit much better. Every time he leaned forward, it fell over his eyes and he had to push it back to see. If Sallie were a few feet farther from their table, she wouldn't be able to tell them apart.

"I wonder why DeLille and Truffaut aren't sitting with the honoreds on the daïs," Sallie said. "The Maestro at least, if not his student. Truffaut is pretty important in IOFA, isn't he?"

"He probably was invited to sit at the high table," Dani said, "but he's very sensitive about his face. He probably feels he'd be too exposed at the main table."

Sallie nodded. "I suppose that's understandable. I saw his bad side at your master class on Monday. It is pretty gross."

The meal was generic convention chicken with

soggy brussels sprouts and rice. Conversation lulled as the diners addressed their plates. Across the room, someone was playing the Pachelbel Canon. The niche nearest Sallie's table remained unoccupied.

Intent on her food, Sallie didn't bother to consult the program to see who was playing what. An oboe solo followed the Canon. As the music worked its emotional magic, the grim events of the past two days receded, and Sallie again had a sense of pleasure in being away from home.

Dave and Max resumed their conversation, talking about Orlando as if he weren't there. Sallie felt resentment on the boy's behalf.

"I suspected at the time that he had talent," Max said, "but I never anticipated the extent of it." Sallie regarded the topic of their conversation. Orlando's eyes were fixed on his plate.

She was struck again by the boy's good looks, enhanced by evening clothes. He wore a pin in his lapel, but it wasn't a flute. It didn't represent anything she recognized, just a flat circle.

Max was still going on as if the boy weren't sitting next to him. "I fully expect Orlando to become one of the greats."

"What do you think, Orlando?" Sallie spoke more loudly than necessary. "Do your plans include being 'one of the greats?' Do you even like playing the flute?"

The trace of a smile passed over Orlando's lips, but the look he cast at his adoptive father was serious, almost cautious. "I don't know about the 'great' part, but I do like playing the flute. It always makes me feel…" He paused and took a drink from his water glass. "It makes me feel safe."

Again Sallie thought of Mary Thrower. Mary always refused to stand next to her brothers in the school bus waiting area. When Sallie asked her why, all she would say was, "They be messing with me."

"Orlando is on the threshold of a fine career," Max said. "Not at all bad for a young man just turned seventeen." He gave Orlando a long, steady look and finally acknowledged his presence by shifting to second person. "I had hoped to send you on your way with the advantage of a very special flute."

Orlando's expression remained impassive. Max looked across the table and explained. "The flute I obtained for Orlando's going-away gift was stolen from us at King's Cross station." He turned a proud smile on his adopted son. "But Orlando needs no external helps. His talent is strong enough in itself." This time Orlando's expression did alter.

"You are sending me on my way, then?"

"You won the Youth Competition," Max said. "Your future is assured."

"You'll love Prague," Dani said. The youth prize was a place with the Prague Symphony. She turned to Max. "You're going to miss having Orlando around. Our house seemed absolutely empty when Larry and Irene graduated from high school and left Chicago for school and work."

"I'll miss Orlando's company, certainly," Max said, "but the house won't be empty." He turned to Orlando. "Senhor Gomés has brought me good news. The boy I told you about, the one whose parents Gomés was trying to track down for me, turns out to have no relatives who want to take him. I'm flying to Rio next week to complete arrangements."

Orlando said nothing, but Sallie noticed a muscle move in his jaw.

"How wonderful," Dani said. "Isn't that wonderful, Orlando? Another child who will enjoy the advantages you have had." To Max, she said, "How old is this new orphan?"

"About the same age Orlando was when I adopted him."

"Another eight-year-old," Orlando said. "How nice."

The lights dimmed. Cutlery clinked against china as the diners finished their desserts in the darkened room. The moment had come for the final piece, the celebrated *Syrinx* by Debussy. Maestro Truffaut's signature piece when he still had the use of all his facial muscles.

A costumed figure entered the niche nearest Sallie's table. Sallie wondered if hearing DeLille play it would cause Truffaut to feel more pain than pride.

The soloist stood spotlighted in the niche, his face obscured by the ill-fitting wig. The first plaintive notes of the *Syrinx* sounded. At first Sallie was absorbed in the sound, the notes, and the timbre. Imperceptibly she became aware of the flute in the soloist's hands. It shone not silver but gold, a reddish gold under the lights, reflecting a myriad of colors. She looked around to see where the colored lights could be coming from, but the only illumination was the white spotlight. The reds, greens, blues, and ambers she saw were coming from the flute.

The music held the entire ballroom entranced. When the piece ended, the performer dropped his head

273

forward in a bow. The wig fell off. The flutist threw his head back and Sallie saw that that the face did not belong to Benoît DeLille. A much older man stood there, beaming at the audience. Face alight with a full smile where before only a lopsided grimace had been possible, Sylvan Truffaut stood triumphant, in his hand, the Fabergé Flute.

As the people nearest the niche realized who had played the piece, they rose to their feet, applauding wildly and shouting Truffaut's name. Suddenly the spot was extinguished and the room plunged into darkness. Sallie sensed someone move up behind her. She smelled a man's sweat and heard heavy breathing close to the back of her head. Heart pounding, she leaned away, anticipating a blow or even a bullet. The chandelier lights came up. Blinking in the sudden glare of the restored lights, she saw that the menacing presence was Aram the Armenian waiter. He sprang toward her, but not at her. His target was Truffaut, where he still stood in the ivy-covered niche.

Aram snatched the gleaming flute from the Maestro and in the next instant made an amazing leap to the top of the sideboard that supported the kitchen partition. There, he stood flourishing the precious flute in one hand and a butcher knife in the other, shouting triumphantly in what Sallie assumed was Armenian. For an instant everyone was frozen in place. Then things started happening. Sallie twisted in her chair to watch.

DeLille leapt toward Aram and, at the same moment, Tacet, trailing his leash, exploded through the service entrance, Amber in close pursuit, screaming for him to stop.

Dave and Dani scrambled out of their chairs to head off the dog, but Tacet eluded them, hurling himself at DeLille's ankles, snarling and snapping. Aram leapt from the sideboard. The motion of his descent skewed one of the concrete blocks. Knocked off balance by the dog's attack, DeLille careened against the partition, staggered, and fell, hitting the floor headfirst. The partition shook, swayed, and began to topple.

Hampered by his eighteenth-century finery, Dave King dived for the dog's lead and caught it, but Tacet's hatred of DeLille gave the animal the strength to pull free. Dave's momentum sent him sliding facedown under a table.

Helpless, DeLille lay directly in the path of the falling partition.

Behind her, Sallie heard an anguished shout and whirled to see Orlando's face contorted in a display of raw emotion. Uttering a long, anguished "No!" he sprang from his seat, clearly intending to go to DeLille's aid, but Max snatched his antique walking stick from under the table. Sallie couldn't see what he did with it, but guessed that he'd shoved it between Orlando's legs, because the boy staggered and put out his hands to steady himself against the table.

"Don't make a spectacle of yourself, Orlando!" Max shouted. "A civilized man keeps his composure, no matter the circumstances."

Orlando regained his balance and turned on his adoptive father, his beautiful face contorted in the most chilling look of hatred Sallie had seen in twelve years of dealing with adolescent angst in the classroom.

Desperately, Sallie looked for the detectives who

were supposed to be guarding her, but they had gone in pursuit of Aram. Two uniformed police were helping DeLille, pulling the partition off his prone body. On top of Tacet, Dani and Dave were thrashing about in a tangle of lace, paws, and wiggery. Nobody but Sallie seemed to be aware of the drama playing out between Orlando and his stepfather.

"Civilized! *Civilized*! You call yourself civilized, you vile old pervert?" In a graceful motion, more horrible because of its grace, Orlando snatched at the walking stick, yanking Max, who wouldn't let go, to the floor. With a powerful pull, Orlando took possession of the cane and brandished it above his foster-father, as if preparing to beat him with it.

That's when Sallie saw it. On the underside of Orlando's upturned lapel gleamed a flute pin set with tiny colored stones, one of only two like it in the world. One worn by Benoît DeLille. The other taken from Alan Bernini by whoever shoved him to his death outside the hotel. Orlando.

By now Orlando was screaming, but in the chaos, only Sallie heard him. "You imagine that spending an outrageous amount of money on a flute to 'send me on my way' would somehow cleanse you for your next act of 'humanitarianism.' Would you like to know what happened to your precious flute? No one stole it. I let you think that. While you were buying our tickets at King's Cross, I took the flute out of your briefcase and put it in my backpack, along with the spy flute I stole.

"Yes, while you were ransacking the old man's workshop looking for the Fabergé Flute, I was in his museum taking my own souvenir. I gave the healing flute to Benoît for his teacher. To Benoît, whom I love.

He's a better human being than you will ever be."

Max's voice rose from behind the table. "Stop making a spectacle of yourself, boy, and help me up." His face, when it became visible, showed absolutely no emotion. A deadly mistake. The boy was in paroxysms of pain. He needed a response. An apology. Something. Even answering anger would be better than this.

Orlando stopped waving the walking stick and stood still as a statue staring down at his stepfather, the muscles in his jaw working like snakes.

Again Sallie looked around for a source of help but saw none. Maybe she could distract Orlando somehow. Touch his arm or something. Walking around the table would take too long, so she clambered onto it and scooted across, scattering plates and skewing the cloth. "Orlando." She spoke in what she hoped was a calm, soothing tone. "He's not worth it, Orlando. He's not worth ruining your life for."

She slid off the table on the other side and put her hand on the arm holding the cane. Orlando flung it off without breaking the gaze he held on Max.

"I'll give you spectacle, old man!" Orlando pressed the jade handle of the antique walking stick and drew out the blade.

"Orlando, no!" Sallie grabbed at the boy's arm. This time Orlando shoved her away so roughly she fell backward over a chair, wrenching her shoulder with such force she cried out in pain.

Orlando raised the blade over his adoptive father. "I don't care what happens to me. You'll not get your claws into another eight-year-old."

Sallie struggled to her feet. Her stomach clenched and her legs felt weak. Max Paulson lay on his back, half under the table, his eyes staring upward, but no longer seeing. A circular crimson stain spread across the ruffled shirt front under the gaping tuxedo jacket, clashing with the scarlet red of his satin cummerbund. Orlando, violently weeping, all restraint gone, leaned over him, thrusting the sword into the same wound, again and again and again.

Chapter Twenty-Two

Sunday, 1 December 1985, Departure Day

Max was dead when Sallie's derelict security team returned from their unsuccessful pursuit of Aram and took Orlando into custody.

Sallie and the Kings returned to their rooms in silence, too stunned for conversation. The fourth floor also lay silent. Deprived of the healing strains of the Fabergé Flute, Sallie spent a night of disrupted sleep, waking exhausted to her last morning in London.

****

Morris Duby stared at the tiny window in his new surroundings in the nursing home. He didn't know how long he'd been awake. Or even if he'd been asleep. As he stared, the darkness outside began to lift. Morning was dawning. Another morning. How many more would there be for him? He never thought he'd admit it, even to himself, but he was lonely. He wished the American would come and talk for a while. He heard a sound at the door but didn't bother to turn his head. Just one of those irritating nursing sisters who'd address him with the royal We. *How are we doing today, dearie.* He'd like to dearie them.

"Maurice?" A man's voice.

Duby felt his body go rigid. Footsteps approached the side of the bed. And again, the voice.

"Maurice? *C'est toi*? It is you?"

A shape moved between Morris and the window. Expensive suit. Blue serge. Good quality. And a scent. Expensive cologne. Him. It was Him.

Dreading to see the disfigurement the American described to him earlier, Morris forced himself to look up at the face. He stared for a long time before speaking. "Your face, Brother. It is not as it was described to me. You ought to look like the Phantom of the Opera. Yet I see nothing more than the tracks of age."

The man laughed. " 'Nothing more'? Age is not trivial, *mon frère*. But yes, before this week, I was badly disfigured. And then someone brought me the Flute."

Duby scoffed. "And it healed your face, is that it? Fairy tales!"

Sylvan Truffaut sat on the side of his foster brother's bed. "It healed me, Maurice. It healed me, as it did all those years ago. Father never permitted you to see my foot after the accident, so you never realized how bad it was."

"How bad could it have been? You never went to hospital. You just wanted attention. And the Flute. You wanted the Flute for yourself." Morris hiked himself to his elbows. "Where is it? What have you done with it? It's mine. I was the true son."

"Gently, Maurice, gently." Sylvan Truffaut stood, laid his hands on his foster brother's shoulders, and soothed him back onto the pillow. "I do not have it and I am glad. People have died because of it." He pulled a chair to the side of the bed and sat. He told how he'd come to have the flute. How once again, it had been lost.

"It is out of our lives now, Maurice. Join me in thanking God that it is gone. Someone with a greater claim than either of ours has it now."

Morris took a deep breath, preparing to hurl all the old anger and resentment upon the man who had stolen his father's love all those years ago, but suddenly he realized that the resentment was gone. And the anger. All of it. He sighed. "We are old, Sylvan. They've brought me here to die, I think."

Truffaut looked around the tiny room, the meager furnishings, the bilious green walls. "Only if that is your wish, Maurice. You have a house in Marseilles. I never sold it. There we can both go to die. But for a few years, I think, we can live in our boyhood home together, as brothers."

Morris's eyes moistened. He thought of his house in the East End, a gloomy house in a gloomy street. He would not miss it. But his collection was there. What would become of it? Strangely, he didn't care. But there was something even he couldn't walk away from.

"I have a dog, Sylvan. Someone is looking after it, but he will expect me to take it if I l don't have to stay here."

Truffaut shook his head. "I'll do much to make up for the pain I have caused you, Maurice. But a dog? I would rather not."

Morris shrugged. The dog meant nothing to him. He'd only got it because of the Collection. Someone had told him that its barking would deter thieves. "Look there, on the table, Sylvan. You will find a telephone number for the American."

****

Although she'd done most of her packing before the banquet, Sallie still had a few items to deal with when the Kings knocked at her door at seven a.m. As she joined them in the corridor, the phone in their room rang.

"Hang on a sec," Dave said. He unlocked the door and went to answer.

Sallie looked down at the floor. Something was missing. "No Tacet. I guess that means Dave found a home for him."

Dani grimaced. "Yes indeed. And his new home has a 6000 zip code."

Sallie stared at Dani without comprehending.

"Chicago. That's the zip code."

"Oh."

"Mr. Duby phoned at the crack of dawn. He's leaving the nursing home."

"Oh, no. After all Dave's labor in moving him."

"He phoned to say he can't take back the dog." Dani shook her head. "It's my own fault," When I told him about Duby's connection with Truffaut, Dave lost no time telling the Maestro where he could find his long-lost brother. Duby's going to live with Truffaut in France."

"France doesn't have a quarantine," Sallie said. "Why can't they take the dog?"

Dani shrugged. "Who knows? Maybe Truffaut's allergic."

"Then where's Tacet?"

"Sedated and reposing in the most expensive dog crate known to man. Dave got the desk clerk to locate a travel crate. Not easy or cheap on a Sunday morning." Dani sighed. "The Queen's corgis don't have a crate as grand as this one."

Dave emerged from their room in time to hear Dani's last remark.

"Admit it, darling, you've grown fond of the creature. Deep down, you're relieved that you won't have to part with him."

"Hmph," Dani said. Then, "Who was on the phone that time? Someone with a pony to unload?"

"No, my dear. Chief Inspector Garrett wanting to know how much longer we'll be at the hotel. I told him we're going to have breakfast before leaving for the airport."

"Did he say anything about DeLille?" Sallie asked. "That partition must have weighed a ton."

"Broken collarbone is all. He may have to face charges of receiving and possession of stolen property—except that without the flute, there's not much of a case. As for why Tacet hated DeLille, I was right. DeLille was in the workshop when Duby collapsed."

Dani gasped. "What kind of person would leave an old man lying on the floor?"

They took the elevator to the lobby.

"Don't be too hard on him," Dave said, as they entered the restaurant. "DeLille phoned 999. He says he tried to stay with Duby, but Tacet was having a fit and trying to chew his feet off, so he went outside to wait for the ambulance. Too agitated to stand still, he paced on the sidewalk. He was a few doors down when he saw Max and Orlando go into Duby's place. Before he could catch them to warn them not to call another ambulance, he saw them hurry out again and scuttle off in the direction of the tube station. About then, the ambulance got there and DeLille figured he could leave."

A thought occurred to Sallie. "What about Duby's flute collection? Will he take it to France with him? Or will it be sold off?"

Dave beamed. "Better than either. Before he died, Bernini mentioned the collection to a friend of his at the British Museum. Truffaut doesn't want to mess with the collection, so he let the BM folks look it over." He turned to Dani. "Remember the flute Duby always said was made from a dinosaur bone?"

"Yes," Dani said. "I never believed it."

"Well, it wasn't. But it *was* made from the wing of an extinct vulture. Turns out it's one of the oldest flutes known."

"How old?" Sallie asked.

"I think he said 30,000 years. The entire collection is going to the BM after all."

For the last time, Sallie and her friends joined the buffet line in the Hunter's Den. It was Sallie's last chance to try the kippers. She picked up the serving tongs, but then put them back down. She couldn't do it. Not that she didn't like fish. Just that it seemed such a strange thing to eat first thing in the morning.

They ate for a while in silence, lost in their separate thoughts. Sallie's mental movie camera replayed the terrible scene in the banquet hall. "Poor Orlando," she said.

Dave scoffed. "Poor Orlando made mincemeat of Max's heart with that swordstick."

"And he tried to kill you," Dani said. "Three times, I believe."

"Four," Dave corrected her. "The shot that killed

Kassim was meant for her."

"Orlando was eight years old when Max took him in," Sallie said. "He went from being a throwaway child living on his wits in extreme physical deprivation to being a pampered sex slave. What chance did he ever have to develop a stable mentality? All he wanted was to feel safe and loved."

"I'm no psychologist," Dani said, "but I suppose that when he hated Max the most, he still wanted to be loved by him."

"Yes," Sallie agreed. "And the Fabergé Flute symbolized Max's rejection of him, a pay-off for services rendered. Max was the closest thing to a father that Orlando had. On one level, he hated him, but on another, he didn't want to be cut loose."

"So, how do you two amateur psychologists explain where DeLille comes in?"

"That's easy," Sallie said. "DeLille was kind to Orlando. When DeLille showed concern, Orlando misinterpreted it as love. He stole the flute from Max and gave it to DeLille as a love offering. He didn't mind when DeLille gave the flute to Truffaut, but Bernini was a different matter. Orlando was jealous of Bernini."

Dani frowned. "DeLille must have known that it was Orlando who snatched the flute from Bernini in the alley. Why didn't he do something then?"

"DeLille was torn between loyalty to Bernini and loyalty to Truffaut," Dave said. "He figured Bernini would insist on turning the flute over to the authorities. He deceived his lover for the sake of his beloved teacher. He never intended to keep the flute. He just wanted to heal Truffaut."

Dani's expression remained disapproving. "He should have come forward when Bernini was killed."

"That's where it gets complicated," Dave said. "At first, DeLille thought that Bernini's death was the result of a traffic accident. And, actually, it probably was an accident. All Orlando intended was to snatch the flute case and run with it, same as when he took it from Bernini behind the pub. When the handle broke, Bernini fell backward into the path of the taxi."

"What about the lapel pin?" Sallie asked. "I can't figure out how Orlando managed to get the jeweled flute pin off Bernini's lapel. I mean, he didn't have time to stop and take it after snatching the flute."

"He got the pin at the same time he got the flute," Dave said. "Orlando told Garrett how it happened. Bernini wasn't just carrying the flute case by its handle. He did have the handle in his hand, but he was also clutching the case across his chest with his other arm. Orlando had to pry the case away with both hands. When he did, his fingers caught on the pin and pulled it away."

"Nonsense," Dani said. "He would have just dropped it in the street as he ran."

Sallie shook her head. "No. He must have known that the pin was a love token between DeLille and Bernini. He would have recognized what it was as soon as his fingers touched it."

Dave went back to the line for a second helping of bacon and the women went on with their breakfast in silence.

"There's something else I'd like to have explained," Sallie said when Dave came back to the table. "Why didn't Orlando take my flute case with him after he'd put the Fabergé Flute in it? Why did he leave it in my room?"

"He was interrupted," Dave said around a piece of bacon. "Orlando took the flute in the old case straight to Truffaut's room on the fourth floor, but Truffaut wouldn't open the door. Next, Orlando went to the elevator, intending to go up to his room, but when he heard the people who got off say that Bernini was dead and the police were looking for a flute case without a handle, he panicked. He knew he had to get rid of the case the Fabergé Flute was in. Instead of getting into the elevator, he headed for the stairway at our end of the hall, passing our rooms on the way. When he saw Sallie's case through the open door, he decided to swap cases and ditch the one the police were looking for."

"How do you know all this?" Dani asked.

"Garrett pieced it together from his interviews. Orlando never intended to leave the flute in your room, Sallie. He was interrupted by DeLille."

"Wait a minute," Sallie said. "I saw Orlando running up the escalator about the same time the desk clerk saw DeLille go into the stairwell. Wouldn't he and Orlando have gotten to the fourth floor almost at the same time?"

"Probably would have," Dave said, "if DeLille hadn't been waylaid in the stairwell by a devoted parent. DeLille was one of the judges for the Hoffman Prize. The woman the clerk saw follow DeLille into the stairwell was the mother of one of the prize contenders. She cornered him on every landing. He finally shook her off at the fourth floor, just about the time Orlando switched the flutes and was leaving Sallie's room."

"So why didn't he just hand the case holding the

Fabergé Flute to DeLille then and there?" Dani asked. "You said he took the flute to DeLille after snatching it from Bernini behind the pub. Why not just give it to him this time?

"This time was different," Dave said. "This time Bernini was dead. Orlando didn't dare admit that he was the one who caused his death. DeLille was still talking to the woman as he opened the stairway door. When Orlando heard his voice, he left Sallie's case on her dresser and rushed into the hallway with the empty case."

Sallie flashed on the image of DeLille exiting the elevator after she'd thrown up in the restroom. "Now I know when DeLille got his red scarf back."

"How did Orlando explain the empty case with the broken handle?" Dani asked.

"He lied," Dave said. "He told DeLille he'd just found the empty case lying on the floor in the hallway and was on his way to take it back to the Maestro."

"And DeLille believed him?" Dani demanded.

Sallie recalled the boy's instant fabrication to Alice Pinkerton at the National Portrait Gallery. "He's a very convincing liar."

"It wasn't much of a story," Dave said. "The only reason DeLille didn't question it at the time is that he was afraid some harm had come to the Maestro. He snatched the case from Orlando and rushed to the old man's room. Truffaut told him he'd voluntarily given the Fabergé Flute to Bernini, who was taking it to the British Museum. When he heard that, DeLille rushed downstairs, hoping to catch Bernini before he could deliver the flute. That's when he learned Bernini was dead."

Dani frowned. "Why didn't DeLille give the case to the police?"

"He didn't want to do anything that might help them find the missing contents," Dave said. "He could see that the Maestro's face was in the process of healing. He wanted to find the Flute before the police did. And he was certain that Orlando must know the Flute's whereabouts. He wanted to get to him first. To buy time, he tossed the case into the dumpster."

Dani groaned. "My head is beginning to hurt with all the ins and outs of this. Orlando left the Flute in Sallie's room. Sallie took what she thought was her flute to the security room. How did Orlando even know whose case he'd put it in? And how did he know to go look for it in the security room and not go back to her room?"

Dave laughed. "All in good time, my love." He leaned back in his chair and wiped the bacon grease off his chin. "Orlando knew the case belonged to Sallie because her name was on it in big gold letters."

Heat rose to Sallie's face. She knew at the time she branded her case with the gold foil letters that she was being stupidly vain, but she'd been so proud of her new flute.

"Orlando knew that Sallie had checked her flute into the security room because he saw her playing with the chit when he and Max stopped by the table where she was sitting with Kassim after the accident."

"So how did he get the Flute back to Truffaut?" Dani asked.

"When he was sure that DeLille was in his hotel room, he hung the Flute in a bag on the doorknob, knocked, and hid. DeLille took it back to Truffaut."

Dave signaled the waiter for more coffee and Sallie took another sip of her tea. Her thoughts returned to the cup she enjoyed the day of the long stroll to the bottom of Charing Cross road and the National Portrait Gallery. The memory prompted a new question. "Do you have any idea why Orlando wanted to kill me?"

"The first time," Dave said, "because he thought you were working with Bernini to recover the Fabergé Flute. The next two times, in the security room and the Exhibit Hall, because he thought you'd seen him shove Bernini in front of the taxi. The third time, outside the theater, because he realized from your remark that you must have seen him kiss DeLille on the bus. He was still conflicted enough about his feelings for Max to want to keep you from reporting what you'd seen to him."

Orlando's face, with its various expressions, flashed into Sallie's mind. The dazzling smile, the venomous look, the emotionless stare. "What will become of him?"

Dave shrugged. "He's been taken to a psychiatric facility. He's young. Maybe he can be helped."

"I wouldn't count on it," Dani said. "Exceptions exist, but for the most part, offenders who have been messed up as children usually stay messed up."

Sallie thought fleetingly of Amber's plan to learn what not to do before having children. Not such a bad idea.

"We've got company," Dave said.

Sallie looked up to see Inspector Garrett approaching.

Dave pulled out the fourth chair for him.

"Sorry to interrupt your breakfast," Garrett said.

"Seems I've still a bit of unfinished business."

"Not at all," Dave said. "Have some coffee with us."

A waiter brought another cup and topped up Sallie's teapot with hot water. The waiter made her think of Aram. "Do the police have any idea where the Fabergé Flute is now?"

"We think the Armenian waiter took it to Armenian House," Garrett said. "It's not far from here. He could've got there on foot."

"Can't they search the Armenian place?" Dani asked.

Garrett shook his head. "Insufficient cause. My guess is that when and if Armenia wins independence, the Fabergé Flute will make its way there in a diplomatic pouch."

Sallie poured herself another cup of tea. She was glad that Aram was the one to end up with the flute. Kassim would have approved.

Garrett placed an envelope and a small paper bag on the table. "I could have left these to the post, Miss Dunbar, but I thought you might like to have them straightaway. First, this."

Garrett handed the envelope to Sallie. She opened it, took out the contents, and felt her mouth drop open.

The detective laughed. "It's a reward. The IOFA and other music associations were offering $10,000 for information leading to the apprehension of the persons responsible for the instrument thefts that have been plaguing music conventions for the past several years. You gave us Slocum and his confederate. That's a cashier's check on a US bank. Cheers."

Sallie felt weak. Ten thousand dollars. She couldn't

begin to imagine what that would mean to her. Ten thousand dollars. Her own place. Out of her mother's basement.

Next, Garrett handed her the small paper bag. "We've been holding these as evidence, but now that the investigation is complete, I can give them to you."

Still dazed by the reward money, Sallie tried to focus on the white bag. It was printed with a store name and an address in Hatton Garden. She held it open and saw a folded piece of paper and a little black box, the kind jewelry comes in.

"The note in there is one of several drafts we found in Mr. Kassim's room," Garrett said. "All but one were crumpled in a wastebasket. The one in the bag was on the writing desk. The box was delivered to the hotel desk on Friday. We learned that Kassim placed the order early Wednesday morning and paid a premium to have it ready before the end of the conference."

Sallie felt her throat contract. Kassim had ordered a gift for her the morning she saw him with Dave in the coffee shop. "Excuse me," she said. "I need to go back to my room for a few minutes."

Sallie sat on the bed to read what was written on the hotel paper. First came one of Dr. Johnson's epigrams: *The basis of all excellence is truth: he that professes love ought to feel its power.* More writing followed.

Dear Sallie Dunbar,

When my assignment here is finished and I am able to explain everything to you, I hope that you can forgive my deceptions. My feelings for you after such a short acquaintance are difficult to understand, but impossible to ignore. As our mentor Dr. Johnson has wisely observed, 'Life, however short, is made still shorter by waste of time.' If your feelings in any way mirror my own, let us begin again on a basis of truth.

Please accept this small token of my esteem. I hope you will approve its dimensions.

Your devoted friend,

Kassim

Crying softly, Sallie opened the black box. A rosy golden flute, about two inches long and set with semi-precious stones for the keys, gleamed against the velvet. The flute was attached to a gold chain. With a feeling of sadness mixed with happiness, she placed the chain around her neck. It felt warm against her skin. Kassim had not been using her. He'd returned her feelings. That's why he hadn't come directly back to the hotel the morning she'd felt so betrayed. He'd gone from his meeting with Dave in the coffee shop to Hatton Garden, the London street of jewelers where customers can take their own designs and have them executed by the craftsmen there.

When Sallie could cry no more, she went to the bathroom, washed her face, and blew her nose. She made a last check of all surfaces, drawers, and the wardrobe to be certain she wasn't leaving anything behind. One of her two wheeled suitcases was already downstairs. The other lay open on the rack, its contents rising several inches above the edge. One reason for the overflow was that the case now contained the shoulder bag with her flute and stand.

Sallie pushed down on the bulging contents with both hands. The intractable pile had grown because of souvenir catalogues and brochures, but the biggest culprit was the chenille robe Mother had swapped for the negligee.

Motivated by a sudden surge of exasperation, Sallie pulled the robe out of the suitcase and smashed it into the largest of the room's three wastebaskets. Next she tossed all the catalogs she'd accumulated, the flannel pajamas, the duct tape and, finally, the Ace bandage. The note from Kassim, and the box the necklace had come in, she tucked into her carry-on bag.

Zipping the suitcase without difficulty, she left the room without a further look behind.

Sallie and the Kings shared a taxi to Victoria Station. From there they took the train to the airport and waited together until time for takeoff. The sedated Tacet had gone with the luggage in his luxurious carrier.

Dave grinned at Sallie. "After all this excitement, how can you stand to return to your boring classroom?"

"My students are never boring," Sallie said. "It's the grownups who wear me down." She thought of her last meeting with Amber earlier that morning when she took one of her suitcases down to the desk in the lobby. Amber's pouting look had gone. She gave Sallie another rib-crushing hug. "Daddy wasn't mad at all," she said with an air of wonder. "He said I should have told him ages ago."

At an intersection where the corridors led to different departure gates, Sallie rested her shoulder bag on the floor. "This is where we go our separate ways. Me to DeSoto Springs, and you to Chicago and your exciting life in the big city."

"Back to traffic jams and snowstorms," Dani said.

"We like what we do," Dave said, "but sometimes we wish we could do it somewhere quieter and warmer."

"Sounds like a description of DeSoto Springs," Sallie said. "Usually quiet and definitely warmer. Come check us out."

"We just may do that," Dani said.

With hugs all round, the friends parted company.

As Sallie walked briskly through the boarding tunnel, she experienced a wonderful sense of freedom. Part of the feeling came from the fact she was carrying only one shoulder bag. Part was a sense of emotional freedom.

For the return flight, Sallie asked for an aisle seat. Room to extend one's legs, she'd decided, is more to be desired than a window from which very little can be seen. She leaned back, happy in the thought of the cashier's check tucked safely in the money pouch beneath her clothing. She sensed, rather than saw, someone stop in the aisle beside her. She looked up. A man holding a boarding pass had found his seat number. She stood to let him enter the row, but he made no move to take his seat.

"Thanks a lot, little lady," he said. "Maybe you'd like the window seat better than the one you're in. I know how you ladies like to look out at the clouds. How come a pretty little thing like you is traveling all by her lonesome?"

Sallie took in the man's flushed face, his condescending grin, his gaudy bolo tie, and thought of Harry Slocum. Thought of Nick. And then she thought of Kassim. She smiled. Kassim told her how he avoided unwanted conversations with tedious travel companions. "I just start speaking Turkish or French or something other than whatever language they speak.

Works every time."

Sallie remained standing and smiled graciously. "*Je regret, Monsieur. Je ne parle pas anglais.*"

The red-faced man sidled past and folded himself into the window seat. Sallie settled back and closed her eyes, pleased to know she'd learned more on her London trip than just how to pack.

A word about the author...

Maeve Maddox combines an academic background with an enthusiastic interest in popular culture.

A longtime contributor to the international language site DailyWritingTips, she writes about English language and literature, online and in print. Her academic writing appears under the name Margaret Joan Maddox.

The Fabergé Flute is set in London, where the author studied and taught for seven years, graduating from the University of London with a degree in English.

Maeve makes her home in Northwest Arkansas with two black cats and a border collie.

Thank you for purchasing
this publication of The Wild Rose Press, Inc.

For questions or more information
contact us at
info@thewildrosepress.com.

The Wild Rose Press, Inc.
www.thewildrosepress.com